Selina realized now that she should never have accepted her father's decision that Jack Ramsay give her lessons in music. True, Ramsay was startlingly accomplished as a music master for a man reputed to be the premier rakehell of the realm. But now, despite herself, her heart beat wildly as she felt his eyes upon her while she apologized for her lack of talent, saying, "You must make all effort to erase from memory the dreadful sounds I produced."

"Ah, but the memory of you at your instrument appeals to a sense other than my ears, Selina," Ramsay said.

Selina could only blush.

Ramsay pressed the point. "I have been thinking we should undertake lessons of a more advanced nature."

She stared at him as he leaned slowly, inexorably closer to her. She closed her eyes at last only as his head sank to hers, and her lips yielded to his.

He had told her that someday he hoped to play with her—and now she realized what he meant. . . .

The Rakehell's Reform

Elisabeth Fairchild

A SIGNET BOOK

SIGNET
Published by the Penguin Group
Penguin Books USA Inc., 375 Hudson Street,
New York, New York 10014, U.S.A.
Penguin Books Ltd, 27 Wrights Lane,
London W8 5TZ, England
Penguin Books Australia Ltd, Ringwood,
Victoria, Australia
Penguin Books Canada Ltd, 10 Alcorn Avenue,
Toronto, Ontario, Canada M4V 3B2
Penguin Books (N.Z.) Ltd, 182–190 Wairau Road,
Auckland 10, New Zealand

Penguin Books Ltd, Registered Offices:
Harmondsworth, Middlesex, England

First published by Signet, an imprint of Dutton Signet,
a division of Penguin Books USA Inc.

First Printing, February, 1997
10 9 8 7 6 5 4 3 2 1

This book is dedicated to

Barb Yirka, Laurel Hanson, and Victoria Hinshaw,
who kindly offered up their Lincoln Center
programs for the scribblings
of inspiration,

and to

Ralph Kirshbaum,
who made love to his cello with
a little help from Haydn,
inspiring the character Jack Ramsay

Chapter One

Down the snow-white marble stairs at Brooks's he headed. It was fitting that he went down. When one has single-handedly lost almost every penny to one's family name, the direction one heads should be down.

Jack Ramsay paused on the third step to look back. The song of Lester Fletcher's triumph followed him. The old man was laughing—laughter that set him to coughing—great, gut-wrenching coughs that hurt just in listening to them. Fletcher had spent most of the evening coughing and winning: choking coughs in his drink; wheezing great cloud-coughs of smoke from his infernal cigars; barking uncontrolled, unstifleable coughs behind the shield of his cards; and, as if an angel sat upon his shoulder comforting him, with every cough he won. The fat, asthmatic blowhard now hacked phlegm over all that remained of the Ramsay family's fortune, his handkerchiefs a pile of promissory notes signed by Jack Ramsay's hand, in his brother Charles's name.

Jack turned his back on the evening and all that had gone wrong to the tune of those coughs. The stairs stretched before him, dizzying in their whiteness. The wind had been knocked out of him. If he were to take a step unassisted, he would go cartwheeling, ass over teakettle, down the unforgiving length of marble.

Grabbing the cold, cast-iron balustrade, he steadied himself. Strange, as many times as he had taken these stairs he had never noticed the curling vinelike S pattern in the black balusters. What did those S's stand for? *Stupid*? *Simple*? *Sapskull*? Or was it no more than support for the shorn shagwits who did not know when to quit betting before their pockets were completely emptied? He had never required the use of the banister before. Today he did not think he could make it to the bottom of the stairs without the support, his legs felt so weak. Terror did that to a man, and he was completely terrified.

Lord help him, how could he have lost, and gone on losing, until there was nothing left to wager? Nothing!

Two men were coming up the stairs as he headed down. The one in the lead, young and dapper, seemed in a great hurry to reach the Subscription Room. He passed Jack with such energy that Jack felt as if some part of him, some indiscernible bit of his essence, was swept up the stairs after the man. *Slow down,* he was tempted to call after the fool. Time enough to lose everything. No need to hurry.

The second, less hearty man, who came puffing in his wake, was Lord Ware, Lester's crony. Rushing up to make sure the coughing spell had not killed Lester, no doubt.

Jack held his tongue until they came together on the landing, but then he could not resist remarking bitterly, "A pity your friend will not live to enjoy the fortune he has won tonight."

Ware passed him without dignifying his insult with a reply. He offered no evidence of having heard the taunt at all, save a withering look of utter contempt, a look Jack had long since grown accustomed to witnessing. You are a wastrel, the look said, unworthy of either my time or the breath it would take to offer a reply.

There were two occupations in which Jack excelled—two occupations in which he gave lie to such looks. One was gambling, for until tonight he had considered himself a dab hand at games of chance. The second was playing the cello.

Now he had not even the comfort of believing himself a good gambler. He *was* a wastrel, unworthy of the love of his family, unworthy of the trust his elder brother, Charles, had bestowed upon him. He had betrayed that trust, betrayed it completely. Nothing left but to put a bullet in his brain and his disgrace would be complete.

To the bottom of the stairs he made it without sinking to his knees—almost to the outer door without another encounter. But Hugh Stuart came in as he was donning his coat.

"Leaving, are you, Jack?" He sounded disappointed. "I had hoped you and I might play a hand or two. It is one hundred and fifty pounds I am determined to win back, don't you know."

"Tapped out." Jack did his best to sound nonchalant. Every word he uttered, every move he made this evening would be gossip fodder tomorrow, when all of London would know of Lester Fletcher's run of good fortune against Jack's bad. Half a dozen of the club's patrons hovered nearby, curious witnesses of his reaction to tonight's overwhelming losses.

"Where are you off to, then? Not the mushroom's ball, I'll wager." Hugh made the remark innocently, cheerfully.

There was no innocence or cheer left in Jack. Hugh sounded to him the complete fool. He responded, without thinking, out of habit, as he always did when the question of a bet was raised. "How much would you risk?"

And yet there *was* a difference. He had risked all, lost all! Everything gone in the turn of a card. There was only a single worthless Welsh penny left upon his person, the only coin he valued too much to risk. The enormity of his losses was numbing.

Oblivious to his concerns, Hugh promised blithely, "I'll lay you a monkey you would never set foot in Avery Preston's house, much less waste an entire evening twiddling your thumbs at his daughter's coming-out ball."

Distracted, Jack heard no more than the words "lay you a monkey," and "ball." Nothing else penetrated the fog of his despair. "A ball?" he repeated stupidly, sliding the one coin still in his possession from the little pocket in his waistcoat, where he never failed to carry it. Negligently he tossed it into the air, palmed it, tossed it high again. "Is there a cello to be had there?"

Hugh laughed. "A cello? I've no idea. I would suppose so. Would you play cello at the mushroom ball?"

Jack nodded. "Yes. Crowns I will play cello at this mushroom ball, castles I go home and shoot myself."

"Crowns it must be then," Hugh said affably.

Careful not to fumble the toss, Jack launched the coin, caught it, slapped it against the back of his hand, and peered at the outcome.

"Damn!"

Hugh frowned. "Castles is it?"

"No, crowns. Where is this ruddy ball being held?"

Hugh laughed, clapped him on the back, and called jovially to anyone within shouting distance, "Splendid! Come on, you lot. Do you hear? Jack means to play cello at the mushroom ball!"

The ices were melting, raspberry and lemon, a consequence of her father's insistence there was nothing better for cooling overheated dancers. A tower of them graced the table, mouth-wateringly arranged around a sculpted block of ice, also melting. Selina Preston stood at the window that looked out over the street rather than watch the pink and yellow puddles expand in the expensive crystal bowls her father had purchased for this very purpose. She felt too much kinship with the ruined ices. Dressed in the shimmering richness of her father's own intricate jacquard silk, her sleeves and bodice dripping scalloped lace, she felt overly ornamental for the echoing emptiness of a ballroom more populated by musicians and servants than by guests.

In her uneven reflection on the windowpane, she, like the ices, melted. Not that there was anything wrong with her appearance. To the contrary, she was tonight as near to perfection as could be rendered at the hands of a fashionable Parisian modiste and the most popular hairdresser in London. All of this primping done with but one goal of her father's fashioning—to win her a husband of noble birth.

Nobility of name did not matter to Selina as much as a nobility of mind and manner. She had confided as much to her mother on leaving for London. Her mother, of course, had nothing to say with regard to the matter, but her stepmother, Mrs. Preston, had been very vocal.

"You have been far too well indulged, Selina," she fussed. "I tried to warn Avery. He would not hear it. 'Too much freedom to participate in business and too much schooling in subjects uncommon to the typical female's education have not brought your daughter happiness,' I told him. 'She has traveled the world, and in consequence comes home dissatisfied with every eligible bachelor in the county!' "

"Would you be happy to see me shackled to a gentleman of inferior intelligence, provincial thinking, unschooled manners, and empty mind?" Selina had asked.

"Only listen to yourself." Mrs. Preston had thrown up her hands in defeat. "And now to London, where there is no telling what sort of people you may meet. Perhaps, as my husband hopes, a titled gentleman will be pleased with you, if not your parents. He will not want to live in Cheshire. And so, your father and I will lose you to his own scheming which began, I am told, even with your birth, in his choosing to name you."

The story was as old as Selina. Her mother had wanted to name her Marianne. Her father had insisted his daughter should not be dubbed anything so ordinary.

"A pompous name and presumptuous," her mother had complained. "The girl will think too much of herself."

"Salt of the earth," her father had argued. And so Selina meant, in Latin. He had often reminded her, that she might not, as her mother and Mrs. Preston feared, think too much of herself.

There was a grim truth to Mrs. Preston's complaints. Selina, salt of the earth, was no more suited to country turnips who had seen nothing of the world than to the all-too-worldly, well-educated, and well-traveled gentlemen of London. Peers of the realm negotiated marriage with care and forethought, exposing themselves and their hearts to none but the chosen few who revolved in the same circles as themselves, circles whose boundaries she could not leap. The women these gentlemen sought possessed connections of bloodline, history, and common acquaintance, along with an equity of power, pounds, and property. She was hopelessly outmatched. The only titled young men who would look twice at her, the wealthy daughter of a tradesman from Chester, were the sort who gathered here tonight—desperate men, fortune hunters. They would take her for her wealth, for money alone, not for the richness of her imagination or the resources of her excellent mind. Certainly not because they loved her. She fit no more comfortably their world than she fit her own of late.

She could be happy, as her mother had been, as Mrs. Preston was, with a good man, a kind man, a man who would love her for herself, not her background, education, or the size of her pocketbook. But Selina believed in obedience to her father. She had agreed to this ball as readily as she had applied herself to study with the best tutor to be had in Cheshire county, as obediently as she had gone away to the finest French boarding school, as agreeably as she had spent eight months traveling Europe in the well-paid company of Mrs. LaRue, who saw to it she was impeccably fitted with the very finery she wore this evening.

Inside and out, all of her life, she had been coaxed, teased, molded, and shaped. Miserable as she was, she could have greeted her guests, had there been any, in flawless French, Italian, German, or Dutch. But there were no guests. There were no carriages lining the street below, letting down a steady stream of passengers.

No one had come, just as she had warned her father. No one of consequence, no one who mattered, no matter how gilded the invitations or how fine the wine. The sounds of the orchestra echoed hollowly in virtually empty rooms. The food on the sideboards, beautifully prepared and presented, grew stale.

"I am sorry, Selina," her father said softly, coming up behind her.

"Sorry, Father? You have nothing to be sorry for."

She tried to explain, her throat thick with memories of her loneliness at school, of her ostracism when it was discovered she bled red rather than blue. "It is my fault. I did not make the right connections. Did not, as they say, 'take.' Too much the bookworm and not enough the social butterfly."

"There is Arabella."

She smiled. On the far side of the room, Arabella sat between two other female guests, eyeing the disreputable gentlemen browsing the delectables.

"Arabella's friendship is a blessing beyond measure. A lone

baron's daughter does not, however, secure my position among the ton. She was no more popular than I at school."

"Reminds me of your mother—would that she could see you tonight."

"And Mrs. Preston, who would not come with us to London."

"Doesn't care for crowds."

"Nor does Arabella. She is shy, retiring, with very little self-confidence."

He did not want to listen, would not see truth until it dripped itself into his consciousness by way of a tower of uneaten ices. Poor Father! This was not at all what he had intended for this evening. He wanted the world for his only daughter. He was ready to spend every penny he had to buy it for her. The approval and acceptance of the ton, however, were not for sale. He had not wanted to believe her when she had informed him that this evening had been dubbed the mushroom ball.

"Call me a mushroom, do they? Why?"

She was surprised he did not know, reminded afresh that a great deal that was commonplace to her, due to her schooling, was an utter mystery to her father. "For your suddenly risen fortune," she explained.

"Do they think a lifetime of hard work and canny decisions sudden?"

"Unfortunately, and unfairly, yes. Your fortune, father, is unrooted. We have no laudable family tree, no crest, no shield, no title—not a single ancestor to refer to in De Brett's peerage."

His face had reddened in his outrage. "You come from honest, sturdy, yeoman stock."

She gentled him with a hand on his arm. "I know. And not a single wastrel or scoundrel among them, unless, of course, Allan means to set a new standard with his wilder habits."

"No harm in Allan. He but cuts his teeth on life."

"As do I this evening," she claimed, unwilling to argue about Allan. "You must not be sorry, Father. You planned a beautiful evening, a perfect evening, a bit of magic."

"Magic gone awry," he muttered, forcing a rueful smile. "Care for another raspberry ice?"

She shook her head, stared blankly out of the window, and prayed for a miracle.

Beneath her, movement in the fog-bound street. A dark carriage pulled by dark horses halted at the curb. Two shadowy figures got out. The first, awaiting the second, seemed to sense her staring. He looked up, his face pale and troubled beneath a tall, dark hat. She felt foolish to be caught standing in the window, waiting for miracles. There was no doubt he saw her. He stared, as if he had never seen a woman standing in a window before. She made a move to go. He tipped his hat. In so doing, he stopped her retreat, for in the light from the carriage lamps his hair glinted like flame, a miracle of bright color in an otherwise gray landscape.

"Come, my dear." Her father took up her arm. "You must dance."

Chapter Two

"Are you sure this is the address?" Jack asked as Hugh emerged from the carriage. "There is not a vehicle to be seen on the street, and the house has a stillness about it that does not seem right."

Hugh laughed. "You wanted the mushroom ball. This is it. No one but fortune hunters who cannot afford carriages. The mushroom has money but no connections. You know the type. He thinks he can foist his frumpy, Friday-faced daughter on the first gentleman who gets wind of his wealth. No one of any great standing will present themselves at such a gathering."

Perfect company, given the circumstances, Jack thought. "A frump, is she? Not the porcelain doll at the window?"

"Doll? What doll?" Hugh craned to look up at the windows, but the woman was gone.

Jack shrugged. A brief glimpse of beauty framed in a window had nothing to do with his current dire straits. Mere woman could not lift his spirits. They dragged too low for that. It was a cello he craved in his arms at the moment, not a female. "How did this Avery Preston mushroom his money?" he asked.

"Salt," Hugh said uncertainly. "Or was it silk? Something with an *S*."

"*S*'s again," Jack muttered.

"What?" Hugh regarded him blankly, but there was no time to explain. The door was opened to them and they were ushered inside. Behind them, in the night, another carriage pulled to the curb. Laughing, the occupants got out.

The interior of the town house was quiet but for the sound of the orchestra—too quiet. Jack hesitated. Were they the only guests save the woman in the window? Perhaps this was more folly on a night of far too much of it.

"Come on, then." Hugh was not one to hesitate or lower his voice out of politeness. "Cello has to be this way. I hear the music." He chortled merrily. "Nothing to stop me from hearing it. I must say, this place is quiet as a tomb."

"Must you?" Jack murmured, uncomfortably eying a rank of footmen who stood, staring blankly into space, feigning deafness, ready to attend to carriages that did not come.

They proceeded to the dining room, took in the sight of tables piled with almost untouched food, and through a connecting doorway caught sight of a few people ranged awkwardly along the far wall of a ballroom in which no one cared to dance.

Voices stopped them in their tracks, lowered voices they were not meant to overhear. A gentleman's voice, coaxing. Hugh smiled wickedly, put a finger to his lips.

"Dance with the fellow, my dear. It is not right that you do not dance."

A young woman responded, her voice heavy with protest. "The man is a gazetted fortune hunter, without talent or prospects to recommend him except perhaps at losing money. I will not lower myself, dishonor you, or offer such a fool expectations by dancing with him."

Her companion's sensibilities were not so fine. "The question is, my dear, is he a titled fool? I would not be averse to your dancing with him has he that much to offer."

"I would," she said bluntly. "These men come to eat your food, drink your wine, and wheedle their way into my affections, and thus your fortune. How could I begin to feel respect and affection, much less passion, for such a knave?"

"None of them please you, then? I will admit the pickings are slim." The voices faded.

Hugh sniffed. "Bloody bad ton, that."

"Mmm," Jack grunted. He no longer knew what good ton was. Certainly they could lay claim to none in coming here.

He stepped into the ballroom, Hugh at his heels.

"Baldwin!" Hugh grumbled. "Might have guessed he would

be here. Finding a rich mushroom for a wife is all that's left to him, after all. Heaven help the unfortunate chit, whoever she may be. With his luck, he will run through her fortune as quickly as he divested himself of his own."

Jack flinched to hear such a cold assessment. Would Hugh say the same of him in six months' time? Baldwin, fellow gambler, fellow loser, was a mirror in which Jack saw his own future. Will Baldwin had lost a fortune at cards no more than five months ago. He had lost everything, including his friends, who had grown tired of spotting him loans that were never repaid. Was the only avenue open to such a man marriage to a monied mushroom's daughter?

The beautiful young woman from the window was staring at them as they crossed the echoing ocean of space that was meant to be swimming with dancers. She had a disconcertingly direct gaze. Wide-eyed and unblinking, she examined them. No simpering, shy, empty-headed miss, despite the doll-like beauty. She seemed, to the contrary, to challenge their presence, as if well aware that they had not been invited. Embarrassed, Jack focused intently on the musicians seated behind a screen in an alcove to her left, sawing away at a contra dance no one saw fit to dance to.

For the flicker of an instant, it occurred to Jack that what he did, in coming here, was both rude and uncalled for. He added, in his own way, insult to injury at this dismal failure of a coming-out ball. And yet, while the thought registered, enough guilt or emotion to stop his progress did not. He was numb to caring whether he hurt this, or any other, young woman. Completely numb. He had, this evening, gravely wounded those nearest and dearest to him. What did it matter if he risked the esteem of a perfect stranger when he had plunged his entire family into penury?

With little more than a dull twinge of remorse, he made his way to the musicians' corner and stepped behind the screen. Thank heavens, there was indeed a cello to be had.

The gentlemen Selina had glimpsed from the window entered the room as if sure of their welcome, as if, in truth, the ball had been arranged more for their entertainment than hers. Sleek, well dressed, and handsome, their aristocratic noses raised, in search of odors too faint for ordinary olfactory senses, she disliked them on sight.

As the focus of this dreadful ball, she expected the gentlemen to make themselves known to her. If not to her, then to her father, who owned the house through which they strode uninvited. The first gentleman rudely did neither. Of thinning hair, indifferent posture, and biscuit-colored attire, having eyed the assembled company through his quizzing glass with a bored look, he appropriated a chair, sat himself down, and proceeded to take snuff. The second gentleman paused as well, his gaze passing in a cursory, almost a dazed fashion over their meager gathering.

He was handsome, tall, and well proportioned, with thick, shining red hair falling over a high, pale forehead in rakish strands, penny-bright lines that led to guarded gray eyes, an unabashedly freckled nose, and a mouth that hovered on the edge of a smile without breaking into one. As an attractive woman, Selina was used to men, handsome or otherwise, regarding her with interest, with smiles, even with open leers. This gentleman was different. Dispassionately, obliquely, he examined her, as if only a small part of his mind cared to recognize her at all.

He walked past her without batting an eyelid, a humiliating snub, his goal the screen behind which the musicians were housed.

"Who in Heaven's name is that?" she demanded of Arabella as the violins squealed to a halt.

"A Ramsay!" Arabella was completely flustered. "One of the notorious Ramsay brothers! Dear God, Selina! What can have possessed him to come here? Did you invite him?"

"You have yet to tell me who he is."

" 'Rakehell.' "

" 'Rakehell'?"

"Yes. I believe he is the one. There are five Ramsays, all of them redheads, all referred to by scandalous nicknames." Arabella's eyes glowed with excitement. "A wild and wicked set, from all I have heard."

"And this one? In what way is he wild? Does he go uninvited to a great many balls only to stop the musicians from playing?"

"No. It is an honor, in a way. He plays, you see, with extraordinary talent. The cello, I believe. It is an odd instrument to favor, I am sure you will agree, but favor it he does. And when he plays, rather like the Pied Piper of Hamlin, he draws enormous crowds."

"Crowds?" Selina laughed outright, the sound of her amusement echoing. "Perhaps he has the wrong address." Yet even as she said so, a party of young men with whom she was not familiar made their laughing way into the ballroom.

The sound of violins warming to a new tune drowned them out. Repetitive, like dancers engaged in the same pattern of steps, the sound echoed from behind the screen. Eight times the same notes measured tone and tempo before a slow, throaty, mournful voice overrode them, rising—anguish personified—a cello. More alive than the violins, stronger, sadder, more emotional. Purposeful yet languid, the wrenching exploration of the strings unexpectedly touched answering chords in Selina's heart. She closed her eyes against the unanticipated burn of tears, so overwhelming was her sense of melancholy.

"This is not Bach," Arabella whispered petulantly. "He usually plays Bach."

It mattered not to Selina what he usually did. It mattered only that the sound should keep filling her ears with an all-encompassing understanding of this evening's disappointment, humiliation, and loneliness. Drawn by the music, she crossed the room.

At the edge of the alcove, her perch a window seat, she fastened her attention on the bright, bent head of the mysterious gentleman known to her only as Rakehell Ramsay.

The notes melted into one another, pain poured upon pain. Emotion troubled this Rakehell's expression as he played. He winced and frowned and bit his lip. With each movement of his fingers the throaty voice sang on.

As if the cello were a much-loved woman that he allowed to weep on his shoulder, he cradled it between his knees. Eyes closed, russet lashes fanned against pale, freckled cheeks, brow furrowed, the better to listen to the sad song he provoked, he slid ginger-dusted fingers gently, with a lover's touch, along the slender black neck of his instrument while his bow rode the taut strings of her belly.

Gooseflesh, and the increasing tempo of her fan, stirred the hair at the nape of Selina's neck. Like the ices, she felt overheated.

Through the cello Jack wept. Tears never scalded his cheeks; they burned through vibrating strings, through the sawing motion of the bow, falling in deep, wailing notes from the open mouth of the cello. Whenever life disappointed him he made a point of pouring himself and his feelings into the instrument by way of the genius of Bach. Tonight he made an exception. Tonight he played a little-known work given him by Princess Esterhazy, who knew he was always on the lookout for pieces featuring the cello.

"Written by the piano instructor to Count Esterhazy's children," she had said in offering it up to him. "It is a sad little piece, but I think you will like it."

Sad and moving, Jack had decided in learning Herr Schubert's piece—so moving, so perfectly akin to his sensibilities, that he had carried it with him everywhere for the past few weeks in hopes of running across a chamber orchestra skillful enough to perform, on sight, the background of violin accompaniment.

Here, at the mushroom ball, he had found such a gathering of musicians. Unerringly the violins followed the repetitive score, while into the cello he poured his sorrow for the evening's fiasco, opening up his shuttered heart, his cloistered soul, his shattered psyche. He gave them all a musical airing.

Images, buried and forgotten, burned through his mind with sudden fierce clarity when he played. A sky so blue it hurt the eyes flashed by, seen through the window of a moving carriage. A countryside blanketed in blinding white snow. A sickening thud, a sudden tumbling sensation, and images of blue and white as he was airborne, limbs flailing, to the tune of a woman's scream and a wounded horse's shrill whinny. Then the winded shock of landing in the snow on his back, breath knocked out of him, the sky reeling dizzily overhead. His life had, in an instant, on an icy road, become the visual equivalent of the sad-voiced tune he heard nowhere so clearly as in the anguished cry of his bow on strings.

Chapter Three

Applause, too much of it, roused Selina from a breathless reverie so narrowly focused on Rakehell Ramsay and his music that she had not noticed that behind her, the room was filling with strangers—dozens of them—all come to hear not the Pied Piper of Hamlin but the Rakehell Cellist of the Mushroom Ball.

Ramsay lifted his bright head, opening his eyes in response to the enthusiastic flutter of gloved hands, and looked straight at her.

For an instant, a powerful connection bridged the distance that separated them. Sadness they shared, despair too, a wisp of anguish so tenuous she could not be sure she had seen it before Ramsay hid all feeling in the satirical arch of one coppery red brow and the quirk of lips that found the world, even its tragedies, amusing. He looked, for a moment, Panlike, a freckled woodsprite without a care in the world. So fleeting was the impression of emotion Selina might have questioned its ever having been there, had not the haunting memory of his music still echoed in her ears, still burned in her heart, left her aching with unnamed need.

"More!" came the shouts.

"Bravo."

"Play another!"

Two gentlemen took it upon themselves to remove the screen. Ramsay and the roomful of unexpected guests were unveiled to one another. The cries for more intensified.

The accolades could not be ignored. Ramsay smiled, a tight, lopsided, cheeky smile. With a self-deprecating gesture of his bow he stood, his free hand bracing the cello. The applause hushed only when, with a flourish of tails and a word to the other musicians, he sat and bent his head, bow poised on the strings.

He played, losing himself in the playing. His eyes closed and with their closing, the woodsprite slept. It was a sad gentleman in gray who bent his head reverently over his instrument, subdued but for the sliding sheen of bright hair that hid his expression. For the better part of an hour and a half, he held the ever-growing crowd rapt in the spell of music. With an unusual intensity Selina studied what was to be seen of his features. Whenever he turned his head the curtain of his hair revealed him: every expression, every line, every freckle.

His jaw was squarish; a dimple showed on rare occasion in his right cheek. The lower lip of his expressive mouth was fuller than the top. The russet dusting of his freckles faded to nothing in the hollow beneath each cheekbone. The gleaming burnt sienna fan of his lashes matched in color exactly the silken arch of each brow. She knew the beat of the faint blue vein that pulsed in his left temple and every satin-smooth shade of lively color that graced his hair by the time the gathering around them swelled to such a size that her guests' very closeness to one another made them restless.

He stopped and threw back the veil of hair, his woodsprite smile firmly fixed in place. Bow in hand, he waved his biscuit-clad companion to his side and said something that had both their heads nodding.

While the roomful of restless guests watched, Mr. Biscuit crossed the dance floor that he might speak to Arabella. Arabella listened intently, blushed, ducked her head, and said something that had both of them looking in Selina's direction. Biscuit recrossed the dance floor.

Bowing before her, he said, "Miss Selina Preston?"

She nodded, and in nodding felt a little dizzy. She had been waiting for something to happen, her expectations heightened by moving music and a few burning glances.

"Hugh Stuart at your service." He clicked his heels smartly together.

A Hugh Stuart was not what she had expected.

"Do you care to dance?" he asked. "Jack means to play a waltz that will soon have everyone on their feet."

Jack, she thought. His name is Jack. A devil-may-care rakehell named Jack who played the cello like a fallen angel.

"I should love to dance," she said, accepting Hugh's hand.

A spritely waltz, they began in front of the musicians, and with a quick, direct look into the eyes of a rakehell, Selina was sent whirling into the crowd, which stirred itself like leaves blowing in the wind.

The dance was exhilarating, despite its being conducted in the arms of the wrong man. Hugh's company was surprisingly pleasant. It was a setback to discover in passing the musicians, that a dark head now bent over the cello, not a penny-bright one. No trace of Rakehell Ramsay was to be seen.

"Has he gone? Your friend, Jack?"

"Wouldn't surprise me," Hugh agreed pleasantly. "The waltz was a decoy, don't you know."

"No. I did not know." Selina felt a stab of regret. She had anticipated an introduction to Jack Ramsay, had been sure they were meant to exchange more than mere glances. "There is a great sadness in him," she suggested, "to produce sounds of such heartfelt grief."

"Do you think so?" Hugh sounded surprised. "I have never noticed any great sadness in Jack. Would not hang about the fellow if he were mopish and melancholy, now, would I? But he and his family have good reason to mourn. Lost his parents as a lad, did our Jack. Witnessed their deaths, didn't he, now?"

"Did he?"

"Of course, he did. Money trouble as a result of it, too. Not to mention his brothers. Rue losing his leg in battle. Roger nasty with pox, and Rip likely drinking himself into an early grave. I would be a sad dog indeed, if my family were mired in such a muddle."

Enough was enough, Jack thought. He could not immerse himself any longer in the voice of the cello. It did not suit the mood of a ball—even a mushroom's ball. Neither did he.

Shouldering his way down a stairway thick with the smell of expensive perfume, crowded with satin- and superfine-clad guests, heavy with questions he had no idea how to answer, he plunged through the front doors into the fog-cloaked night, busy now with arriving guests, their mouths opening on more questions, the same questions.

"Have we missed your playing?"

"Is it true Lester Fletcher beat you at cards?"

"Were your losses as heavy as rumored?"

"Who is this mushroom, anyway? Have you met his daughter?"

"So sorry. Must dash," he fobbed them off.

Purposefully he made his way to the street, and yet on reaching the curb he hesitated. Which way to go? What to do? His life seemed directionless at the moment, devoid of purpose. He took a deep breath, more content with breathing in the damp smell of coal fires and steaming horseflesh than pomade and perfume.

His club was out of the question. The place would be abuzz with his losses. He had neither the strength nor the desire to explain, as he would doubtless be expected to explain, over and over again, just what had happened. He had no great desire to go home, either. Sleep was unthinkable. He was too staggered by what he had done to sleep.

Jack nodded to the tall, broad-shouldered footman who stood curbside, waiting to open carriage doors. The man stiffly returned the nod. "Shall I summon your coach, sir?"

"No, thank you. I mean to walk."

"Very good, sir." The man knew better than to press the issue or to ask questions. He returned his attention to the street. Another carriage approached.

"I say," a voice called from the doorway behind them. "Are you leaving?"

Jack pretended not to hear. He could not face more searching questions, searching looks. He turned right. One should take the right direction when everything else one did was wrong.

Footsteps slapped the pavement behind him. A little winded, the voice persisted. "I say, there, hold on."

He turned. A gentleman of affable expression, stoutish stature, and graying hair was doggedly following him. The fellow was a stranger, the face not at all familiar.

Jack headed off questions with a question. "Had enough of the mushroom ball, have you?"

"Mmm, well, not exactly. Merely wanted to get a breath of fresh air. I shall have to go back, but wanted to thank you for the privilege of hearing you play. Mind if I walk with you a bit?"

Without waiting for a reply, the man fell into step beside him. Jack cast a peeved look at the window in which he had earlier spied a bored beauty in amethyst silk. The window stared blankly back at him, empty of life but for shadows on the ceiling that spoke of a room now filled with dancers.

The man at his elbow sighed. "Tedious, these come-out balls."

"This one more tedious than most," Jack said dryly.

The gentleman coughed and then choked on the cough, reminding Jack of Lester Fletcher and his similarly troubled lungs. He pounded the stranger briskly between his shoulder blades until he caught his breath and held up a hand.

"Thank you," he gasped. "Doubly I thank you. The whole affair this evening would have proved unbearable had you not arrived to stir things up."

Jack eyed the doorways and windows of the houses they passed. Neat, orderly, prosperous looking. The opposite of his life. "Nothing more than a bit of rudeness, really."

"Rudeness? How so?" The man sounded genuinely interested.

"I was not invited, you see. I am no more acquainted with the mushroom than I am with you, sir. Do forgive me, for failing to introduce myself earlier." He thrust forth his right hand. "I am Jack. And you?"

The man grabbed his hand to pump it vigorously. "Preston," he said. "Avery Preston. The mushroom himself, at your service."

The mushroom? Jack stared at him blankly a moment before he burst out laughing. Preston began to chuckle as well.

Jack gave the man's hand a friendly squeeze and clapped him companionably on the shoulder. "Preston, is it? Thank God you've a sense of humor, sir. I do apologize. I had no idea to whom I spoke."

"Gathered that, young man. Apology accepted—but tell me, Jack, the rest of your name, that I might thank you for the bit of rudeness, as you call it, that has turned my daughter's come-out flop into the crush of the Season."

"My name, sir? Just call me an idiot, and I will not argue, a complete and utter fool and I will bear you no ill will. The name is Ramsay, sir. Jack Ramsay."

"Pleased to meet you, Jack Ramsay, and your way with a cello. Brought tears to my eyes, young man. I am fond of good music. Cannot play a note myself, but I am a good listener. Collect instruments, you see. Have every hope my daughter will one day master the playing of them."

"Has she talents in that direction, sir?"

"No. None at all. No aptitude, she tells me, though her mother was talented. I have hope for her yet. Well educated in every other regard. She is quick to learn most things, but no one in Cheshire can teach her a note. Can you recommend a tutor?"

"Perhaps she, too, is a good listener," Jack suggested.

"Aye. She is that. Good at most things, but I do long to hear music about the house. I am willing to pay handsomely to any-one mad enough to come all the way into the hinterlands of Cheshire. Don't suppose I could convince you to take the posi-tion?" He chortled. "I wager, with your talent, she'd be mak-ing music in no time."

It was the word *wager* that brought Jack's head up with a jerk. "I am sorry to say, sir, I cannot take you up on any wa-gers—sworn off all forms of gambling this very evening."

Odd, he had not known such was the case until the words burst from his lips, but he could feel the truth of it, deep within. He had to make an end of gambling before gambling made an end of him.

"Pity," Preston said. "But a pleasure to have made your acquaintance. If anyone else should come to mind, please notify me before the end of the Season."

Jack shook Avery Preston's hand. "I shall keep you in mind, sir," he said, though before the man's back was turned he had already forgotten his idle promise.

Down Berkeley toward Piccadilly Jack trudged, the voices of violins and a single sad cello in his head. His fingers tingled with the memory of vibrating strings. Deserted, Piccadilly was yet well lit, lined as it was with coaching inns and hostelries. The smell of horses, manure, and the ripe, wet, stink of the Thames was strong. One could hear the occasional bells from passing ships. Fog clung to the basement steps and mews, veiling the need for fresh paint and a good street sweeping.

He chose his route with care. Piccadilly was named after Piccadilly Hall, where Colonel Panton had once won such an enormous sum of money in a single night at cards that he gave up gambling entirely and invested his windfall in buying and developing land.

The developments included Albany Court, which Jack passed without a glance. London's more fashionable bachelors took rooms there. He had never been able to afford the place. The Museum of Natural History was the Colonel's work as well. There one might witness the unnatural history of a living skeleton, Siamese twins, and a two-headed nightingale. Great Windmill Street also figured into the Colonel's scheme. Across from the Haymarket dwelt London's less fashionable, Jack Ramsay among them.

The "street of adventure," as the Haymarket was dubbed, never really slept. Nighthouses, inns, taverns, oyster bars, and dancehalls abounded. For blocks one could smell the thick, fermented odor of spilled ale in trampled hay. Whoops of drunken laughter and roisterous merrymaking cut bluntly through the fog.

Barnes's, Croft's, the Nag's Head, the Cock, the Unicorn, the George—Jack had raised his glass in all of them at one time or another. But it was Shaver's Hall he was most familiar with—another of Colonel Panton's creations. Strange that a man who had given up gambling should build a gaming house.

The play at Shaver's was not what one might call upper cut. Jack felt the siren's call nonetheless. Without a single farthing left to wager, he longed to weigh a deck of cards in the palm of his hand, to hear the rattle of dice; he longed to feel the sweet rush of anticipation that never failed to possess him when bids were cast. The right hand of cards, the right pips on the dice, and life would come right again. It would settle on the table like a well-cast die, an orderly square of black and white, not this terrifying foggy grayness that threatened to engulf him.

At the corner of Coventry and Great Windmill, a lamplighter, perched on his narrow ladder, was wrestling with the cast-iron cover of the guttering streetlamp.

Jack paused, considering the idea of turning his back on his bed. There was a good chance someone he knew would be at Shaver's. He might cadge a handful of coins. A handful was all it took if luck turned in one's favor. Colonel Panton was evidence of that.

"Good evening, guv," the lamplighter called gruffly from his perch. Flickering light threw his begrimed face into garish relief, dancing in the red stripes of his oil-stained jacket and gleaming on the metal protruding from the canvas apron at his waist: the snout of an oilcan, the handles of a pair of scissors.

"Evening," Jack agreed. He could not bring himself to call it good.

From St. James's to the south and Golden Square to the north he heard, faintly, two voices of the watch calling, "One o'clock, and all is well."

They had it wrong. All was not well.

"Shed a bit o' light on things, I do," the lamplighter said, even as he cast the ill-lit corner into darkness by carefully lifting from its glass housing the wick bowl. "There's mischief about at this hour, when lights are out."

Eyes adjusting to the sudden dousing of the light, Jack blinked and said, "You must see a great deal of mischief in your line of work." He made the remark offhandedly, still caught on the horns of his dilemma. Could he win it all back again? As Panton had. As Lester Fletcher had. Dare he try?

The lamplighter was chuckling. In the dark, his scissors snipped at the wick, trimming it for a more even burn. Something in his laugh sounded familiar. Jack peered keenly at the man, but without light he was no more than an unkempt silhouette.

Jack yawned. Fatigue weighed heavy on his shoulders, dragged leaden at his bootheels. Absentmindedly he pulled his found penny from its pocket and flipped it. Crowns he would stop at Shaver's, castles it was home and to bed. The coin, cold and heavy, slapped familiarly against the back of his hand. Castles. To bed, he thought. Luck had completely slipped his grasp tonight. He would look for it in the morning. Thrusting the coin into his otherwise empty pocket he turned into the dark stillness of Great Windmill.

"Night," he said absently to the lamplighter.

The man, carefully refilling the oil reservoir, murmured, "Have a care."

The words held an unmistakable note of warning. They seemed to presage danger. Beset by an uneasy gut feeling he had relied on throughout the course of his life as a gambler, Jack shrank into the shadows that gathered around the steps of the house on the corner. Warily, he crept three steps down the yawning stairway that led from street level into what was probably servants' quarters.

The deep shadows around his doorway, halfway down the block, weren't right. He searched the darkness, ears straining for untoward sounds. Stealth rewarded, a flicker of movement caught his eye. Almost imperceptibly came the murmur of a voice. A second murmur answered the first.

Under his breath, he swore softly, his heart beating loudly enough he was sure it must give him away. Who lurked in the dark awaiting his arrival?

Clinging to the shadows, he backed along the face of the building and stealthily rounded the corner into a blinding pool of light—the streetlamp, freshly lit, no longer guttering. Jack closed his eyes against the glare.

"Good show, Jack. Spotted them, did you? Been there all evening, they have." A changed voice emerged incongruously from the mouth of the lamplighter—a familiar voice. Jack scrutinized the unfamiliar halo of black hair, the scruffy mustache and beard he was ready to swear he had never encountered before. The man's eyes, however, could not be disguised. They were an all too familiar shade of Wedgwood blue.

"Roger? Damn! Rog, is it really you? Gave me a bloody start. You look like trouble, you do. What dark business are you about, traipsing the streets in that ghastly peruke and stage whiskers? And why not bloody well tell me the constable's men are on my doorstep?"

"I did warn you," Roger said coolly, languidly, as if they spoke of nothing more important than the need for an umbrella.

"Warned me?"

"Have a care, I said. And you did. You proved to me you are not entirely stupid. I had feared otherwise."

"What?"

"Well, really, you have to be fairly stupid to have the constable's men after you. Are you sure that's who they are?" Roger peered around the corner from his perch on the lamppost. "I thought they might be moneylenders' thugs."

"Either way, they mean to clap me in irons and cart me off to debtor's prison."

"No more than you deserve if what I have heard is true." Roger climbed down from the lamp. Picking up his ladder, he headed back the way Jack had just come. "Lost all of it this time, haven't you? Every bloody penny. What are you going to say to Charles?"

Jack could not answer, would not answer. He deserved worse than debtor's prison, far worse. The idea of facing Charles made his stomach turn. For an instant his mind went blank as fresh snow.

He thought Roger meant to walk away from him without another word. That, too, was no more than he deserved.

But Roger turned. "Grab an end," he ordered. When Jack

merely stood there, gaping, he said it again, this time impatiently. "Grab an end. Come on. I've business to take care of."

The ladder! He meant the ladder. A shudder of unadulterated relief coursed down Jack's backbone. Feeling strangely dizzy, he picked up the end of the ladder and clung to the rungs. Perhaps, with Roger's help, he could find a way out of this mess.

"Ready," he said. "Where to?"

Chapter Four

Roger set the pace briskly. "I am on my way to a look-see . . ."

"A what?" Their footsteps, forced to fall in perfect tandem in the toting of the long, narrow ladder, echoed hollowly in the deserted street.

Roger ignored his question. "I am late." His haste and tone would seem to indicate he blamed Jack for his tardiness. "Things might get a little tricky. I had hoped you might watch my back?"

"That should be easy enough. Just lean me against a lamppost and I shall be happy to tell you to have a care."

Roger laughed brusquely. Shifting his hold on the ladder, he dug into his apron.

The ladder banged Jack's shin. "Ow! Watch it!"

"Pardon!" Roger stopped, put down his end of the ladder, and turned, holding out a pistol so diminutive in both barrel and grip it seemed more toy than weapon. "Know how to use one of these?"

Jack rubbed at his shin. "I say, what is this look-see that I should require a pistol? Are you engaged in something nefarious? If so, I'll have none of it."

"Take it, Jack. It is tap-action. You have the benefit of two shots. I should not like to be responsible for you getting yourself killed."

Jack dropped his hold on the ladder. It thunked on the pavement.

Roger frowned.

Jack backed away from the pistol. "Keep it, Rog. You're going to need it far more than I will. Call me a coward, but I mean to head in the opposite direction of anything that might get me killed."

Roger shrugged and tucked the pistol away. "I see I was mistaken in believing you enjoy a bit of a gamble now and again."

"I gamble with money, not lives."

"You deceive yourself. You risk a great many lives in losing Charles's inheritance."

No one could sound more chilling than Roger.

He made a shooing gesture. "Go on, then. By all means preserve your own skin. Think nothing of mine." With surprising strength for a gentleman troubled by ill health, he hefted the stepladder and started off alone.

Jack watched him go, feeling as worthless as a fly on a dung heap. How could he refuse Rog a hand? Rog, who was wasting away with the pox. Rog, who might not have long on this earth because of it. If anyone was meant to take a bullet this evening, surely it must be him, not his brother.

Roger was halfway down the block when Jack trotted up behind him and hoisted the tail end of the ladder. It yawed between them until he fell into step. "I shall never forgive you if I am hanged for this evening's work."

Roger shrugged and waved his free hand. "More likely you will be shot."

Jack sighed. "Hand over the bloody popper, then."

Roger delved into his pocket. Folding his arm into the small of his ill-clad back, he handed over the pistol without breaking stride, without so much as looking over his shoulder. He led the way south into St. Martin's Lane.

"Where do you take me?" Jack asked mildly, tucking the pistol into his jacket pocket, resigned now to whatever fate Roger led him to.

"Waterloo, Monsieur Bonaparte," Roger said.

Fog hung thickly around Waterloo, hiding it from them. Like otherwordly fumes it swirled along the Doric-columned elegance of the new bridge, clouds of Fate obscuring a glittering span across the River Styx. Their footsteps, their voices, trapped in the stuff, sounded muffled, their origin deceptive.

Hoofbeats approached. With a rattle of harness and the groan of heavily laden wheels on pavement, a wagon plunged out of the pale clouds, flashed past, was swallowed up in ghostly luminescence again.

Shoulders aching, Jack shifted the weight of the ladder. "How long do you mean to keep me in the dark about this business?"

Before him Roger, too, seemed mystical and otherworldly in his lamplighter's guise, his hair the wrong texture and color, his posture and clothing unfamiliar. "Some of the Admiralty's supply ships are docking in, short of goods."

"Goods?" Jack asked. Why should Roger concern himself?

"Hemp, cording, canvas, timber. You name it, it has gone missing, generally on nights when the moon is on the wane."

There were no moon, no stars, no world at all beyond two good strides. Their footsteps took on a hollow ring as they set out over the water. The air smelled dank and moist.

"Perfect night for mischief," Jack murmured warily.

"You would know," Roger said with a trace of his customary sarcasm.

Losing Charles's fortune. That was what he hinted at. Guilt punched at Jack's abdomen like a fist. His mouth went dry. Emptiness stretched grayly above and below, before and behind him; emptiness echoed grayly within. He tried to fill the emptiness with words, to find something normal in this completely abnormal night. "What do you want with these goods?"

"I don't." Roger hitched the ladder a little higher, his ground-eating stride testing the limitations of their befogged boundaries.

"Who does, besides the Navy?"

"That's the question."

A bell rang beneath them, unexpected and close. Jack tripped on an unevenness in the pavement. "You're not here to steal the goods, then?"

Roger stopped abruptly. Jack's arm jerked violently on the rung he clutched. Ladder scraping, Roger whirled to face him, a dirty lamplighter in worn clothing with the indignant bearing of a prince accused of treason. "You take me for a thief?"

"You do seek their company."

"I number doxies, beggars, thieves, and chronic gamblers among my acquaintances, but I'll have you know I am not given to fornication, begging, theft, or the losing of fortunes."

The remark stung. Jack responded in kind. "Doing it a bit brown, aren't you?"

"How so?"

"Not given to fornication? You would not have the pox were you not given to it."

"Right you are," Roger said softly, even emphatically, as if Jack had hit upon a point of profound truth. He gave no sign that he took offense. "Abstinence is the very best way to avoid such embarrassments. Just as avoiding the gaming table would seem the best way to avoid losing an inheritance."

Jack sighed. "Too late to hobble the horse that's already bolted. You were better served in telling me what it is you expect me to do rather than what you do not care for, that I have already done."

"Quite right. Call truce," Roger agreed languidly. "What I require is that you should wait for me, pistol at the ready, as I investigate the wharves between Waterloo and Blackfriars. There is a good chance that the supply ships are putting in to offload a bit of their booty at a fat profit."

"They will not take kindly to being observed in the act, if you are right."

"No. Don't suppose they would. You are prepared to fire?"

"Not much good to you otherwise."

They had reached the end of the bridge. The wharves stretched to their left, water lapping against piers, wooden hulls bumping gently. The breeze stank of fish, lye, and rendered hides.

Roger's wary gaze probed the eddying fog. "An hour. Wait no longer. I mean to head this way at a good clip if I run into trouble. If not, be so good as to meet me at the Turk's Head in the Strand. If I do not show myself there, assume I have either been taken or killed and inform Collingwood."

"Admiral Collingwood?"

"Uhm-hmm."

Jack was dismayed. It had never occurred to him that Roger was working on behalf of the Navy in this matter. While his own efforts had been futilely fixed on cards and dice, his brother had grown up, had become more than he had ever anticipated, a worthy individual he no longer knew as he had known the rampaging, risk-taking boy of his childhood. To discover that one's sibling was a mystery of magnitude and worth, only moments before he stepped into the night, perhaps to die, was enormously disturbing.

In the distance, he heard muffled voices. The wharf shuddered beneath their feet, a ship misgauging docking distance in the fog.

The two exchanged a look.

"Right. I'm off."

Roger would have left him then had Jack not caught him by the sleeve. "For God's sake, don't get yourself killed." Their gazes met briefly, fell away. "I should hate to have to explain to Charles how I lost you the same night I lost all else."

"Mmmm," Roger chuckled. "It would almost be worth dying to place you in such a predicament." Without another word, he hefted the ladder and faded into the night, his footsteps so quiet, there was a ghostly quality to his leave-taking.

Jack paced the fog-fettered darkness, listening, every nerve stretched like the strings on a cello. Too tightly, fingers cramping, he clenched the pistol.

He had just made up his mind to follow Roger rather than stand a moment longer, when a muffled shout met his straining ears, then the high piping of a sailor's whistle, followed by a splash, the crack of a pistol, and more shouting. He ran toward the noise, the coppery taste of fear souring his mouth, his heart beating so fiercely he thought the world must hear.

An ominous silence brought him skidding to a halt.

Closer now, a clatter, a crash, the sound of someone cursing, footsteps pounding on the dock. From the fog Roger burst, wig flapping. Hard on his heels, scrambling to retain his footing on the slick planking, came a burly fellow swinging a cudgel.

"Shoot him!" Roger shouted.

Jack raised the pistol, hand shaking, his fingers stiff. An unsteady shot might down Roger instead of the man who followed him.

"Shoot, damn you!"

The cudgel caught Roger a brutal blow on the shoulder, driving him to his knees.

Jack squeezed the trigger. A deafening roar, a whiff of cordite. Smoke stung his eyes. The cudgel-wielding gentleman dropped his weapon with an oath to clutch a bloodied sleeve.

"Go!" Roger barked grimly. "He's not alone." Wig askew, face contorted with pain, he scrambled to his feet and ran for the bridge.

The man with the ruined sleeve scuttled, like a crab, out of firing range.

"Come on!"

Jack followed Roger's disembodied voice. At the end of the fog-bound bridge he hesitated, gun at the ready. Footsteps approached. One set clear. Farther away, muffled, what sounded like dozens more. A shadow loomed. Jack lifted the pistol. One shot left. He took careful aim.

To his surprise, an officer, unmistakable in navy jacket and white breeches, appeared, a heavy pistol brandished in each hand. It never crossed Jack's mind to shoot. Not so the officer. A puff of smoke and a roar from one of the pistols. Something struck Jack's leg. Instinctively, he fired. Glanced down. Blood soaked his pant leg. Looked up again. Pain seared his thigh, but that pain was as nothing compared to the pain of recognition that struck him, heart and gut, as his assailant sank abruptly to his knees with a shocked expression, a blooming crimson stain flowering the chalk-white lapel of his uniform.

"Jack. That you?"

"Dear God! Nicki!"

"Damn!" Nicholas Caldwell swayed, blinking in disbelief at his blood-drenched lapel. "Improved your aim," he murmured weakly as he pitched face-first into the street.

* * *

Roger emerged from the fog, urgency in both voice and gesture. "Damn it all! Come on!"

Jack could not move. Nicki's still form held him spellbound. He wanted him to stir, willed him to. "I have shot him!" The words were no more than a whisper.

Roger grabbed him viciously by his neckcloth and yanked him, limping, onto the bridge. "Yes. I can see you have. This way. Now! Or we shall be next."

"No!" Jack struggled to go back. "Good God! It's Nicki. I cannot just leave him."

Roger seemed ready to choke him rather than loose his hold. Like a yoked oxen, he led Jack deeper onto the bridge. "Hisst! They're coming!" He released his hold, and put finger to lips. In his frizzy, off-center wig, he had the look of a madman.

Behind them came the noise of what sounded like half a dozen men arriving on the scene. Jack felt as if he were caught in a dream, a nightmare. Voices floated, ghostly, from the fog.

"The lieutenant. 'E's been shot, sir."

"Can he tell us who shot him?"

Jack's left hand rose to his mouth. The gun jittered in his right.

"No, sir," came the blessed response.

Relief flooded Jack. Too soon.

"He's dead, sir," the voice went on, shattering Jack's sense of relief, loosening his hold on the instrument of death.

"Shit!" Roger hissed, lunging to miraculously catch, one-handed, the falling gun, before it struck the pavement.

"After the fellow, then," one of the voices bellowed. "He cannot have gotten far."

"Quiet, sir!"

"What?"

"A noise, sir. I heard a noise."

Quiet fell, a dangerous, waiting quiet.

Roger and Jack stood frozen in the blessed blanket of the fog. A rat appeared, paused to sniff the blood that dripped from Jack's leg, scurried past. Water dripped from the bridge.

Water, a subtler sound, the steady pulse of the river, surged against the bridge's piers.

Jack's leg burned. His eyes burned. Deep in his chest, it felt as if a great weight had settled, crushing his heart. Nicki dead? And by his hand? The truth of it was too big, too awful, too painful to comprehend. He wanted to scream, to shout, to wake himself up, but even the pounding of his heart was too loud in the expectant stillness. With each thundering pulse of it in his ears, he was reminded that he lived, that he wanted to live, that Nicki did not.

Oars splashed downriver, creaking in oarlocks. Voices murmured upstream. In the distance a bell rang.

At last, a voice. "There! That way, sir."

Jack and Roger eyed one another uneasily. Had they given themselves away?

"Go, then. You three. After him. Syms, Neery, take up the lieutenant's body."

They waited, achingly silent, expecting discovery at any moment. But the footsteps headed away, not toward them. They were left with the sound of the two men given the task of carrying Nicki's body. A bumping, groaning sound.

"Mind his head," one said.

"Mind my back. He's heavy."

"Damn it. Mind his head. Can't just drag it in the street."

"He's past caring."

Jack closed his eyes, bit shamefully on his tongue, and allowed a tear to course, unheeded, down his cheek. He and Roger waited, unspeaking, until there was no sound at all but their breathing and the bounce and lap of the water beneath them. With a jerk of his head, Roger indicated his intent to move again. Without a word, their steps guarded, they crept across the bridge. It seemed to stretch forever. Only when they reached the north bank of the Thames was their mutual pact of silence broken by the noise Jack made in leaning over the edge of the bridge to retch.

"Sorry about Nicki, Jack. I—" Roger meant to soothe.

Jack whirled, furious, the bitter taste of regret fouling his mouth. "Sorry? Good God, Rog! I could wring your neck. Did you know that Nicki was involved? Did you arm me, knowing that there was the slightest possibility I might shoot him? How could you?"

Roger kept his voice low, his right arm wrapped around the left, as if to warm himself. He looked utterly harmless in his lamplighter's disguise. His posture was slope-shouldered, almost meek. "I knew there were officers involved, Jack, but had no idea Nicki was one of them. Must believe me."

"Believe you? Why should I believe the master of deception?" Jack spat the words. "You told me nothing going in. I had no idea there was a possibility I . . . Good God, Roger! I have just killed a friend. Shot him point-blank. He *knew* me, knew *I* had killed him, even as he fell."

"He was a thief against the Crown."

As if that made it all right! Jack ran agitated fingers through his hair.

Standing so still, Roger, his voice even and quiet, seemed completely unmoved. "He shot first, did he not? Might just as well have killed you as creased you." He nodded at the blood-soaked hole in Jack's breeches.

Jack hit him—hit him hard—busted his knuckles in hitting him. He had to stop Roger spouting any more logic. There was no logic to the killing of a friend.

Roger fell back, folding up like a useless hand of cards as he careened into one of the grand pillars marking the end of the bridge. "Shit! Watch the arm," he croaked from the ground, his face pasty.

Jack flexed stinging benumbed fingers and asked sarcastically, "What's wrong? Have I bruised you?"

"Not bruised," Roger groaned, propping himself against the base of the column. "Dislocated my shoulder, the blow that fellow gave me back there."

"Good God!" Jack forgot his hand. "Only now you think to mention it?"

"You had not abused it until now."

"Hell! What's to be done about it? Do we wake a bone-setter?"

"Could. Might be better if you knocked it back into place."

"Me?" Jack backed up a step. "Hell, no! I have done quite enough damage this evening, thank you very much."

Even prostrate, Roger sounded cool, calm, collected. "It would be better for both of us if you did."

"Hell! Bloody damn hell! I won't."

"I beg you will. This is not the first time the shoulder has given me a bit of trouble. I can tell you how it is done."

Jack sighed and closed his eyes. "Will it hurt?" he asked tersely. He hoped the answer would be yes. In that moment he wanted Roger to suffer as he suffered.

"Did the last time. Devilishly so." Roger's reply was irritating in its nonchalance, as if he were all too accustomed to pain.

"All right." Jack's voice was gruff, petulant. He sounded as if he was a child again, as if he and Roger squabbled over spillikins. He had always been taller than Roger, stronger, but Roger was smarter, quicker, more handsome. There had been much to squabble about.

"Think I deserve it, don't you?" Roger tried to laugh. It was not a convincing sort of amusement.

Jack held his tongue. Roger knew him too well.

"Should I faint, take me to number sixty-seven Tweezer's Lane."

Jack was surprised. "The nunnery?"

"Yes. A woman name of Peg will see to it we get a bed."

"Of course she will," Jack said bitterly, angry with himself, angry with Roger, angry with Nicki for putting himself in harm's way. The anger was an ugly thing, and he was filled with it, possessed by it. Rage coursed through his veins like too much wine. "What am I to do?" He forced the words through clenched teeth.

"Kneel down. Take my hand."

He knelt, but even as he reached to take up the injured arm Roger snatched at his wrist. "Gently," he said softly, unexpected force behind the softness, unexpected strength in his grasp.

Their eyes met, Roger's bloodshot, glazed with pain, overshadowed by dark, flyaway strands of the wig. There was no anger in the Wedgwood blue, no hint of rage. There was only sadness, a great, compassionate, brotherly sadness, the strength of which robbed Jack of his anger.

What right had he to puff up like a game cock? He had destroyed lives this night—a score of them—and none of it Roger's fault.

"Lift my arm," Roger directed. "Parallel to my good arm. Like so." He stretched out his good arm, placed it solidly on Jack's shoulder, as if to offer courage. "Give it a nice, steady pull. You will hear it pop into place. I shall try not to faint, but no promises, mind."

Jack hated what he was about to do. He had spent the evening doling out pain in every sense of the word. To be asked now, begged even, to provoke more pain seemed a hell-begotten sort of justice.

"Time's wasting." Roger sagged, his voice fading.

Jack took a deep breath. Pulled.

Roger bit back a high, animal-like yelp.

It seemed an anguished eternity, but the shoulder ground into place.

With what breath he had left, Roger, ashen, murmured, "Splendid."

Jack caught him as he fell, this marvelously brave, mysterious brother of his. With the last remnants of the energy his former anger had generated, he lifted Roger in his arms, a fourteen-stone rag doll. Staggering under his burden, his leg still bleeding, he headed east, along the embankment, toward Tweezer's Lane.

Chapter Five

Blue and white, sky and snow, the world tumbled before Jack's eyes until, with a terrific thump, he landed flat on his back, the wind knocked out of him so that he thought he might never draw breath again. From his lungs at last came a whisper that should have been a shout, clawing its way, tearing at his throat, resounding in his head while nothing emerged from lips shaken by the cold sight of his mother, beside him in the snow, pale as porcelain, crisp curls clustered at brow and cheek. She lay utterly still, staring, unblinking, her right hand unfolding, ever so slowly, its grip on his coin.

"Mother?" he cried.

The corpse rose, leaned over him, curls bouncing.

"Sorry, love. Wake up. My turn at the bed! It's Peg, not your mother."

Jarred from the nightmare, heart pounding, Jack opened his eyes to the white of sheets, not snow, to a sleepy stranger, redolent with heavy perfume and the heavier musk of sex, who peered at him from green eyes, not blue. Peg. Roger's friend. The prostitute. Without seduction or embarrassment she slipped an elegant, low-cut evening gown from her shoulders. Green velvet slid to the floor, revealing the pale, pendulous moons of rosy-nippled breasts. He had called her mother.

"No," he agreed, feeling the perfect fool. "I don't suppose you could be."

The woman frowned. She stepped free from the fall of velvet, from the rustling stiffness of starched petticoats. Flinging the dress and undergarments onto a chair already pyramided with clothing, she wrapped her arms around bared shoulders, covering bared breasts. Anger colored her cheeks. "Do you mean to be insulting me?"

"Not at all." He sat up, his back to her, rubbed his eyes, thrust his legs from the warmth of the covers. The floor was cold. "She's dead, you see."

"Is she? Sorry, love." Lifting the covers behind him, she dove into the warmth he had just vacated with a contented sigh. "I'd no idea. Me own mum is pushing up daisies. I'd not be doing this line of work, else."

He reached for his shirt, pulled it over his head. "How was the opera?"

"Told you where I was, did they?" He heard her yawn. "It was lovely. My escort, old dullard, fell asleep. Had to give him a prod whenever he started to snore." She sighed. "Gave me the prod back, he did, when the singing was over. I would far rather have given in to snoring myself at that point, but he was feeling quite rested, don't you know. Heard you were busy last night, yourself."

What had she heard?

"An extraordinary night," he agreed, wincing as he tested the leg in which he had received the flesh wound.

"I should love to hear you play sometime," she murmured. "Fond of music."

She was referring to the mushroom ball. It seemed part of a far-distant past. For a moment he dwelt on the memory of it, the only bright moment in an evening of great darkness. For a moment he thought of another woman, framed in a window above him. "What time is it?" he asked.

"Not quite noon." Drowsily she plumped pillows.

He stepped carefully into torn breeches and bloodstained boots.

"Waiting for you, he is. In the hallway. Asked me to wake you."

Throwing yesterday's crushed neckcloth around his neck, Jack did the best he could to retie it. "My thanks, Peg, for the use of your bed." He allowed himself to take his first good look at her in the mirror. She was a pretty, well-endowed, pudding-faced girl with glossy golden curls. Nothing like his mother.

She chuckled warmly. "Think nuffing of it, my dear. I'm rather in the habit of sharing my sheets. Would do anything for Roger. Pity about the pox." Her voice rose wistfully as her head sank to the pillow. "I would bed him for free were he not so open about the taint of it. Doesn't want anyone else to suffer as he does, he says. A true gentleman, your brother. The accountable kind."

A mysterious gentleman, Jack thought. The secretive sort.

Roger stood waiting in the mean, ill-lit hallway, looking very much the way Jack was accustomed to seeing him, apart from the sling about his arm. All traces of the ugly lamplighter were gone. In his place lounged a refined, clean-shaven gentleman, in Wedgwood-blue superfine and a nattily striped waistcoat, sleek auburn curls gathered in a queue at the base of his neck. Roger cultivated the rather romantic appearance of a beau from a former century, with a froth of old-fashioned lace at throat and wrists, and patches, two of them, provocatively near his mouth. The patches were a clever affectation.

"Disguises all evidence of my affliction, when it flares up," Roger had once explained with a devil-may-care wave of his hand.

Jack closed the door behind him.

"Roused you, did she, dear Peg?" his brother drawled suggestively.

Jack ignored the innuendo. "Yes. Kind of her."

"Peg is free with such kindnesses."

"She would far rather it had been you warmed her sheets, but then that has always been the case with the ladies, has it not?"

Roger shrugged. "Women no longer trouble me."

"Is it true, what she told me? You practice abstinence?"

Roger yawned and started down the stairs that led to the ground floor. "My condition can be rather off-putting."

"I daresay." Jack frowned. Roger was not in the habit of discussing details of his physical complaints. He always seemed annoyed when asked. "How do you do on that front?"

Roger shrugged. "Not to worry. I spend far more restful nights than I did in my youth. How about you? Sleep well?"

Jack had not slept well. Exhausted as he had been, the night's cumulative events were too incredible to allow for dreamless sleeping. He had tossed about for hours, staring at the ceiling, thinking of Nicholas, of Lester Fletcher, of the mushroom ball. He could not gripe to Roger, who rarely so much as mentioned his own deadly complaint. "I slept well enough, for a penniless murderer," he said dryly.

Roger's tone was vaguely sympathetic. "Shame about your friend."

Jack responded vehemently, the words uttered hoarsely. "I should never have gone with you."

"Forgive me if I disagree, but it would be me dead this morning and not Nicki, had you not." Roger clapped him on the back. "As a token of my appreciation, I sent a lad to get you these."

He pointed. At the bottom of the stairs stood two leather bags, Jack's own.

Jack bounded down the last few steps and bent to open the larger of the two. A mad tangle of his belongings had been jammed inside. "Brilliant! A change of clothes. Fresh neckcloths! I don't suppose my cello is hidden in here?"

Roger seemed in no mood to be amused. "No. It would not fit through the window."

"The window?"

"The lad could not go through the door."

"No?"

"Word is out as to last night's losses. Your front step is knee-deep in creditors."

"Oh. Of course. It would be. Do I owe this lad of yours as well?"

"No. He has already taken payment."

"You paid him? Good of you."

Roger adjusted the lace at his throat. "I gave him leave to take whatever silver he might chance to come across in your quarters."

Jack looked up from the cases. "You what?"

"Told him he was not likely to find much. That you had probably sold or pawned the majority of your valuables in order to cover past gambling debts. Was I in error?"

Jack felt like punching Roger smack in the middle of his even, white teeth. "No," he said wearily. "Did he find anything?"

Roger yawned, studied his nails. "Mentioned a card case, collar studs, a telescopic pencil case."

"He is satisfied?"

"Yes. Are you?"

Jack wrenched the neckcloth from his throat, plucked up a fresh one, and snapped both cases shut. "Completely. There are several changes of clothes here. Soap, brushes, a razor. All of the comforts of home. The lad was thorough."

"Told him to bring all that you might require for an extended absence. No good setting out on a long journey emptyhanded."

"Journey?" Jack blindly struggled with his neckcloth. "Are we going somewhere?"

Roger waved aside his hands to tug and prod at the neckcloth. "Not we. You."

"Me?"

Satisfied with the arrangement of the knot, Roger said calmly, his voice low, "You shot an officer of the Royal Navy last night in front of a witness, an action for which you may yet be held accountable if said witness is given opportunity to identify you."

"But you caught this witness in the act, stealing things. Will he not be up on charges?"

"Yes, and ready to do or say anything he can to have those charges reduced. We would not like to have you hanged for murder as a consequence of saving me, now, would we?"

Jack fingered the knot at his throat. "Preferably not," he agreed.

Chapter Six

Selina began to think herself obsessed with Jack Ramsay. She had no desire to be obsessed, certainly not with a gambler, a desperate man with little more to recommend him than a way with music. He was, after all, completely responsible for the week of social hell that followed her ball. Callers came in droves, the well-bred strangers who had crowded into her father's house for no other reason than to hear Jack Ramsay play cello. Like a flock of scavenging rooks they had descended on the ball, picking platters and bowls clean, dancing until dawn, some of them falling beneath the tables with the consumption of too much of the excellent wine they had poured in rivers down their throats.

As harsh-voiced crows, they returned in the days that followed, bright-eyed and inquisitive, calling cards in hand, hungry this time for gossip, not food. Complete strangers claimed to be unable to live with their own rudeness in having taken advantage of her ball, in having arrived uninvited. Nor could they leave her in peace until they had discussed all there was to be said about Rakehell Ramsay.

"Lost everything to Lester Fletcher." More than one guest made a point of whispering the shocking truth. "The self-same night he played the cello at your gathering."

She made her callers comfortable, offered them coffee or tea.

"He has gambled for years."

"His mother died when he was no more than a lad."

"Carriage overturned in a snowstorm."

She nodded thoughtfully. Arabella, who, often as not, was in her company, could be counted upon to cluck sympathetically.

"His father drank himself into an early grave, pining."

Selina felt a strange combination of pity, contempt, and fascination for Rakehell Ramsay.

"Charles, the eldest, has gone to China to revive the family's flagging fortunes. Due back any day, he is. Rash Ramsay, people about town have begun to call him, a consequence of his having been so foolish as to leave his finances in the Rakehell's hands."

"Rupert, the youngest, lost a leg at Waterloo."

"Roger, God bless him, is dying of the pox."

"Aurora—she is the only girl—runs after life in a wild, unladylike fashion. Can you blame her, amongst such a rough crew?"

Selina's curiosity and empathy for all of the Ramsay family increased incrementally with each fresh tidbit.

"Only fancy the Rakehell coming to your ball for no more reason than to play the cello. He did so on a bet. Did you know?"

She did not know, knew nothing until it was poured into her waiting ears. Her ignorance was not to be believed genuine, however. How was Jack Ramsay's odd behavior in playing at her ball—of all the gatherings he might have indulged—to be accounted for otherwise?

"I have no idea," she responded politely to this rudeness. How was she to account for a man's madness when she had not so much as exchanged a word with him?

Her reticence was interpreted as obstinance. The callers did not linger. A relief, really. They were a tiresome lot, more interested in gossip and Jack Ramsay than in her or her family. They left their cards, encouraged her to call on them, said their adieus, and had no more than made it down the front steps before she was met by a fresh wave of callers, cards, and questions.

She should not have found anything to interest her in Jack Ramsay, much less to like about him. And yet, against all sense, she became a trifle consumed by the tidbits of information she gleaned as she was besieged by the curious. Like a puzzle, she tried to fit him together, to create a whole person out of odd bits. She longed, in fact, to know more. His music lingered in her memory, as did his face, haunting and sad. Expectancy beset her, nameless and troubling.

A note arrived from Jack Ramsay.

"My dear Miss Preston," it began. An immediate affront. She was not his dear and yet her fingers shook to be so addressed.

> *There is no sound reason you should accept profound apologies from a complete stranger for rudely intruding upon your come-out ball, uninvited and unannounced, but extend the olive branch I hereby do.*

She found him rather civilized for a Rakehell, strangely eloquent as well.

> *Will you understand that I found myself in dire need of a cello at the time and yours the closest available? I think not. Such an excuse seems completely nonsensical, even to me, to whom it made all the sense in the world at the time.*

Perversely, she did find sense in it. Who could not find some higher sense of order in such music as Jack Ramsay produced?

> *Can you find it in your heart to forgive an irredeemable rakehell bent on more mischief than is good for anyone whose path he crosses? I hope so. I trust chance will offer us the opportunity to further our acquaintance in a more mannerly fashion. It was a pleasure chatting briefly with your father. Give him my best.*
>
> > *Yours most humbly, Jack Ramsay.*

She was surprised by the note, surprised, too, to learn that her father had spoken to Ramsay. She longed to beg him to repeat every word exchanged, but satisfied herself with his, "Pleasant fellow. None too high in the instep. Told him how much I enjoyed his music."

To no one else did she mention the missive, not even to Arabella. It seemed a private exchange. That there should be something private between her and Rakehell Ramsay was oddly pleasing.

She cherished most the line in the note that referred to making her acquaintance in a more mannerly fashion. That they must eventually do so was, in her mind, a given. An invitation to some spot where she was likely to encounter the Rakehell was to that end required. She set about returning calls.

Arabella was invited to accompany her. Calls were conducted, as was expected, within the obligatory time frame and between the hours of two and four. Arabella seemed pleased to have been asked along. A new bonnet and fresh gloves were purchased just for the occasion.

It was a wasted expenditure, for few saw them. A great majority of the doors upon which they knocked remained, in every way that mattered, closed to them.

Lord and Lady Whosits and Mr. and Madame Whatsits were not at home to visitors, a score of high-nosed butlers informed them. Did they care to leave their cards?

They did not care to, but pretended they did, extracting silver card cases with practiced ease, politely turning down corners as was expected of them, and dropping the carefully printed squares onto countless silver salvers.

"I am very sorry, Arabella," Selina said with a sigh as they turned their backs on the eighth brass-knockered doorway from which they had been turned away.

"Sorry? Whatever for? Lady Reems was probably conducting calls herself."

"Along with Mrs. Benson, Lady Beemish, and the Misses Troy? I am not convinced. Can you not hear the sighs of relief that follow our every exit? More than once I have seen, from the corner of my eye, the curtains twitch as our leave-taking is furtively observed."

"Undoubtedly the servants."

"Undoubtedly," Selina said with a level of sarcasm that flew right over Arabella's head. Linking arms with her, she led the way out of North Audley and into Oxford Street.

"This is not the way to the Herveys'," Arabella observed.

"No." Selina paused on the busy street to look in the window of a shop that sold lamps, chandeliers, and the modern gas fittings. The gleaming array of lights blurred for a moment as she straightened her hat, smoothed her hair, and fought to regain her composure. It did not matter that no one saw them. She did not want a husband, after all, and that was the reason for the ball that had spurred the stupid calls that had to be returned to people she did not really know well enough to care about. She knew she did not care for the temple curls her hairdresser claimed perfectly framed her face. They made her look frivolous. She was not frivolous. She did not enjoy being treated as if she were. She would not give in to this entirely unwanted and completely unexpected welling of tears.

"I would much rather do a bit of shopping than endure another . . ." Snub, she was going to say, but the word stuck in her throat.

In her reflected view of the street, among the passing drays and carts, phaetons, curricles, and gigs, a lone horseman approached, the slope of his shoulders, the tilt of his head familiar. He wore a hat. What she could see of his hair looked red.

Rakehell Ramsay!

Heart racing unreasonably, she whirled to be sure, her sudden movement drawing his attention. His gaze found hers, registering recognition, registering something else as well—something indefinable that had flashed between them before when their eyes had chanced to meet. He doffed the hat, his hair blazing a burnished copper in the sunshine. Reining his horse to a stop, he stepped down from the saddle, his boots as glossy as his hair.

"Miss Preston, you received my note?"

His voice was deeply resonant, as she had expected, his tone polite, but he addressed Arabella, whose jaw dropped unbecomingly.

"Note?" Arabella snapped out the word as if it pained her.

"I did," Selina said, gravely disappointed that Ramsay did not know her. She had little reason for such a strength of feeling. They had never been introduced, after all. Nonetheless, her chagrin was acute. "It was kind of you to write." She managed to sound polite.

His blue-gray gaze shifted in an expression temporarily confused. "*You* are . . ."

"The mushroom's daughter." She spoke smoothly, her smile brittle.

"Ah!" He met her words with the devil-may-care smile of a gentleman more inclined to play a cello than mourn the loss of his family's fortune. "It would seem you have yet to forgive me, Miss Preston." His very contrition was charming, if perhaps a little too well practiced.

She had no rejoinder.

"I do beg your pardon," he went on. "I am inclined to make a hash of everything of late. Perhaps you have heard?"

She wrapped her arm around Arabella, as if around an anchor, that she might not be swayed by charm. "May I introduce you, Mr. Ramsay, to the Honorable Arabella Mendip?"

Arabella blushed a painful red and bobbed a half curtsy.

"You are related to Baron Mendip?" He was all politeness, except, perhaps, for the occasional wavering of his attention as he spoke, his gaze flickering from Arabella's shyly downcast face to Selina's and back again.

Arabella nodded, her chin biting into her neck, her blush deepening. "My father," she whispered.

"A pleasure," he said, but got no further. A gentleman had stepped from the haberdashery across the street and was hailing him.

"Ramsay! I say there, Ramsay!" he shouted.

Ramsay glanced over his shoulder, frowned, and moved toward his horse. "Excuse me, ladies. I've pressing business elsewhere."

The gentleman waved, tried to cross against the traffic, and was very nearly run down by a chaise.

Ramsay swung with nimble speed into his saddle. "Please forgive my haste. On my way to visit an old friend. Mustn't delay."

Then he was gone, the horse gigged into a brisk trot, the hat dousing the flame of his hair, the moment over, but for the gentleman who defied death, dodging between the chaise and a heavily laden cart to shout after him, "Stop! Damn it, Ramsay. You owe me money!"

"The Rakehell!" Arabella said breathlessly. "Dear Lord, Selina! We have been acknowledged upon the street—busy Oxford Street, at that—by none other than Rakehell Ramsay!"

"Do we make ourselves notorious?"

"I suppose we do." Arabella sounded rather thrilled by the notion.

"As notorious as a gentleman who is chased down the street by angry tradesmen?"

Arabella was watching Ramsay's escape, eyes shining. "Reputations are either made or ruined by such a thing. Do you think our own have been scarred by the encounter or enhanced? I cannot decide. He had cases tied to his saddle. Did you see?"

"Leaving town, no doubt, to escape his debts." Selina knew she sounded prudish, but she was in need of a moment's prudery. Her cheeks felt hot. Her back and neck were stiff. Her head was far too full of the memory of coppery highlights in sun-touched hair and the indefinable intensity of a pair of incomparable gray eyes. She did not want to remember Rakehell Ramsay so favorably. She did not want to be bewitched, as Arabella was, by the romantic danger of a gambler who had nothing to his name but a reputation—and an unsavory one at that. He had not recognized her! Had not known who she was at all! The ignominy of it hurt, even angered her, far more than she might have expected. The bruise of it could not be salved, not even by the fact that he openly acknowledged her in the street on a day when no one else seemed inclined to do so.

Both of the gentlemen who had made sport of the mushroom ball meant to make peace with the mushroom's daughter. Hugh Stuart came to call that very afternoon.

Arabella was preparing to leave when he was announced. She removed her hat immediately and professed stoutly she should not, could not, would not leave her dear friend Selina to face the rude Mr. Stuart alone.

Contrary to expectation, Mr. Stuart proved not at all rude. He was, in fact, affable, even edifying.

"Seems to have disappeared off the face of the earth, does our Jack," was how the most interesting bit of their conversation began. "No one has seen hide nor hair of him for the better part of a week. Thing of it is, I owe Jack a bit of blunt. A bet he won off me. As it would seem his pockets are to let, I cannot help but feel he may be in dire need of the five hundred pounds."

"Five hundred pounds?" Selina was astounded. How could anyone foolishly risk such sums on nothing more than a bet?

"A great deal of money," Arabella said solemnly.

Hugh shifted uneasily in his chair. "Don't suppose he has come to call?"

"No," Selina said. "Nor do I think it likely he will."

"We have just seen him in Oxford Street, on his way out of town," Arabella hastened to explain.

"He told you he meant to leave town?"

Selina shook her head. "Not precisely. He mentioned visiting a friend."

"There were cases strapped to his horse," Arabella said helpfully.

He responded with gratifying interest. "Cases? Perhaps he is rusticating. A shame, really. I have news for him. Two deaths of which he would surely wish to be informed."

"Deaths?"

"How dreadful!" Arabella was shocked.

"Yes. I do beg pardon for mentioning the matter. No nice way to put such a thing, after all."

"I am so sorry for your losses, Mr. Stuart." Selina was moved enough to stretch out a hand to him. "Were these dear friends, or relatives?"

"Selina!" Arabella, stricken, shook her head in alarm. It was not, after all, polite or proper to have introduced such a subject, much less to encourage it.

Hugh Stuart took no notice. He seemed quite happy to divulge the whole. "A mutual friend, a Lieutenant Caldwell, has been shot. Jack would want to know."

"Of course he would," Selina agreed.

"Dear, dear!" Arabella fanned herself nervously.

Selina dared not turn her gaze in Arabella's direction. She was sure to receive a censorious frown for asking, "How did such a dreadful event occur?"

Hugh blinked rather rapidly, his eyes bright with the desire to divulge what he knew of the tale. "Word has it he was shot trying to stop a thief from stealing supplies from one of His Majesty's own ships. Brave fellow!"

"Brave indeed," Selina agreed. "I am sorry. Had I known this afternoon I would most assuredly have advised Mr. Ramsay to consult you for details."

"Yes. But perhaps it is best, after all, that he has fled London until this whole Fletcher business is settled."

"Fletcher." Selina could not pretend herself unfamiliar with the name. "Is he not the gentleman who beat Mr. Ramsay at cards?"

"Was," Hugh said emphatically.

"Was?" she and Arabella parroted.

"Yes. Popped off as well, poor devil."

"The second death of which you wanted to inform Mr. Ramsay?" Selina said.

"Precisely! And just as Jack said. No time to enjoy his winnings at all. Truly proved to be Jack's ill luck, if you ask me."

"How so?"

"Had Fletcher seen fit to cock up his toes a week or so sooner, Jack would never have lost the family fortune to him."

Selina was in no mood to be charitable toward Jack Ramsay, who had attended her ball, sent her a note, and accosted her in the street without so much as knowing who she was. "Would he not have been just as likely to lose it to someone else?" she asked. "I have observed that committed gamblers keep on gambling no matter how much they lose in the process."

"Obsessed with gambling, you mean?"

"Yes. Your friend, Mr. Ramsay—is he as obsessed with gambling as he can be about the playing of a cello?"

Hugh shrugged, apparently baffled by the question. "He is fond of games of chance, but so are scores of my acquaintances. Do not ask me to judge. I delight in the tables myself."

Chapter Seven

In the entrance to Robert Galdough's modest Elizabethan home, Jack stood quietly, methodically tossing his Welsh penny in one hand, hat and gloves held in the other as he listened to the wailing of a baby. A newborn, from the strength and pitch of it. Women's voices, crooning, sought to soothe the cries. In direct contrast to their gentle ministration, another female voice, ear-piercingly shrill, cried out, "Good God! You refine too much on the matter. If you will not take Nanny's advice, come up with a viable alternative to gin tits. You must do something to shut up this infernal noise or I shall go right out of my mind."

The wails escalated. A door slammed. Footsteps pounded along the corridor above. The crooning intensified. Jack pocketed the coin.

"Terribly sorry, sir." The maid who had opened the door to him trotted down the stairs. "Did not mean to leave you holding your hat, sir, but as you can hear—"

"The baby," he said. "Have I arrived inopportunely? Perhaps it would be better if I—"

"No, sir. Colic, sir. Poor mite's always wailing. Cannot say it would be any better were you to come back later. Master Galdough will be right down, sir, if you care to wait. His face lit up, sir, when I handed him your card. If you will just step in here, it will prove a little more peaceful."

"In here" proved to be a sitting room, comfortably, if not very tastefully, furnished with chairs and a sofa in the new stripework that was all the rage. There were also a needlework frame and a pianoforte.

"I'll just be going back upstairs now to see if I can help."

The door closed behind the maid, muting but not eliminating the piercing noise of the baby's cry.

Jack paced the room, stared out of the window, and sat on the bench before the pianoforte. Rob would appear to have done well for himself—new house, new wife, new baby, new pianoforte. Jack splayed his hands across the dark keys, his gaze rising to the ceiling. Would music soothe or serve to exacerbate the unhappiness upstairs?

He withdrew his hands from the instrument. His sister, Aurora, had been troubled by colic. He remembered the disturbance of her cries. He remembered, too, that his mother had, at times, soothed her not with gin tits and shouting matches, but with a hushed, darkened room and lullabies. Closing his eyes, he leaned his head back and began, ever so softly, to play.

Quiet and soothing came the notes, familiar as nursery rhymes, soft as swan's down, the ghostly echo of his own childhood. The first song he had learned to play had been this lullaby, his hands riding the backs of his mother's as she played the phrases over and over until he knew them by heart.

"You have a knack for it," she had said.

Her words had filled him with pride.

Above him, as the music swelled, the baby's cries softened, slowed to hiccups, stilled entirely. He smiled. Perhaps, after all, he had, this day, accomplished one worthwhile objective.

Footsteps sounded on the stairs. The door to the sitting room swung open as the final notes of the piece trailed away. Rob swept into the room, brash and brave, his hair grayer than Jack remembered, his face a trifle haggard from exhaustion, his voice low that the baby might not be roused.

"Good God, Jackie boy! Is it really you!"

Arms wide, they engaged in a shoulder-squeezing, back-pounding embrace. Rob's eyes had a damp look about them when he held Jack at arm's length. "Bless you for the music." He crossed to a sideboard, where he poured them each a finger of brandy. "Worked a charm on the wee one. Have you come, then, to lull him to sleep every time he wails? If so, you have got your work cut out for you." He laughed softly at the idea.

"As a matter of fact, I am hoping you would not mind putting me up for a night or two."

"Stay with us?" Rob's expression betrayed, for an instant, dismay. "You've no intention of actually sleeping then, have you? The house is always in an uproar." He downed the brandy, poured himself another. "Of course you're welcome. Stay as long as you like."

The lack of true conviction in his tone hurt.

"Never mind," Jack said awkwardly. "I can see that the last thing you need is someone intruding on your privacy with a new baby at hand. Did not mean to bother you."

"No, not at all." Rob tossed back half his second glass of brandy in a single swallow. "Do stay."

"I had thought I might look up Val."

"Val?" Rob's face went pale. The haggard pinch of his lips forbode dire news. "You have not heard?"

"Heard what?"

"Val shot himself."

"Dear God. He didn't."

"Wish I could tell you otherwise. Gone to Hell, he had. Lost nearly everything he owned. Living on tick. Debt so huge he knew not what to do. Hadn't a decent pair of shoes to his name, Jack. Drank to excess, which only made matters worse. I cannot tell you how many times I found him on my doorstep, reeking of rum, dirty as a street urchin."

"Dear God. I had no idea."

"Of course you hadn't. How could you? Christ, Jack, you turned your back on us when you went to London. How many letters have I sent you? I have lost count. How many were answered? I can tell you. Not one."

"I am not much of a scrivener. Besides, you only wrote to ask for money, Rob. I had none to spare."

"A miserable lot, are we not?" Rob stared morosely into the bottom of his snifter. "Too much to drink and the foolish conviction that fortune lies in the turn of the dice or the faces on a card. It came home to me in watching Val deteriorate. Oh, I cleaned him up each time he appeared, offered him loads of advice, and gave him enough pocket change to send him on his way. Merry as a cricket he could seem. 'A bit too much sauce,' he would say. 'Too drunk to find his way home,' he claimed. Never told me he no longer had a home to go to."

"His brother refused him entry?"

"Packed up and moved to Spain. Escape from Val's creditors. Never so much as came home for the funeral."

"So you set yourself straight and fell in love. You would seem the wisest of our lot, Rob."

Rob's face contorted. "You think me wise?" He fairly growled the words. "Did you not wonder that my wedding was such a quiet, family affair? Come. I will show you wisdom."

Thrusting through the door to what had to be his study, judging from the hunting prints on the wall and piles of sporting news on the desk, he pointed bitterly at a chair. "Have a seat. Gaze upon my wisdom."

The chair faced the desk. Behind the desk loomed a portrait that dominated the room, the painting of a sumptuously dressed woman whose coarse, unhappy, frog-eyed, mastiff-jowled features seemed all the more unfortunate, surrounded as they were by a setting of refined elegance.

"My wife." Rob leaned down to whisper the epithet in Jack's ear, as if the portrait might hear him and raise a howl. "No love match, my boy, but an arranged marriage."

"Do you not care for the woman at all?" Jack asked in disbelief. "You have fathered a child on her."

"I *value* her." Rob stressed the word. "Her father is a wealthy banker with presumptions of grandeur. He was enormously generous in his marriage settlements. Paid off all my debts, and they were considerable. Provides me with a quarterly sum. Enough to keep the house, the land, my horses. I am even allowed out, on occasion, on a tether, to go to the races. In return, I do my duty by her when lights are out and enough rum in me to forget how disgusting she is to me. She and her children have benefit of my name, connections, country house, and my apartments in London. I conduct any liaisons of pleasure discreetly on the side. She knows her place. I know mine. In short, Jackie, my boy, I stew in a broth of such misery that I long, on occasion, for Val's end in preference to my own."

"Bertie!" A thin, petulant cry came from somewhere above them.

"Christ!" Rob leapt from his chair, crossed the room, flung up the window, and sprang out into the shrubbery with such speed and dexterity that it appeared this was not the first time he had taken exit of his house in the same manner. "Quick!" he snapped. "This way, while there's still time."

"Berrr-tie!" The cry increased its querulous intensity, and with it this time came the renewed howl of the baby.

Jack made an exit in the same manner Rob had. "Bertie?" he whispered. "She calls you Bertie?"

"Refuses to call me anything else." Rob quietly slid the window shut behind them. " 'A verb does not a proper name make,' she tells me."

"Is she the real reason you hesitate to offer me your hospitality?"

Rob sighed, parted the shrubs, checked that their course was clear in both directions, and set off briskly toward the stables, brushing leaves from his jacket as he went. "You've nicked it, old man. Has me pinned, she does, quite firmly, you see, under her thumb. Rules the roost, as it were, along with the purse strings. Never marry, old man, certainly not for money. Speak to me of other wisdoms, if you will. Tell me how you get on? Have you seen Nicki of late? I think you have missed your mark, you see. He was the wisest of our little band of merry men—marrying the military."

Jack felt as if his chest had collapsed. His mouth seemed all too dry. He could not tell Rob the truth. Could not explain that Nicki had resorted to thievery. That he had shot him. That he was destitute, like Val. That he had lost his brother's inheritance, every penny.

"Nicki's dead, Robbie."

"No! You can't be serious." Rob's pace slowed. He looked old squinting against full sunlight. "How did it happen?"

Jack slid the penny from its pocket, tossed it into the air, caught it, tossed it again. "I wish I knew." He said it softly, the words heartfelt. Slap. The penny found his palm. "It just happened." Slap. "I had a strong desire to come see you as a result."

"Daresay you did."

Jack clenched the penny, stilling it.

"What has become of us, Jack?"

He rubbed the coin beneath his thumb. The image of crown and feathers was shiny with past rubbing. "You have become a husband, a father. Can't say just what it is I have become."

Rob turned impatiently, his arms spread wide, encompassing his estate. "We were a drunken, irresponsible, unaccountable crew of ruffians, Jack, with little concept of consequences and far more to lose than we ever appreciated. God help us in reaping the seeds of our folly."

Jack pocketed the coin. God help them indeed!

He put Rob and his recently delivered wife behind him. To Oxford he went that very afternoon, booking a room near his college, at an inn where he had often gambled as a student. Not that he wanted to gamble. He had put all of that behind him. He had no intention of ending life as Val had.

He went at once to his room to count out what Roger had given him. He had money enough to last a month. Then what? His lack of prospects was daunting, deepening the sense of melancholy that had possessed him since the night of the mushroom ball. He thought of that night in those terms—thought of the mushroom and his unexpectedly charming daughter, of the wonderful music he had coaxed from a cello—not in terms of lost fortunes and a lost friend.

He had told the mushroom that he had given up gambling, and in the moment he had said it he had believed his vow. It occurred to him that he was little suited for other pursuits.

Hungry, he went downstairs to look for a bite to eat. What he found was a game of Matrimony in progress, and with the clinking of coins and the slap of pasteboard on the game board an insidious, insatiable hunger to shuffle a deck and turn a card possessed him. It quite overrode the growling of his stomach. With a modicum of luck, after all, he reasoned, he might double his meager funds. One might win big with only a small bet in the game of Matrimony.

He tossed his penny to decide the matter.

He proved himself right. By midnight he had tripled his purse. But luck toyed with him as a cat toys with a mouse. Once begun he could not call halt to his indulgence. He went on playing the cards, throwing his coins haphazardly good after bad. Even when he began to lose, he convinced himself that with just a few more face cards he would win it all back again. By dawn, he had lost every copper in his possession, everything but the clothes upon his back and the horse Roger had given him.

Luck had turned against him. He knew it had. And yet he could not push himself away from the cards, away from the table, away from the promise of winning it all back again.

He played yet another round.

Another man rode away on the horse.

Chapter Eight

Sunlight streamed into the nave of Oxford's Cathedral Church of Christ the King, arch-shaped shafts of evenly spaced brilliance that turned honey-gold some of the walnut pews, and set dust motes whirling like tossed flecks of bullion. Selina stepped into the light. She felt for a moment as if God himself stretched fingers through the high windows to warm her face, to illuminate the exquisite pendant vaulting that arched above her head like a mass of lace carved from wood and lath. It was the lierne vaulting she had come to see. When she had been a child, her mother had described it in detail as a treasure worth viewing. That and the Becket stained glass.

Deeply she inhaled the candlewax-scented splendor. Head thrown back, arms spread wide, like a little girl she slowly pirouetted, bathing in the light, glorying in the magnificence of massive Norman columns rising to the airy marzipan confection of the ceiling. Dust motes floated past her fingertips. Her slippers whispered on the marble flooring, her skirts whispered around her legs.

"Beautiful!" The word, softly spoken, echoed, rising like a prayer toward the manmade cobweb of a ceiling, a reverent compliment she hoped might reach the ears of the fifteenth-century artisans who had crafted such a marvelous tribute to God.

She thought she was alone. She would never have abandoned herself so much to her thoughts and the beauty of the place had she known she was being watched. He sat so still in the shadows, head bowed. She did not see him, did not sense his presence at all until he raised his head and the light caught the copper of his hair.

"You!" she whispered, jerking to a halt.

"You," he said, so low she was not intended to hear.

Their voices, in unison, had unexpected strength.

She blushed. "I thought I was alone."

"Always in windows," he murmured.

"Windows? Did you come to see the Becket?" Her words were rushed, a trifle breathless. She had convinced herself she was never to encounter Rakehell Ramsay again.

He squinted against the light, held up his hand to shade troubled gray eyes, stared at her for a moment with a dazed look. "Becket, Miss Preston?"

He remembered her! Remembered her name! A small thing, really, but she was extremely pleased.

"Thomas à Becket," she said.

"The assassinated cardinal?"

"You mentioned windows."

His brow wrinkled in confusion. "Do you believe God answers prayers, Miss Preston?" His voice echoed in the stillness. His question, so far removed from Becket, and windows, surprised her.

"I do." She said it earnestly, for indeed she did believe prayers were answered. Perhaps her own had just received answer in Mr. Ramsay appearing here, of all places.

"I hope you are right," he said. "I begin to believe you may be."

His ambiguity troubled her. "You have had a prayer answered?"

"It would seem so, Miss Preston, as little as I may deserve my prayers be answered."

"You are an irredeemable sinner, then, sir?"

His coppery brows rocketed abruptly.

She smiled, her remark made in jest.

"Undeniably a sinner." He responded in all seriousness. "It is the irredeemable part I wrestle with."

She wondered at his meaning, stared into his eyes looking for answers as he rose from the pew and came out of the shadows to stand beside her in the block of brilliant sunlight. Stubble darkened his chin. There were lines about his shadowed eyes. Evidence of another line had begun to etch his forehead. He looked tired—no, world-weary—as if his eyes had met with too many dreadful sights ever to feign innocence or naïveté again.

And yet her heart floated, light as a dust mote, that he should stand so close to her, should regard her so intently. She forgot all mention of sins—all knowledge of those he had committed—could think only of the shine of him, the glinting lights in hair, lashes, and brow; the mischievous, Panlike gleam in his eyes; the soft, sensual sheen of his lower lip. He looked marvelous to her, absolutely breathtaking.

He held out his arm, as if he expected her to take it. "You mentioned windows? Will you show me?"

She nodded, afraid to smile, afraid almost to speak, definitely afraid to take his arm.

What did this man pray? she wondered. How had his prayers been answered? Breath catching in her throat, she entwined her arm ever so carefully with his, fearful of the closeness of him, the heat, the darkness. There was a darkness about him, despite the brilliance of his hair. He was a dangerous fellow. She had known it from the first moment she set eyes on him, had disliked him on sight because of it. He was too charming, too intriguing, the type to break hearts and empty pockets wherever he went, with no more than a smile or the notes from a cello. A woodsprite with red hair. She would not be so easily won, could not allow it. She would be wary of Jack Ramsay.

His angel of deliverance hesitated in taking his arm. Jack could not blame her. Fortune should hesitate in linking arms with misfortune. He had begun to think himself beset by misfortune, but what could be more fortunate than this encounter with the mushroom's daughter? It could not be sheer coincidence that he opened his eyes from the most profound and heartfelt prayer he had ever delivered up to God to find her cavorting in sunbeams. He had sworn to Heaven, upon his honor—for honor was all that was left to him—he would never gamble again, sworn he would do penance to those he had wronged, sworn to make amends in some manner for the shooting of Nicki. He had prayed for deliverance and deliverance stood before him.

She led him to the stained glass. He did not explain that he had begun to associate her with windows. Every time he had encountered her, thus far, she stood framed in the light of them.

This time, stained glass colored her pale complexion, kaleidoscope fashion, with the soft gemlike hues of sapphire, garnet, and smoky topaz.

"The windows were almost destroyed," she said, "because they depict the assassination of Thomas à Becket. Henry VIII ordered all such effigies smashed."

"How were they saved?" he asked, hoping he, too, might be saved, and by her hand.

"A very clever cleric removed his head."

"I thought that had been accomplished some two hundred years earlier." He actually felt like jesting in her company.

"His *glass* head," she replied with enough of a smile that he knew he had amused her. "He refilled the spots with plain glass."

Jack tried to imagine what the colorful window panels must have looked like with blank spots where Becket's head was depicted. "Who would have thought that by removing the head, the rest of the man might be saved," he murmured, feeling a strange kinship with Becket. Perhaps by giving his hands up to something other than cards and dice, he, too, might be saved. "Your father is here with you in Oxford?"

"Of course," she said.

"You leave London earlier than was planned. Mr. Preston told me you meant to remain until the end of the Season."

She seemed surprised he should care. "We received word that a broadloom and a silk winder had broken down."

"There is no one there to mend them?"

She frowned. "No, and while Father was quite willing to leave me in the care of Arabella Mendip's parents, I had no desire to remain."

"London did not treat you well?"

Very quietly she said, "It did not."

"The loom." He changed the subject. "Your father has gone to get replacement parts, perhaps?"

Her expression softened. "Nothing so mundane. We have stopped here that he might purchase a kit."

"A kit?"

"Yes. Father collects musical instruments. Old ones. Expensive ones. It is his only indulgence other than his children. One might almost call it his obsession. I am surprised he did not tell you."

"Oh, a kit!" He made a sawing motion at shoulder height. "A dancemaster's greatest friend."

"Yes. Italian. It is said to be sixteenth century. Carved ebony wood with ivory inlay."

"And yet he does not play."

"No. Do you find it odd?"

"Perhaps a little, but we are all of us obsessed with something—or someone—are we not?"

"Are we?" She bent on him a searching look.

He knew he certainly was. He had just been praying for deliverance from it.

"Is there nothing, Miss Preston, that draws you, though you know it is dangerous to be drawn?"

She dropped her gaze and blushed richly. "Perhaps there is, sir, but not to the point of obsession. I have little contact with that which is dangerous, and surely one must be regularly tempted to succumb to the desires that become obsession."

"Little contact," he repeated. "Perhaps avoidance would work to advantage in the curing of all obsessions."

"Do you seek a cure, then, sir?"

"I do."

She studied the vaulted ceiling, her eyes dreamy—bluer than he remembered. "You have come to the right place to find it."

He studied not the ceiling but the fine, symmetrical oval of her face. "I believe I have," he said softly. "I pray that I have."

Selina sat staring at him from the coach window, her pencil busy, recording the shape of his face, the fall of his hair, the molding of his mouth. The limber grace of his hand as he non-chalantly tossed a coin again and again into the air fascinated her. The rhythm of his movements was so even, the spinning wink of metal so regular, that, like a metronome, he mesmer-ized. Heads bent together as amiably as if they had known one another for years, Ramsay and her father discussed the merits of the newly acquired kit. She had told him she had little con-tact with that which was dangerous. Yet now she made a per-manent image of it. The danger was Rakehell Ramsay. He would soon part ways with them, she was sure of it, perhaps never to cross paths with them again. Yet she felt compelled, against her better judgment, to take a rendered memory of him away with her, a reminder that their strangely moving en-counter in Oxford's intimate cathedral had actually happened.

Was it obsession to dwell, if only in graphite, on the set of his shoulders, the line of his jaw, the way his hands moved when he spoke? Was it obsession to consider it unfair that her father should have more discourse with Ramsay than she did?

At last the conversation ended. The two shook hands. Un-willing to appear too interested, she took a long, last look, im-printing Ramsay as firmly in her mind as she had in her sketchbook. Leaning back from the window, she put the fin-ishing touches on her drawing. It pleased her. She had cap-tured him rather nicely. There was the sense that something was missing in the absence of color in his hair and eyes. Be-yond that, she could not judge her rendering too harshly.

The door opened. The coach rocked as bootheels rang on the iron step. A shock! Rakehell Ramsay's red head poked in, not her father's gray one.

In a flurry of pages, Selina hid her drawing.

Ramsay paused, his gaze on the sketchbook, then, briefly on the empty place beside her. Bounding into the coach with unex-pected energy, he took, instead, the seat underlings were gener-ally relegated to, his back to the horses. Coach swaying uneasily, they stared at one another. What they had done and said in the cathedral hung between them like an unfinished song.

She could not look away. Something was changed in him. She could not put her finger on it—perhaps it was no more than a trick of the light—but the lines in his face seemed softer, the worried look less pronounced. The woodsprite, bright and burning, peered at her from beneath the dark copper veil of his lashes.

She opened her mouth to say something, anything that might snap the overstretched string of tension between them, but he spoke first.

"Draw, do you?"

She nodded, clutching the book a little tighter, afraid he would ask to see what its pages contained.

His brows rose. The suggestion of an impish smile curled his lip.

Dangerous! God help her, he was dangerous.

"And I foolishly thought you kept staring my way because you found me handsome."

Her jaw dropped.

That he should make such a blatantly self-centered remark, that in so doing he revealed he had known all along she sat staring at him, struck her dumb. She had begun to like the man, to like him far more than was prudent or proper. Yet with no more than a dozen words he rendered himself both arrogant and annoying.

Her father's entrance could not have been better timed. "Ah, my dear. We are ready now." He settled himself beside her and leaned out of the window to shout, "Drive on."

The coach lurched into motion.

She looked away from Ramsay, refused to allow her gaze to be drawn back to him. How to address the man, after such a cocky overture. "He means to travel with us?" she asked her father, as if Ramsay were either deaf or invisible.

"He does," Ramsay murmured, far too pleased with himself, more Panlike than ever.

Her father sat back, equally self-satisfied. "I have convinced Mr. Ramsay to come with us, love. For your sake."

"My sake?" He could not have shocked her any more had he struck her. "Whatever do you mean?"

He wagged a finger at her. "Do not tell me you were not greatly touched by this fellow, Selina. I saw the way you watched him the night of the ball. There was a tear in your eye. No denials, now."

She blushed, staring at her father in disbelief. There were moments, like this one, when the machinations of his mind completely baffled her. She looked to Ramsay to make some sense of it. The woodsprite had a guarded expression.

"I touched you, Miss Preston?" The way he asked made it sound as if he had physically touched her.

She met his watchful gaze defiantly. How did one reply to such impudence?

"You made the cello cry."

"You are too kind." His gaze delved deeply into her eyes, revealing no hint of what he thought or felt.

"Prettily said, pet." Her father sounded well pleased. "But it is Mr. Ramsay who proves kind beyond words, in agreeing to accompany us all the way to Cheshire, with no more reason than to share with you his genius."

What he said made no sense to her. "His genius?"

"Your father is convinced I can teach you." Ramsay paused, brow arched, his eyes gleaming dangerously. "Fingering, stroking, or strumming, Miss Preston. Whichever you prefer, I am at your service."

She blinked at him in astonishment. Knew his tongue no bounds?

He was not yet done. Amusement brimmed richly in gray-blue eyes, the only element in his ruddy, freckled coloring with any sense of coolness.

"I mean to teach you to *play*, Miss Preston," he said, his subtle emphasis deliberately suggestive, designed to provoke a response.

"To play, sir? Was it wordplay you had in mind? Or some other game?"

For the first time since she had laid eyes on him, Rakehell Ramsay smiled, really smiled, his entire face engaged—lips curving upward, eyes sparkling with delight—the charming woodsprite in full force. He was very handsome in his amusement, far too handsome. She could see why he had charmed so many, so long. She steeled her lips that they might not smile back at him.

"I am to be your master," he drawled.

"My master?"

"Yes. Together, we are destined to make wonderful music."

"I would not bet on it, sir."

"No?" He studied her intently, seemed almost hungry for her reply.

"No. There is a hidden card in this hand you have been dealt. I haven't a musical bone in my body, sir. I do love to listen to it, but have neither the patience nor the passion required to learn its playing. Many have tried to teach me. All have failed."

"And would you declare me a failure before we have so much as begun, Miss Preston?" As with everything else he said, there seemed double meaning to his words. The subdued tone of his voice in asking, the intensity of his gaze, reminded her of the Ramsay she had engaged in private and revealing conversation in Oxford's cathedral. Here was the troubled young man who had bared some part of his heart and soul to her, the man beneath the Pan.

She was stumped for a reply. She could not tell Jack Ramsay to his face that indeed she thought he was a failure. There was too great a part of her that hoped him otherwise.

Chapter Nine

"**B**ombyx mori!" Avery Preston uttered the word as if it were an incantation. "He's our energetic little Far Eastern lad. What would we do without him? Gives us a single continuous thread when he wraps himself up in his little white shroud. Did you know that, sir? One continuous thread?" He made an unwinding motion in the air, his face alight.

One thread. Jack had not known. There was much he did not know as far as Preston's world was concerned. Bored, he palmed his penny, playing with it a finger game, a singlehanded passage of the coin from knuckle to knuckle at lightning speed.

Preston rattled on. "That's why we have to unwind the little bugger's wrappings. It's called a greige, you know. The East India Company brings them to us by the boxload."

He had not known, did not want to know. Bombyx bombast! Far too much excitement over a worm, as far as Jack could see.

"A great deal of our work involves the cleaning of the greige. Soak it in soap and oil we do, to soften the gumtacks."

"Gumtacks, sir?"

The mushroom's daughter watched him, watched the lightning-fast passage of the penny from knuckle to knuckle.

"Hard sticky spots with which the silkworm holds his threads together. He goes to a great deal of trouble to stick them all together and we go to equal trouble to unstick them. If we could just convince the little fellows to dispense with the gluing, we should all have a much easier time of it." The worm meister laughed at his own joke and rambled on, with Jack only half listening. Bobbins, pirns, throws, warps, and skeins—this was a language too foreign to keep straight.

The mushroom's daughter scowled a little at the movement of his hand and made a point of responding in an intelligent and eminently boring manner to whatever nonsense it was her father had just spouted.

Jack sighed and pocketed the coin. It seemed unreal and languid, this strange, meandering turn his life had taken, a gentle dream from which he must wake. And yet there was a price, other than boredom, inherent in this odd respite taken in the company of the mushroom and his testy daughter. He found himself caught in a position he had never before suffered—firmly beneath another man's thumb.

Mr. Preston controlled conversation within the confines of the coach as it left the lofty golden spires of Oxford behind them and barreled north across the Cherwell River. He was a cheerful, self-important, talkative man, given to exuberant explanation of the things he loved best—his collection of antique instruments, the salt collection process, and the spinning and weaving of silk.

All the way to Banbury he prattled, past sleepy cottages, gray limestone, and honey-yellow ironstone, past grazing sheep, windblown cornfields, gentle streams, and wide, flat meadows dotted with tree-topped knolls. And while he talked, Jack had time—far too much of it—to ponder the folly his life had become. He had lost everything! He had shot Nicki! He was now posing as a music master. His life seemed too big for the confines of the coach, too knotted to untangle, too horrendous to calmly share small talk with the likes of Preston and his daughter.

She stole an occasional look at him from beneath her lashes, as if he were the industrious silkworm wrapped up in his single strand of gumtacked thread. He liked to think she meant to unravel him.

Preston ceased his conversational spate only when they paused to eat at the inn where the horses were changed, and then only because his mouth was full of cheese, bread, ale, and Banbury's own cakes—flaky puff pastries thick with spiced fruit filling. He partook of food with the same gusto with which he spoke.

They ate, al fresco, at a table beneath an oak tree. A brisk breeze fanned their faces, teasing Selina Preston's fair hair and plucking at her bonnet. Jack could not help but be reminded of his circumstances. It was not his place to suggest they step inside, out of the wind. He had not the means even to feed himself without Preston's assistance. The older gentleman paid freely for all that was required along their way, an unending stream of coins pulled from an intricately woven silk jacquard purse as heavy as any Jack had ever carried.

Jack was not used to being dependent on anyone's largess—certainly not the munificence of a man he barely knew. That he must get used to such a position, perhaps for the remainder of his days, made him feel small, unworthy, childlike. And from his childhood came the odd memory of a nursery rhyme.

"Where is Banbury Cross?" he asked.

"The one every child rides a cockhorse to?" Selina Preston understood his question immediately.

"Yes. How does it go? To see a fine lady."

"Upon a white horse," she joined in. Together they finished it, their voices blending in singsong delivery, even Mr. Preston joining in, crumbs rolling down his chest. "Rings on her fingers, bells on her toes, she shall have music wherever she goes."

They smiled at their own foolishness. Jack felt, for a moment, lighthearted.

"My mother used to recite that one," he said.

"You have never been to Banbury." She said it with authority, as if she knew all there was to know about him without a question asked.

"How . . . ?"

"You asked about the cross. Most people do their first time through. Sorry to disappoint. There is none."

"What? Never?"

"It was destroyed. Years ago, by the Puritans, who disapproved of icons."

"Really? The people of Banbury have not put up another? What a shame for all the children who pass this way."

"I thought so when I was a child." She said it wistfully.

"And now?"

"I have not given it any thought for a long while."

"Singularly appropriate that you should just now," her father chortled.

"How so?"

"Now that you are here, sir," the mushroom said as he waved at his daughter and reached into the case that held his prized new kit, "she shall have music wherever she goes."

He held out the diminutive violinlike instrument, as if Jack were an organ-grinder's monkey, ready to play on demand.

Jack hesitated. The kit was a delightful piece, beautifully inlaid with the mellow gleam of ivory, its neck magnificently carved in the shape of the torso of a goddess.

The mushroom stared at him, no doubt wondering why he did not readily take the instrument.

"The strings, sir. They may be too old." He had to say something.

Preston waved the bow at him. "Check the strings, then. We will make a point of buying new ones in Warwick, if needed."

At the behest, then, of the mushroom who was now his master, Jack cradled the kit in the hollow where his neck and shoulder met and drew bow across strings that squalled in protest. It was a strange feeling, to have one's talent, one's joy, at the beck and call of another. And yet adjustments must be made, just as adjustments were needed in the tension of the strings. He twisted, plucked, and plied the bow until the strings hummed their approval.

High angelic voices these strings possessed, like the shorter strings on a harp. Sweet, if a little thin. He closed his eyes and played Vivaldi, the "Winter" largo from the *Four Seasons*. Fingering was tight on an elfin instrument, designed to fit more comfortably in a man's pocket than on his shoulder. The first few notes stumbled out awkwardly, but before long the kit had settled into Jack's hands like a willing woman. Eyes closed, he played her, swept away by Vivaldi's measured tones. The sweet, vibrato sadness carried him high above all worries, all cares. There was a blessed release in the music. His soul lost track of time and trouble and the fact that he was governed by another's wishes. Sound surrounded him in beauty, in sorrow, in the vision of cold, blue skies and pristine snow.

The last note fading on the breeze, he came back to summer with the opening of his eyes. Sunlight dappling her hair, as if she embodied warmth, Selina Preston watched him, her eyes by turns clear, bright cerulean and then, shadows shifting, dark and brooding as a winter sky. In that sky there lay hint of an understanding, as if he had carried her with him, into the ethereal.

He held the kit out to her in one hand, in the other the bow. "First lesson?"

She took the instrument, their fingers brushing. Eyes wide, cheeks flushed, she lifted the kit and positioned the carved goddess perfectly, beneath her jaw. "I know the scales, if you are prepared to suffer them."

"Bless me. Not the scales, my dear." Avery Preston vacated the bench he had been warming and made haste to place some distance between himself and his daughter.

"You may want to stick your fingers in your ears," she cautioned Jack. "I am truly dreadful. Cows refuse to give milk when I play. Chickens stop laying. Most people beg me to stop."

He shrugged. Everyone sounded dreadful to begin with. "Show me."

She began in a rush, her right hand too heavy, her left lacking proper pressure on the strings. Notes emerged awkward and tuneless, strings squalling protest as the bow scraped and sawed. A head poked out of the window above them. Beyond the wall of the courtyard a dog began to howl.

Jack's hand darted out, encircling Selina's arm, just above the wrist, gently halting the movement of the bow.

She flinched, let go.

He caught the bow as it fell.

"I warned you." She reclaimed her wrist and stepped away from him, her face flushed crimson.

"Do it again," he said. "Slower this time."

She glanced uneasily at the woman leaning from the window above. "You are a glutton for punishment. Do you intend to set all the dogs in town howling?"

He smiled. "Indulge me, Miss Preston. One note, if you will. Just one note. Sustain it as long as you can." He handed her the bow.

Repositioning the instrument, she would have struck the note had he not stepped in behind her, his hand on her arm again.

She shrank from him.

He frowned. Never had he encountered a woman who responded to his touch as if it scalded her.

"Angle the bow, this way." Bare flesh soft and warm beneath his fingers, he pivoted her wrist slightly, felt the flutter of her pulse beneath his thumb and tried not to inhale too deeply the sweet cloud of perfume that rose from her hair. "Play on the edge of the horsehair. Like so."

She froze, allowed him to manipulate her wrist as he would, seemed in fact, incapable of any other movement.

"Show me," he said, releasing his hold, but not yet stepping away. He wanted to look over her shoulder, the better to see exactly what she did, the better to determine if the expensive blended perfume she wore was more jasmine or rose, the better to judge if he had completely paralyzed her with his proximity.

In an arthritic fashion, she lowered bow to strings exactly as he had indicated. An unhappy noise issued shakily from the kit. Her hound dog accompaniment chimed in. Selina's complexion, cheek and throat, bloomed a decidedly rosy hue.

"The kit is a difficult instrument to master." He wished to set her at ease. "The fingering is cramped for a beginner. Bow sounds dry as well." He darted away. "Aha!" A small wad of what he required resided in a felt pouch at the bottom of the instrument case.

"Do you know how to rosin?" He held out his find.

"No. But I wager you mean to show me."

He took the kit from her hands and gently set it aside. "As instructor to you, Miss Preston, and as an expert in the matter,

I would highly recommend you avoid wagers. They will only lead you into trouble."

Their eyes met. He read surprise in her regard, and was it pity? He did not want her pity. There were any number of things he might like to read in those deep blue eyes. Pity was definitely not one of them.

"Take the bow in your right hand. Draw it across the rosin in your left." Hands on hers, he demonstrated. "Start here. Near the frog. Now, rub the wad firmly along the string, several times here, where the stroke starts."

Together they stretched, hand against hand, arm against arm, rubbing, stroking, their movements, the language, highly provocative. Provocation to which she seemed completely oblivious.

She was far too clever, he thought, and at the same time naive. He could tell by the very stiffness of her posture, that she was as much a novice with men as she was with music. "Loose wrist." He pivoted the joint between his fingers. "Bow hand should be loose, relaxed. You are not at all relaxed, Miss Preston."

"No. I am not, sir." She sounded predictably prickly. "I am not at all used to gentlemen hovering over me, breathing down my neck, grabbing at my person."

He ignored her waspishness, far more interested in the quickened rise and fall of her breast, the increased rate of the pulse beneath his thumb. There were decided advantages to playing the part of a music master. Her perfume was definitely more jasmine than rose. He released his hold, reined in his burgeoning desires, and adopted his most professorial tone. "Show me you understand."

Obediently, she demonstrated.

"Yes. Better, but keep the bow parallel to the bridge. Just so. Now, everything we have discussed thus far. Put it together. Show me."

She took a deep breath, played a note, wrist limber, the bow sufficiently angled. The sound she wrenched from the strings was no better than before. Two dogs keened. The woman in the window above them withdrew, slamming down the sash.

The innkeeper stepped through the archway to the court-yard. "What's all this noise?"

Rousing himself to the defense of his daughter, Mr. Preston went to speak to the man.

"Bother!" Selina said irritably, and would have stopped and put away the kit had Jack not encircled her arm again with his right hand, and leaned in close to her ear.

"No forcing it, now. Positioning is important. Closer to the bridge. Like so." His hand guided hers.

Again, the instrument complained.

She laughed. "Are you sure you can teach me, Mr. Ramsay? The dogs hear no progress in my tune, no matter how well positioned the bow."

His right hand still piggybacking hers, he reached around so that his left did the same.

"Sir!" She sucked in the word abruptly.

"Miss Preston." He maintained the tone of an instructor. "Your left hand, as opposed to the looseness of the right, must be taut, firm." He rode her fingers into the strings.

"Ow!" She shook his hand away.

"Have I injured you?"

"You mashed my fingers," she snapped.

"Terribly sorry. Perhaps you would care to mash mine in return." He nudged her fingers away from the strings. "Go on. Reverse positions. Mash away."

She hesitated, but could not resist temptation. Placing her fingers boldly atop his, she did her best to squash them. He had hoped she might.

"Stronger than you look, aren't you?" he whispered, his cheek brushing the softness of her hair.

"You take pleasure in teasing me, don't you?" she said tersely in an undervoice, that her father might not hear. "I daresay this music master business is no more than a pretext for getting your hands on a foolish female."

"I am not at all attracted to foolish females, my dear. To the contrary, my goal is to demonstrate to a rather clever one how to apply the proper pressure. Once you have mastered pressure, I am convinced you will garner as much enjoyment out of *playing* as I do."

"I would not bet on it, sir."

"Are you so eager to gamble on our mutual failure?"

"Failure?"

"Yes. Mine to teach and yours to learn."

"I am not a gambler. I have seen and heard what damage it can do to those who play at it unwisely."

"You are not a gambler? But that's a bold-faced lie, my dear. We all gamble at life, if not at the gaming tables. You and your father have just gambled away a Season in the hopes you might snare a title, did you not?"

She stiffened and pulled away from him. "And you gamble now, sir, that you will not lose the position you have just secured by so insulting me."

"I wager that you are that rare sort of female who can look the truth in the eye without flinching," he said.

She bit her lip. "Is that what you think of me? That I would give myself into the hands of a man for no more reason than who his ancestors happen to have been?"

"I think," he said quietly, his eyes searching hers, "that we were discussing pressure."

"Yes," she agreed thoughtfully. "It was pressure."

"Do you have it?"

"More than you may realize," she said sharply.

"Show me," he said, not at all sure what pressures she alluded to.

Her gaze strayed, toward the tree beneath which her father stood talking to the innkeeper. With a determined look, she carefully positioned the goddess beneath her jaw, mimicking all that he had thus far demonstrated to her.

"Excellent!" he said. "Now, all together, what have you learned? Give it a go."

She exhaled heavily and played a single note, the sweet, singing sound a vast improvement on what she had accomplished in the past.

Mr. Preston and the innkeeper stopped their discussion to look in their direction.

"Very good. Try again."

Expression intent, Selina Preston made music. A trifle unsteady, an occasional hiccup, but it was undeniably the scales. The village dogs held silent.

"Bravo!"

Preston startled them.

Selina, slightly dazed, looked up from her concentrated efforts. But it was not to her father she looked first, eyes glowing with pride. She smiled at Jack, as if together they had surmounted a great obstacle.

Chapter Ten

Into the heart of the Midlands the carriage carried them, across the Avon into Warwick, where the ancient, walled magnificence of Warwick Castle blotted out the sun entirely as they rattled past. They stopped at a comfortable inn on the north side of town. There, in his room, as he readied himself for bed, Jack was interrupted by a knock on the door from Mr. Preston, who let himself in with a polite, "A word, sir?"

"Of course. Do come in," Jack said.

Preston gave the room and its view a keen look before he sat himself in a straight-backed chair and said, in the politest of tones, as if he discussed the weather, or the airing of sheets, "I'll not have you defiling my daughter, sir."

Struck dumb for a moment, Jack collected himself enough to reply with the same nonchalance Preston maintained, "Such was never my intention."

Preston barked a laugh. "I have heard the road to Hell is paved with the best of intentions. I do not mean to offend you, Mr. Ramsay, but neither will I play the fool. You have a reputation with the ladies and I have seen the two of you together and listened closely enough to how you speak to my girl to know I raise a valid point."

Jack was offended, the man rude beyond words! "Do you wish me to leave, sir?" he asked stiffly. "Have I enjoyed your hospitality too long?"

"No. To the contrary. I've no objection to you wooing my only daughter if you do so with purpose."

"Sir?" Jack had been certain the man could no longer surprise him. He was mistaken.

"Do I surprise you? Selina shows interest in you—more than she has evidenced in any other fortune hunter who has dangled after her."

"Fortune hunter, sir? I must protest."

"Must you?"

Jack kept close rein on his disgust and waited for the man to go on. He would undoubtedly go on.

"If I am a mushroom, and willing to admit as much, will you not be as honest in allowing that you are in search of your fortune?"

"I am, sir, a loser of fortunes," Jack admitted wryly.

"Aye, the gambling. I have heard of your losses."

"You have heard that I lost everything and still you invite me to your home, and now invite me to pursue your daughter?"

The old gent eyed him narrowly. "Do you mean to go on gambling? Could you lightly lose another fortune to bad habits?"

"No!" Jack said emphatically, so much so it surprised him.

"That was my impression. You seem a man who has been made recently aware of the idea of consequences. See you do not forget, Mr. Ramsay. I shall hold you accountable otherwise."

"Do you groom me, then, sir, as candidate for a son-in-law?"

"You are a frank fellow. I like that, but I groom you for nothing. I would, of course, like to have Selina married, and happily so. I would like to know there is someone to take over management of salt and silk production when I am gone, but Selina must decide who she will or will not marry, and while she has shown interest in you, I will not have her so compromised that she has no choice but to say yes to someone she does not love. Are we of an understanding?"

"We are, sir."

"Good." Preston rose and made his bow. "I wish you good night, then."

Jack closed the door on him scowling, almost sick with disgust. He considered packing up his bags that he might take a different road than this aggravating mushroom and his daughter, but abandoned the idea because of the late hour and his complete dearth of funds. How did one display one's pride when one had nothing left with which to display it? A man who had been made recently aware of the idea of consequences, Preston called him. The mushroom hit too close to the truth. That annoyed Jack no end. The irritating feeling had not abated by the following morning.

Freshly annoyed in watching Preston pay his reckoning, order their breakfast, and instruct that the inn's best team of horses should be led into the traces of his carriage, Jack found it difficult to willingly ensconce himself in the luxury of Avery Preston's carriage, where he must submit to the road and direction Avery Preston wished him to go, without alternative or recourse. Consequences indeed!

It was a richly wooded and picturesque area they passed through. Mr. Preston found it pleasing, as did his daughter. Jack had little to say. Mr. Preston, therefore, governed all conversation except the unspoken language of stolen looks that Selina sent in Jack's direction. Preston was right. She was interested in him. Could not keep her eyes off of him. Yesterday it had pleased Jack. Today it was an irritation.

"The Ladies of Lichfield." Miss Preston interrupted her father's unending discourse to point out of the window when they reached Lichfield, a charming town, dominated by the three-tiered spires of its cathedral.

"Who?" Jack asked impatiently, unwilling to indulge her with so much as a polite response now that it was her father's intention they should be very friendly indeed.

"Not a who, a what," she said, with a puzzled look, as if his curt tone confused her.

They hit a rut in the road, bouncing their knees together. She jumped whenever he touched her. He rather liked it that she did. What he did not care for at all was his heightened sensitivity to their every exchange—not out of any great feeling for her, but because her father so closely observed all that transpired.

"Beg pardon," he said.

"It's nothing," she murmured, but the spots of bright color in her cheeks told him otherwise.

Avery Preston must needs involve himself in the exchange. "The towers of the cathedral, young man. *They* are referred to as the Ladies of Lichfield. Can be seen for miles on a clear day."

Without so much as a word of direction to the coachman the coach was driven straight to the cathedral, where the door to the coach was flung open by the footman, and Miss Preston, clutching one of the mysterious sketchbooks she guarded as if they contained great secrets, was handed down without discussion. When Jack moved to exit the coach as well, Preston plucked at his sleeve.

"I mean to go elsewhere to pick up parts for the loom. You may, of course, stay with Selina—whichever you desire."

The mushroom, or the mushroom's daughter?

There was no question as to his desire and both men knew it. Jack looked from the one whose company he had begun to resent to the other, into whose company he resented being thrust. She waited not for the outcome, advancing up the steps to the cathedral door as if it made no difference to her what he did.

"I should like to see the cathedral," he said and felt as if Preston engaged him in a battle of wills in his very acquiescence and amiability.

"Right. I shall not be long."

Bewildered that the man would, based on nothing more than promises, hand his daughter into the care of a single gentleman known to all London as a rakehell, and yet not at all inclined to inform the man that he gambled unwisely in so doing, Jack climbed down from the coach, snapped shut the door, and watched the vehicle clatter away.

Inside the cool darkness of the triple-towered church of St. Mary and St. Chad, it took Jack a moment to orient himself, to find that Miss Preston had taken a seat in the nave. Not to pray, he saw, when he slid into the pew beside her. She sketched the beautifully worked stone of the Gothic arcade and triforium arching gracefully above rows of stained glass that painted the pews with colorfully muted gems of light.

"He leaves you alone, then, to wander churches," he murmured.

She kept her attention firmly fixed on the rendering of the arches. Her voice was low. "You can see he does."

He could see, but the truth of it bore clarification. "While he is off conducting his business? Gone, perhaps for hours?"

A flicker of a glance in his direction and she was intent once more on examining architecture, confidently transferring in graphite what she saw to the page. "I am content to work my sketches, and Father believes me safer here than among his many male business associates."

"Are you safe?" he asked.

She stopped sketching long enough to look him directly in the eyes. "Perhaps not. This is the first time Father has left me in anyone but God's company."

He frowned. "Have you not suffered some loneliness, wandering so many empty cathedrals and churches?"

"Loneliness?" Pencil in hand, she drew an arc on air, as if to inscribe the ceiling. "How can one feel lonely in His house? There is a fullness in such places that precludes loneliness. I feel as if I am surrounded by . . ." She spread wide both arms. "By spirits."

"Ghosts?" he asked skeptically.

The word deflated her. Both of her arms sank to a more natural, less exuberant position, her hands balled in her lap, the pencil still clenched between her fingers. "Not ghosts, no. Shades, if you will, of past history." She sighed. "How can I make you understand?" She bit her lip a moment. "I know. Tell me, why do people go to churches?"

"To pray," he said, unsure what she was getting at, sure only of what had recently drawn him to church. "To pray for forgiveness, for guidance, for inner peace."

"Exactly," she said. "And to be married and to christen children and to grieve over lost loved ones. Strong emotions! Important moments! A goodly amount of an entire town's joy and anguish is poured into the confines of one building, generation after generation. I imagine traces of those people, of their thoughts and feelings, hanging like whispers above our heads. Do you not hear them?"

She paused, head cocked, listening. He listened, too, but heard nothing out of the ordinary. Pigeons rustled and cooed from the windowsills. There were creaks to be heard from a few of the pews, the echo of doors opened and doors closed, with the attendant sounds of horses' hooves and carriage wheels as the outside briefly intruded. There were whispers and footsteps, but not from the past. They issued from the mouths and feet of those who came to pray, to meditate, to honor headstones. There was a weight, not of sound, but of silence hanging over the place.

She spoke again when he did not, her face lifted to the light, one hand playing with the pencil, the other reaching out, as if to touch upon the things she mentioned. "There is, too, some essence of the artisans who by the sweat of their brows placed stone upon stone reaching for the heavens and who spanned high ceilings with backbreaking beauty at great risk to their very lives. There is in every bit of carved woodwork, every piece of chiseled stone or leaded glass, a little bit of someone's love and thanksgiving for the gifts with which God endowed their eyes and fingers. The essence of so much creativity is poured lovingly into a place like this. It hangs like a fog in the very air. Do you know what I mean? Do you have some sense of it? I come away from these beloved and holy places filled with the sense of others, generations of others, whose feet have trod the same stones mine do. Never loneliness."

This passionate explanation from the heretofore all-too-quiet mushroom's daughter astounded Jack—so much so that he was for a moment struck speechless.

She set to work again.

"And do you fill your sketchbooks," he asked with dawning understanding, "so that a part of you may survive your mortal form?"

She laughed. "I suppose in a way I do." Her pencil scratches bridged the silence. "It must be difficult for you."

He had just been thinking the same thing. What had he to leave as legacy, other than ruined lives?

"Music is such an ephemeral expression," she said.

He had not even considered his music. It seemed to him such a trivial thing. Yet it ruled large in what little she knew of him. Of course her mind would focus on it.

"Your gift is an immediate one, fragile and elusive as perfume on the wind, while I carry away with me a small piece of each place, beauty, relic, or mystery that I visit."

He held out his hand. "May I see what mysteries the Ladies of Lichfield Vale keep hidden beneath their skirted towers?"

She snapped shut the sketchbook, as though she shut off part of herself, insulted. "This has been a holy place for centuries. Saxons and Normans had churches here. Lichfield has been a center of pilgrimage—"

"As we are now pilgrims." Too late, he tried to soothe her.

She clutched the book to her breast like a shield. "You do not improve yourself in my estimation by making light of this place. Great indignities have been heaped upon these walls. The cathedral came very close to complete destruction in the Civil Wars."

"Hard to imagine." He looked about at the peaceful Gothic arcades, the glowing stained glass, the quiet expectancy of empty pews.

"The windows all smashed, the central spire destroyed, and where it fell, a great hole in the roof. Slates, stone, and wood were stolen for building materials. Tombs ransacked and desecrated."

"The Reformation occurred a long time ago to rouse such passion in you, Miss Preston."

The word brought her head up, glittering brightness in her eyes as if in response to some form of challenge. "I am a passionate creature!" She studied him carefully. "Long ago wrecked, long ago restored, I find this place and all it stands for most moving."

She was an intriguing creature.

"I do not doubt it," he said, and wondered in what way she

had long ago been wrecked. Or was it, after all, only the cathedral she meant?

"Are you not similarly moved, Mr. Ramsay? Or would you claim yourself devoid of passions? I should think you, of all people, would be affected by this proof that even the most horribly ravaged object of desecration, plunder, and abuse can find restoration with hard work and the love of God." Her remarks were as pointed as her looks.

He studied the place, unable to meet the meaning in her eyes. "Do you view me, then, Miss Preston, as a cathedral in need of repair?"

He could feel the intensity of her gaze without turning. "I believe, Mr. Ramsay, that we are each of us God's house as much as or more than any cathedral." She said it softly, her words, carefully enunciated, powerful in their very lack of force. "It is up to each of us to maintain our house, or allow it to fall into disrepair. Have you decided you would rather be a ruin, Mr. Ramsay? A colorful ruin that people like to visit and talk about, but a ruin nonetheless?"

How did one answer such a question? He could not. She dropped her gaze and rose with the intention of exiting the pew.

He blocked her way, raising his hand to grasp the pew back in front of theirs. So sudden was his move, so presumptuous, that his sleeve brushed her skirt, his elbow her thigh.

With a sharp intake of breath, she backed away.

It had not been his intention to touch her, certainly not to come into contact with her so inappropriately. "I beg your pardon," he said. "But I do undertake a reformation of sorts—a rebuilding, if you will, from the ground up."

"You go too far, sir." She looked pointedly at the arm that blocked her path. He released his hold on the pew, lowering his head, unable to meet her eyes. He should not have expected her to understand.

She stepped past him, the sway of her skirts drawing his attention involuntarily, the sway of her hips maintaining his attention, if only briefly. She turned, her skirt still brushing his leg.

Light fell across her shoulders like a multicolored mantle. Her eyes, translucent blue, searched his—for what, he knew not.

"To rebuild from the ground up implies there is little to salvage of the original structure."

"Yes."

Her remark confused him.

"You go too far, sir."

It was the second time she had said as much. But in searching her expression, in dwelling deeply on the feelings she harbored for him behind a veil of lashes, he realized his misinterpretation.

"You see salvageable material, then?"

"Am I wrong to see it?"

He wanted to laugh at her naïveté, but could not. It would be too cruel to laugh. "You know me too little to pass such judgment." He said it gently but firmly.

She studied him a moment longer, unflinching. "I know you are not rotten to the core, Mr. Ramsay."

"Do you?"

"Yes. Otherwise, you would not care about, or even question, the loneliness of a mushroom's daughter."

She walked away from him then, straight backed, hips swaying, her footsteps echoing not so much as her words.

Chapter Eleven

The horse could not have picked a better place to go lame, in Selina's opinion. They had almost traversed the peaceful beauty of Cannock Chase, twenty-six miles of protected moorland and oak forest, once the hunting grounds of Plantagenet kings. Fallow deer, wearing summer fawn, their backs sprinkled with powder white, their palm-shaped antlers no longer covered with spring's felt, bounded away from the coach's approach. Black striped tails flicking nervously, they made for the woods. She would have liked to follow them. There were hundreds of wonderful things to draw in the shaded peace of the trees.

She wanted to draw, needed to focus her thoughts. A few moments alone with paper and pencil and she would remind herself who she was. She needed reminding. She felt rattled today, ill at ease in the cramped space of the carriage, weary of her father's incessant conversation, and horribly uncomfortable in such a closeted space with Jack Ramsay, after the strange and all-too-stimulating day they had shared.

The man invigorated—by his conversation, his music, his very presence. He stirred her in a way she had never been stirred. She felt vulnerable, exposed, as if the world moved too quickly, or not quickly enough.

She watched him. She tried to stop herself from watching; tried to concentrate on her father's words, on the fact that she had no intention of falling for a man with Ramsay's history. She could not stop. Her gaze seemed drawn, as the bow is drawn to play the string, as if she were played in the hand of a greater force than that of her own will. Every time her glances stole in his direction, he felt them, sensed her every intention.

She played a strange tune that only he could hear. His head turned from the window at just the right moment that their gazes might meet. They played a duet of probing, speculative looks. She wondered what he saw when he gazed at her.

She did not want to interest a man who thought of her as nothing more than a mushroom's daughter. He was everything she had promised herself she found loathsome in high society—a glib, coin-tossing wastrel; a gambler; a gentleman of notorious reputation. That she should find his gaze compelling, that it should cause her pulse to race and her heart to pound, that a flush rose to her cheeks whenever they exchanged words as if she were some lovesick schoolgirl, humiliated her own sense of herself. Yet she wondered what it would be like to converse further with such a man, wondered, in fact, what it would be like to be seduced by such a man. Such wonderings shamed, annoyed, even angered her.

He had told her yesterday that she did not know him well enough to pass judgment on him, good or bad. He was right. She knew very little about Rakehell Ramsay. His words were a warning. Rather gracious, if his rep was to be believed. Yet she could not stop thinking of him, looking at him, thrilling when he looked at her. Her nostrils flared involuntarily now and again, the better to breathe in the smell of him—an expensive, subtle sandalwood and cypress scent.

She had to get out, away from him, to put some space between them. She had to make her mind tranquil and settled again by focusing on her drawings. She was therefore relieved when the coach slowed, when the coachman leapt down from his box, came to the window, tugged at his forelock, and informed them dourly, "Stone bruise, sir. Aft fore on the lee wheeler. Shall I lead the creature into Milford, sir, and return with a fresh one?"

"Excellent idea!" her father agreed, opening the door and jumping down to assist in unhitching the team.

Ramsay stepped out as well. Selina sighed with relief to see the back of him. But he stopped—stood holding the door for her.

"Do you wish to take the air, Miss Preston?"

"Yes. Just a moment." She dug into the storage pocket attached to the far door, fishing out her sketchbooks and pencils. Ramsay watched her every move. She selected two of the books, the one bound in green leather, the other in gray, weighed them in her mind, and put away the green one.

"You mean to draw?" he asked.

"Yes. I am rarely to be seen without a sketchbook." She put her gloved hand in his, struck by his warmth, by the size of his palm in proportion to hers, struck, too, by the strange, dizzy tingling that possessed both hand and brain as long as he touched her.

She made haste to leave the coach, to separate her hand from his. "Father!" she called. "I mean to take my sketchbook into the woods."

"What's that?" Her father looked up from the hoof he was examining. "Sketching? Yes, of course. Don't go far."

Jack watched her walk away.

Avery Preston and his footman were focused on—and full of directions for—the coachman as he led away the limping cause of their unexpected delay.

"My good man." Preston startled Jack in throwing an arm familiarly around his shoulder. "What are we to do with ourselves during this unforeseen delay? I have a deck of cards. Perhaps you would indulge me and Thompson in a game? Black Lady Hearts? Penny ante?"

Cards.

The very mention of them brought a tight feeling of anticipation to Jack's gut. There was a certain terror, almost a feeling of panic that he now associated with the idea of gaming. He had sworn to himself and to God that he was through with gambling, even for pennies, of which he had only one, and that too precious to lose.

"I am sorry, sir. Must refuse. I uhm . . . no longer play, you see. Thought I might take a little stroll, stretch my legs, get some air."

"Yes, of course. You did tell me once before you were through with games of chance. Sorry to have tempted you. A walk's the thing." Preston scanned the edge of the forest. "Perhaps you would do me the favor of keeping an eye out for Selina? I do not like to think of her losing herself in these woods."

If not cards, the man tempted him with the private company of his daughter! Who was he to quibble?

"My pleasure," Jack said and set off after Selina.

She almost passed them by, the yellowish cluster of mushrooms she assumed to be the most common fungi of the woods. Something in their color was unusual, a hint of green in the yellow. Steps retraced, she bent to more closely examine them, hastily flipping through her sketchbook to find a fresh page, excited by her find.

Amanita phalloides! She had read about them in her books on fungi. Attractive, umbrella-shaped mushrooms—fleshy, thick, rounded, and smooth—they looked quite tasty. With a stick, she stabbed at a decaying specimen, leaned in for a whiff of its odor, vaguely vomitous. She drew back in disgust. Definitely not the *citrina,* which smelled of raw potato.

Her pencil flew, recording shape, size, and the way light fell upon the pale cluster. She had come to the woods hoping to find mushrooms, determined to remind herself why she scorned the idea of becoming enamored of a rakehell. She must not forget.

A noise stopped her pencil, brought her head up.

A feathery flash of gray-blue and buff, a nuthatch, flew toward her, not away, as it should have. Behind it something crashed through the underbrush, something big. Uneasy, she rose, clutching the sketchbook.

A fallow deer leapt into the clearing and bounded gracefully straight toward her. He froze when they came face to face, his sides heaving, huge brown eyes glassy with fear.

Selina froze as well, her heart racing with sheer exultation. He was beautiful, exquisitely beautiful, ears belled and translucent, pink as the petals of a tulip, legs slender, almost too delicate to hold up the bulk of his body. His head was too fragile for the top-heavy crown of antlers. Eyes huge, dark, and moist, benign in expression, regarded her in an almost plead-ing fashion, while the powder-dusted fawn of his coat looked soft enough to touch.

This animal was no threat to her. He was a gift of God's grace and beauty, brought here, before her eyes, if only for a moment, before bounding on his way again.

But the buck did not bound away. To the contrary, with a grunt, and trembling hindquarters, he sank to his knees, tried to rise again, could not, lay down in the grass and leaves at her feet, as if in obeisance. It was only then that she saw the arrow that protruded from his heaving, blood-stained ribs, a tiny, waving, feathered flag. A hunter's triumph.

Horrified, tears burning in her eyes, Selina moved toward the animal, not away as would have been most prudent. The buck snorted with anxiety as she approached, tried futilely to rise, breath gusty, legs thrashing, no longer possessed of the energy for such effort.

He was dying. There was nothing she could do to stop it. Her very helplessness brought a sob to Selina's lips. The buck's side heaved, his every labored breath a pain to watch as he tried again to stand, haunches trembling. Weeping, stum-bling, Selina ran from the death, too distraught to realize that she was no longer alone in the clearing.

A shadow bruised the pathway. A stench, sour as the stink of old mushroom, assaulted her nose. A man in soiled buck-skin and a black hood blocked her way.

She jerked to a halt, blinking back tears, pulse racing.

He was a stocky man. His eyeholes were crooked, as if the mask had been hastily donned. A bow was slung across his broad shoulders. Arrows tufted from a case at his back. The hunter had come to claim his kill. A poacher, from the looks of his headgear.

Cold fear raised the hair at the base of Selina's neck. Her sobs had long since ceased, her concern for the downed deer fled. She was in danger now as great as any the deer had faced.

" 'Peers to be alone, she does." The hood puffed away from the man's face when he spoke.

"Not a local girl. I've never seen the likes of her."

Selina closed her eyes, knees gone watery. Two more men, also hooded, stood at the far side of the clearing.

"What shall we do with her?"

"Hmm. Pretty lass, alone in the woods. What *shall* we do with her?"

Her plight amused them.

Selina tensed her legs to run, tensed her jaw to scream, but before she could do either, a new sound drew her attention— drew the attention of the poachers as well. First, the unmistakeable click of the hammer of a pistol being drawn. Second, the familiar slapping sound of a coin finding Jack Ramsay's palm.

"You could hand her over to me, before I decide to shoot you."

The sight of Jack, nonchalantly leaning against the trunk of a tree, lazily tossing a coin in one hand while in the other he held a pistol, flooded Selina with a sense of relief. Ramsay's voice sounded sweeter than music!

"You'd be pluck full of arrows before you could get off your second shot," one of the poachers declared.

"Willing to bet your life on it?" Jack drawled. "As I see it, a Jack with an ace up his sleeve beats three masked knaves any day."

"Odds are three to one. How do you figure?" demanded one of the poachers on the far side of the clearing.

Jack replied languidly. "Well, sir, I am an ace shot and this a reliable weapon. Should we resort to violence I will, as you have pointed out, probably end up stuck full of arrows, but I will undoubtedly kill two of you before I am dead. Thus, one lucky fellow is left alive with both the deer and the girl, the one which he cannot carry without the other running away. You must ask yourselves, crown or castle. Is today your day to prosper or to die?"

"You've got a better idea, I suppose?" The man on the far side of the clearing seemed the leader of the three. He did the talking.

Jack laughed, stopped the movement of the coin, and smoothly pocketed it. "But of course!"

Selina was amazed. Ramsay sounded so collected, so reasonable, so civilized!

"What *you* really want is the deer. What *I* really want is the young lady." It thrilled her to hear him say so! "We both walk away with what we want and call it a day. No one dead. No messy bodies in the woods to be worrying about."

"You'd turn us in!"

Ramsay pushed himself away from the tree with a shrug. "And if I did? Who are you to me but three masked men? Being a stranger to the district, I could never identify your voices."

The one who did the talking nodded. "Take her, then. Be on your way. You'd be wise to keep the filly on a shorter lead."

Ramsay made a come-hither gesture to Selina.

She obeyed, stepping past the man at whose hooded head the pistol was aimed. As she did, she could not resist saying, "And you would be wise, gentlemen, not to risk transportation for a few pounds of venison."

An ominous creaking sound followed her remark.

"I wouldn't do that if I were you." Jack shifted aim. A quick look over her shoulder revealed why. One of the poachers, arrow knocked, stood poised to respond to her reprimand with violence.

Jack forced a smile, his gaze steely. "It would seem we are all risk takers, gentlemen, gamblers if you will, in our own way—even the young lady."

"Bitch needs muzzling," the poacher growled, but he lowered the bow.

Selina safely behind him, Jack backed away from the trio, pistol still raised, until the trees swallowed them.

She would have said something then, but Jack laid a finger to her lips, silencing her, his head cocked, listening. Pointing to the trunk of a substantial old oak that stretched its low hanging limbs across their path, he whispered, "Climb."

"Are you serious?" she hissed.

He nodded. "Climb! And quietly."

She handed him her sketchbook, lifted her skirts that she might hitch them in the belt at her waist and with a presumptuous boost on her backside from his well-placed hand, she climbed, stockings snagging, her knees and shins soon bruised and scraped, her hair undone by the grab of twigs and leaves.

Tucking her sketchbook between his shirt and waistcoat, he swung up after her, urging her higher when she might have stopped, halting her with a grab at her ankle. When she turned, prepared to scold him for such forwardness, she froze. His hand on her bared leg seemed the lesser of two evils. There, beneath them, moving stealthily, crept one of the poachers, bow at the ready.

She wanted to gasp, to cry out. Her sweating, shaking fingers wanted to let go her grasp of the tree. He had but to look up, sight the bow, let an arrow fly and she was as dead as the deer. Terrified, afraid almost to breathe, she shut her eyes, concentrating on the alarming sensation of Rakehell Ramsay's fingers clasping her ankle, strangely comforted by the fact that his hand was almost as sweaty as her own.

They remained silent, motionless. The poacher moved on. An eternity, they stood frozen. Not until a woodpecker drummed a nearby tree and a pair of squirrels romped among the leaves below them did Jack release his clasp.

"Stay here," he whispered, and shinnied down the tree.

She watched him go with trepidation, stood listening for his return, clinging to the rough comfort of tree bark. She almost fell into his arms when he called her down and said, "The poachers are gone, along with all trace of the deer. I followed their tracks half a mile or more."

She clung to him when her feet hit the ground, clung as tightly as she had to the oak, her face buried in the folds of his neckcloth, sobs shuddering from her throat when the weight of his hand caressed the crown of her head, while he whispered gently, "It's all right. No harm done. You are safe now. Don't worry."

She was sure she must be a dreadful sight when he put her from him, his hands firmly gripping her shoulders. "Come now. No more tears."

She wiped her face with the handkerchief he offered, plucked leaves from her hair, bent her head that he might assist in the endeavor, and searched her pockets for a comb, hair-pins, anything that might neaten her appearance.

"Never mind," he said, smoothing wisps of hair away from her eyes, his expression so sympathetic she wanted to weep again, wanted to stay enfolded in his arms, his palm cupping the crown of her head.

"Are my eyes terribly red?" she asked, dabbing at them.

"Yes. They are," he said without hesitation. "But you are alive, unharmed. Even your sketches have survived. What so compelled you to draw that you would risk your life?"

She reached for the sketchbook as he pulled it from his waistcoat, would have snatched it from his hand, might have succeeded, but he anticipated her move, blocked her grab, opened the book. "Oh, no, you don't! I mean to see. You owe me that much for saving your pretty little neck. What secrets do you keep in here?"

She would not further disgrace herself by tussling with him over the book, merely sighed and set off ahead of him.

"Mushrooms," he murmured behind her. "Are they all mushrooms, then?"

She did not want to answer him, did not want to explain, not with the memory of his arms about her, still warm. She lengthed her stride.

He came loping after her, grabbed her shoulder.

She flung away from him. "Hands off, sir. We are no longer up a tree, and yes, they are all mushrooms. I thought it prudent to learn all that I could about the objects with which my father and I have been so closely equated."

"You draw mushrooms for no other reason than consequence of your father being called one?"

"I find mushrooms most interesting, Mr. Ramsay." She stopped abruptly, stared coolly at him in an attempt to cool her feelings for him. "Do you?"

He smiled as he looked at her, not the drawings. "Extremely interesting."

"Well, I am glad of it, if for no other reason than that your curiosity has chanced to save my skin." She set off again, her heart thumping ridiculously fast.

"And very pretty skin it is."

"Really, Mr. Ramsay!"

"Yes, really, Miss Preston." He fell into step beside her. "Do you mind telling me where you are going? The carriage is that way." He pointed.

"I want to see where the deer was." She could not explain why, but she had to see, had to reconcile herself to the fact that the buck was gone, that she had very nearly met his same fate. "I will not linger, but I must see. Will you accompany me?"

"Of course." He fell silent a moment as they retraced their steps. "They are really quite lovely."

She looked up, puzzled. "Deer?"

He held out the sketchbook. "Mushrooms. I cannot say I have ever before paid much attention to them, as individuals."

"Until forced by circumstance into the company of one," she muttered as she took the sketchbook.

He laughed. "You are not a mushroom at all, but a hedge-hog, Selina Preston."

His words provoked her. "I have not given you leave to call me Selina, Mr. Ramsay."

"Far better Selina than hedgehog, you must agree."

She was shocked into laughing. The laughter grabbed her, shook her, took over. She laughed on, hysterical, emotionally overwhelmed, until he grabbed her by the shoulders and gave her a gentle shake.

"Enough of that, now. Enough."

She choked back the laughter, fought tears, and lifted her face to look him in the eyes—beautiful, gray-blue eyes, full of concern—she could not get enough of them.

"I have not thanked you, Mr. Ramsay, for saving my life."

"Jack," he said.

"What?"

"You can thank me by calling me Jack. One must, after all, be able to call one's rescuer, if anybody, by his first name. Do you not agree?"

She sighed, unable to think of a single good argument against it with him standing so close to her, the smell of sandalwood and cypress clouding her judgment. "I sincerely appreciate your appearing when you did, Mr. . . . uhm . . . Jack."

"A bit of luck, the timing," he agreed.

They had reached the clearing. He strode in front of her, to the spot where the deer had fallen. "There is some blood, of course."

"Dear God!" she said softly. "The mushrooms! They have taken them!"

"What?"

"They were right here. All gone now. Every one of them."

"Must have thought they would go down good with fresh venison," he said lightly.

"Go down well?" She was stunned. "You have heard, perhaps, of a mushroom called the Death Cap?"

"Poison, is it?"

"Deadly," she said softly.

He laughed. Even though she frowned at him, he did not stop laughing until she turned her back on him and walked away.

Chapter Twelve

"I do not care very much for death," she said, as they headed out of the woods. "It was dreadful having that deer die at my feet with nothing I could do. I don't suppose you would understand."

"I understand far better than you would suppose," he replied heavily, thinking of Nicki.

"And yet you laugh, knowing that those men might die!" She seemed baffled that he should do so.

"Yes. I find an ironic humor, a poetic woodland sort of justice, if you will, in contemplating a mushroom death for men who meant to kill—"

"A mushroom's daughter?" she said. The words hung uneasily between them. "Surely death is excessively harsh and permanent justice, sir."

"It amazes me that you feel pity."

"Of course I feel pity," she said. "Who would not, knowing that this sort of poisoning is both agonizing and slow?"

He would not. The men got no more than what they deserved, in his opinion. They had taken action against Nature and Nature held them accountable. She seemed fragile to him at the moment, fragile, forgiving and noble. He was very glad to have prevented death from touching her. If he could see nothing precious in the lives of the poachers, he could most certainly see it in her continued existence.

Nervously she cleared her throat. "I have avoided telling you something I should have passed on long ago. I thought, knowing something of your history, that death might be a sensitive subject to you. I can see now I was mistaken."

She baffled him. "You have some news of death for me?"

"I do, and I apologize. It is news best delivered from other lips."

Her lips might tell him anything at the moment. "Go on."

"Your friend, Mr. Stuart, came to call."

"Hugh? He brought you this news of death?" Head cocked to one side, he gazed at her, touched that she saw fit to concern herself with his feelings. He almost laughed again at the irony of it. "Came to tell you about Nicki Caldwell, did he?" His voice had a strangeness in uttering the name.

"You knew? He did not think you had been informed. I am sorry, sir, for your loss. Hugh said your friend was a brave man."

"A brave man? How curious he should think so." He said it sarcastically. He found nothing brave in Nicki's behavior. It was too much like his own. They had both, too carelessly, gambled away what life they had in the fruitless pursuit of undeserved riches. It struck him afresh the correlation between actions and accountability. The fallen deer, the fallen body of his friend. "You mentioned two deaths? Was the second Valmont Cormack?"

She shook her head, her brow furrowed. "No. Lester Fletcher."

He expelled his breath in a startled rush. "Fletcher? Are you sure?"

She nodded, her face pulled into lines of concern.

He could not express sorrow and regret. There was none in him. With news of Fletcher's sudden death a tiny flame of hope did in fact spring up within him. "Do you know, by chance, *when* he died?"

She blinked. Shook her head. "No. I did not ask. Does it matter?"

"It might."

They broke free from the woods at that point. Avery Preston, catching sight of them, came loping toward them, his color high. "Selina! Where have you been?"

"Father!" She ran to him, would have launched herself into his arms, but he held her away, his face taking on a purple hue.

"What's this, then? You look a frightful sight, my love."

"Yes, Father. It was dreadful! Mr. Ramsay—"

"Thompson! Bring the whip!" Preston bellowed, drowning out the words ". . . saved me."

Her voice shook. "I feared for my life, but Mr. Ramsay was wonderfully cool about the whole affair."

Preston's gaze settled unfavorably on Jack as Thompson came running. Snatching up the whip, he flicked it expertly, decapitating the grass bunched at Jack's toe. "What have you to say for yourself, young man?"

Jack met the man's blank rage, met the second snap of the whip without flinching. "Poachers, sir. Chased us up a tree. We have only just come down."

"Up a tree, Mr. Ramsay!" Preston bellowed. "You would have me believe such a Banbury tale? Disappearing with my daughter into the woods for upwards of an hour and a half. Bringing her back in such a state. I warned you I would hold you accountable and by God I will! Why, I'll thrash you back to Oxford, sir, unless you get down this moment on bended knee and beg for her hand!"

Her hand!

"Father!" Selina's voice rose in outrage.

"Sir!" said Jack. "Your daughter has suffered no harm."

"I'll brook no argument. On your knees, sir." The whip snapped again, perilously close.

"No, Father!"

"You will stay out of this, Selina. Down, sir! This minute, sir! I would see you grovel!"

"If you will only calm yourself, sir, allow me to explain."

"No explanations necessary from a man too many call Rakehell, Mr. Ramsay. I know the ways of such men."

"Not this man, Father."

"Silence, Selina! No good will come of defending the honor of a man who has none."

"I will not be silent when you impugn my honor and insult the gentleman who has just saved my life! You must apologize to Mr. Ramsay."

"Saved you, you say? Not ruined you? Tell me the truth now, girl. No wild stories."

"I would now be ruined, possibly killed, by three ruffians

had it not been for Mr. Ramsay, Father. Poachers, as he said. Twice he has saved my life this afternoon!" Her eyes sparkled magnificently when she was angry. "Put down the whip and I will tell you everything."

Thus it was that in the leg of their journey that led them through Milford, where the lame horse had been exchanged for a sound one, past Weeping Cross and into Stafford, where they stopped for the night, Avery Preston said not a word, other than to prod his daughter and Jack Ramsay for a completely detailed account of what had happened to them in the woods and to apologize, lavishly and with tedious repetition, to Jack.

Jack wished the man saw fit to apologize half so prettily to his daughter.

In Milford, word was left for the gamekeeper. Three poachers in black masks had been seen taking a buck. The poachers had picked poisonous Death Cap mushrooms.

The innkeeper to whom they spoke laughed about the mushrooms.

"These men may have families," Selina pointed out. "Wives and children who may partake unwittingly of the poison."

"Aye. And a great laughingstock their men will be if they have killed off their families for no more reason than a bit of illegal venison."

In Stafford, a quiet country town on the River Sow, the local constable was summoned. The innkeeper's son set off after the man as soon as the tale of dangerous poachers had been told.

Paper and pens were fetched as well. Jack required them that he might write a letter or two. Miss Preston's attempt to inform undeserving poachers of the dangers of mushrooms had reminded him of a concept he would much rather have continued to forget. Accountability. His own, in connection with the loss of his family's fortune. The first letter he directed to Roger, inquiring into the specifics of Lester Fletcher's demise. Was there any possibility, he wondered, that his debt to Fletcher might get lost in the settling of the man's estate? Another letter he directed to his sister Aurora, whom he knew to be in the company of his younger brother, Rupert, at a sheep shearing in Norfolk. He could not count on a miracle with regard to his debt to Fletcher, after all, and they were in a perfect position at such a gathering to sell off the sheep, cattle, and pigs. He recommended they do so.

He felt like a pig himself when the letters had been written and sealed. How accountable was it, after all, to ask others to pick up the pieces he had so carelessly strewn in his wake?

Asked to explain his rescue of Selina Preston yet again when the constable arrived, Jack kept his story to a minimum. He did not feel heroic. That he should have to tell and retell a story that led others to regard him in such a light seemed nothing short of hypocritical. That he should be clapped on the back and regarded with awe seemed a strange sort of torture. He was heartily glad when the constable went away and he might remove himself from the very wearing company of the exuberant Mr. Preston and Selina, the cloistered daughter he had followed into the woods with every intention of seducing, given opportunity.

Selina looked blankly at her father and nodded. What had he said? Something about a castle being rebuilt at great expense on the site of some ruins? She was too distracted to care, too intrigued by Jack Ramsay's silence to listen. Yesterday he rescued her from poachers, today he ignored her, ignored her father, stared glassy-eyed out of the window, ignoring the scenery as they careened northward through lush farmland, dotted with grazing cattle.

He had spent the evening writing letters, had been no more than curtly polite to the constable of Stafford, had made no attempt to speak to her before taking himself off to bed. Today he made no attempt to make conversation with either herself or her father. He rarely even turned to look at her.

What went on in his head? How had their brush with death affected him? She knew too well how it affected her. She had spent the night tossed by the nightmare that she was a deer, that Jack Ramsay, not poachers, chased after her. With an arrow he had pierced her heart. She had tried to run, but her feet would not obey. She had fallen, dying, at his feet. It had been a gladness to wake, to discover her nightmare no more than that, to open the window on a day of brilliant sunshine and clear skies.

The world seemed a sparkling place, too wonderful to imagine not having woken. The smell of coffee seemed richer than usual, the buttery toast, poached eggs, and sausage tasted almost exotic. A bowl of full-blown roses, pale pink petals drifting onto the sideboard of the dining room at the inn, had moved her almost to tears. As for Ramsay, well, she could not feast her eyes too much on him. He was the reason she enjoyed this morning. Her savior. His hair had never gleamed so richly in the sunlight, the freckles across his nose had never looked so endearing. His hands, the hands with which he had raised a gun to protect her, with which he had boosted her into the safety of a tree, the same hands with which he created wondrous music—they were nothing short of a miracle. She longed to kiss his every finger—longed to feel those blessed, miraculous fingers cradling her head again, plucking leaves from her hair.

The only shadow on the perfection of the morning was that he would not look at her. She had grown accustomed to his regard, had grown to anticipate the synchronous meeting of their gazes. It troubled her that his vision seemed to be turned completely inward today, of all days. Did he not relish the balmy breeze that rifled the coppery strands of hair that drifted across a brow from which she longed to smooth a wrinkle? Did his brooding gray eyes not find the passing landscape wonderfully lush? Did he not revel in the fact that he had saved her, saved himself, that he was alive?

Even her father noticed Ramsay's quiet lack of focus. More than once, he fell silent in his ramblings. He went so far as to try to draw Jack out when they passed through the village of Stone. "You must take a good gander out of the window here, sir," he suggested. "There are excellent views to be had behind us of the Trent Valley."

Ramsay obliged him, leaned out the window, took a good look behind them. "Very nice!" he said. That was all.

Very nice!

Selina wanted to shake him. The view was far better than nice; it was wonderful, and they were alive to enjoy it! His blood ran cold while hers burned in her veins with the heat of a joy so searing it throbbed in neck, breast, and groin.

Into Nantwich they rolled. Dear old Nantwich! It felt good to be back to the familiar sight of quaint streets crowded with beam-and-wattle houses, herringbone-patterned in ochre and brown. Her heart swelled with satisfaction, indeed love, in observing the familiar octagonal spire of St. Mary's poke through a silvery stand of birch.

"We shall just nip in to see how they do at the saltworks." Her father leaned out the window to call to the coachman, to greet the tobacconist, to inquire after the health of Mrs. Tucker's new baby.

Ramsay peered out the coach window as they slowed—the closest thing to interest he had exhibited all day.

What did Nantwich look like to a gentleman accustomed to apartments in London and an estate in the Midlands? In wondering, the familiar seemed entirely new to Selina, new and in some ways surprisingly ugly. She had never before noticed how very yellow was the tobacconist's smile, nor that the doors and shutters of the saltworks could do with a fresh coat of paint.

Jack felt like a strange fish swimming in Avery Preston's pond. The man was known to virtually everyone they passed in the street, or so it seemed from all the hat tipping, head nodding, and forelock tugging that went on in the wake of his passage.

The saltworks was a long, low brick building with a few windows and three doors, all propped open, most emitting steam that gave the breeze a seaside scent.

"Have you ever seen a saltworks?" Selina asked.

He turned from the window, looked at her, really looked at her for the first time that day. Her face had a softness to it he had never noticed before. The light from the window behind him made her eyes shine deep blue, but it was not so much their color that impressed him as her expression. Of all the people in Nantwich, she was the only one who recognized him with anything other than curiosity or suspicion, and appeared to like what she saw. Her complexion had a translucence, her hair a tempting honeyed gleam, her lips a lush fullness. He wanted, in that moment, to lean over and kiss her.

The thought flashed through his mind that he had, in some small way, begun to right the wrong of having taken Nicki Caldwell's life in saving hers.

"No. I have never seen a saltworks," he admitted.

"Would you care to?" She had dimples when she smiled, deeper on the right side of her mouth than the left.

"Do you mean to be my guide?"

"If you like."

"Please." He opened the carriage door and offered his arm. There was a certain comfort to be taken in the firm, hale wholeness of the gloved hand she placed on his sleeve.

The heat was oppressive inside the low building. A bit of Hell. Steam billowed in rolling clouds from great, shallow pans in the center of the room topping a brick kiln into which an aproned man shoveled coal. Three other sweat-drenched men raked with wooden paddles the boiling pans of what looked like nothing so much as dirty water.

"We use cast-iron trays rather than the lead ones that the Romans favored." Selina stood on tiptoe and spoke into his ear, that she might be heard above the noise. The rose bouquet of her perfume was heightened by the heat. "The donkey pump we use to bring the brine to the surface is modern, but other than that, little has changed in the process for years. It is, quite simply, a matter of evaporation."

She, and the cloud of jasmine and roses, led the way the length of the room, calling out a personal greeting to each of the workers before passing into a second room, this one much cooler and free of steam.

"Here the brine is left to cool, that the salt solution might crystallize." She smoothed steam-limp strands of hair away from her forehead. "Hard to imagine that inferno in there produces something so pure, so sparkling white, is it not?" She raked up a handful of the rock salt, her hands fine boned and pale, her pointer finger smudged with graphite. "Rather like life," she said.

"Life?" He did not see the connection. "How so?"

"When life heats to a boil we are reminded of its essence. A single moment of crisis or joy can crystallize for us what is pure and elemental and important."

"And have you had such moments?"

"Oh, yes. We all have, if we will only recognize them."

"For instance?"

"For instance, yesterday, when I stood between three men who were determined either to change my life or take it from me, I realized with great clarity just how precious life was. Into that moment of hopeless realization came the blessed sound of your voice. I can repeat to you every word said, every inflection. And in the moment you spoke, another moment of clarity. The unexpected intrusion of your life on mine seemed suddenly to make the greatest sort of sense, as if the pieces of a puzzle had fallen into place. As consequence of your having been with us, of your having stepped into the forest at that very moment, I did not die."

Rather than burst the bubble of her elation, he said indulgently, "Fortune smiled on you."

She laughed, the sound as rich, soft, and rosy as her perfume. "Not fortune at all. God. He has a plan for each of us, and you are an integral part of mine. Have you no defining moments, indelibly etched in your memory?"

Jack nodded grimly. The memory of Lester Fletcher's gleeful turn of a fateful card was etched in his memory. Clearer still was the moment when Nicki had looked up, recognized him, and coolly remarked on his aim before falling dead at his feet. "All too many," he said gruffly.

She looked at him keenly as she held open the door to another room, revealing more than a dozen white-smocked women ranged around long wooden tables breaking up and boxing the crystallized salt. "Is the salt of your life sprinkled too liberally, sir, to bring such grimness to the set of your mouth, such sadness to your eyes?"

He felt as transparent as crystallized rock salt when she looked at him so knowingly and spoke to the very heart of him. "And if such were the case, Miss Preston? What do you recommend?"

"Less spice, sir."

Chapter Thirteen

*L*ess spice, she had said, as if the recipe for happiness was a simple one. Jack enjoyed talking to Selina Preston, enjoyed hearing her voice, her outlook on life. She perceived the world differently, this mushroom's daughter. He wondered if the fact that she was an artist had aught to do with it.

"May I see your drawings, Miss Preston?" he asked as they settled into their seats in the carriage.

Preston enthusiastically seconded the notion. "Yes, dear, show the man. Very clever with a pencil is our Selina. Draws patterns for the looms, you know."

Jack had not known.

"This is one of hers." Preston patted the silk jacquard of his waistcoat, an exquisite oak-leaf pattern on a speckled ground. "The buttons as well." He turned the thread-covered fastener so that it caught the light. An acorn and oak-leaf pattern designed to match.

It had never occurred to Jack that Miss Preston's drawings might be generated for such practical application. The young women he knew who drew did so for no other reason than pleasure, and the occasional framed work to hang about the house, that everyone might know their talent.

He was genuinely intrigued.

With the look about her of a startled fawn, she handed over the green sketchbook. It contained not mushrooms but page after page of flora and fauna. A red-breasted robin; a beautifully black-hooded, peach-bellied finch; a saffron-tinted yellowhammer. Flowers, the names as colorful and evocative as the drawings themselves—purple, star-shaped columbine; cheerful butterscotch-yellow wallflowers; lush, frog-lipped toadflax. Vines and leaves she had captured, too, ivy, cinque-foil, black bryony, and honeysuckle, oak, chestnut, dogwood, and maple. Occasionally an animal peeped from the pages—a fox, a goose, a horse, a cat. What made the drawings most un-usual was that while each subject was drawn quite naturally on the left side of the page, on the right it was drawn again, the pencil marks firmer, broader, bolder. The subject was reduced to a stylized grid pattern, redesigned and watercolor-tinted with fabrics and buttons in mind.

The patterns were beautiful, inventive, a startling insight into the mind of the young woman he had once dismissed as no more than a female on the prowl for a titled husband. He looked up from the sketchbook. She watched him, doe eyes narrowed, as if she feared he might judge her talents too harshly.

"Splendid!" he said enthusiastically, enjoying the blush his praise brought to her cheeks. "Are there more? Have you done the same sort of thing with your architectural studies?"

She nodded.

"Show me. Please!"

Shyly she pulled another sketchbook from its hiding place.

This book was thick with stained-glass windows; vaulted ceilings; rainspouts in the shape of angels, of women, of grin-ning gargoyles. Page after page of wood carvings depicted first biblical scenes; then, more amusing, a dancing bear, an elephant, two monkeys. Marble statuary, too, graced the paper, crypt covers and tombstones. Angels, saints, and a few brass rubbings of knights and ladies brought to life bygone days on folded onionskin. The book fairly exploded with imagery. In rifling the pages, Jack felt he rifled the pages of Selina Pres-ton's mind and spirit.

"A carving?" he asked, intrigued by an unusual drawing of a young woman in a cloak offering something to what looked like a fox garbed in a monk's robes.

"A misericord," she said.

"A misery what?"

"Misericord. Seats of pity. Both beautiful and functional. It is a carved lip attached to the bottom of the seat in a choirstall. When the choir stands to sing and the seat is raised, it serves as a place to lean, that the singers might appear to be standing without forever burdening their feet. The ones in Chester are the most beautiful I have ever seen."

"As these drawings would seem to prove. Most impressive, Miss Preston."

"She is rather a dab hand, is she not?" Her father beamed with pride. "You have yet to see her portraiture."

"Father, no! Mr. Ramsay has surely seen enough of my handiwork for one day."

"Have I?" He got the feeling she wanted him to say he had, regardless of his true feelings in the matter.

"You must excuse her reticence, Mr. Ramsay. She is very sensitive about her portraiture. Rarely shows anyone the red book. She is very good with faces, you know. One can identify who it is she has drawn immediately. Says she has trouble with hands and feet, however."

"You will not show me?" Jack asked. "Not even if I swear, upon my honor, that I will not judge too harshly your hands and feet?" He looked at her hands as he spoke, then her feet, his gaze rising slowly the length of her anatomy to meet her gaze. "Or anything else in between?"

The frightened fawn was back. She frowned.

"Of course she will show you." Her father exhibited far more assurance than did she.

Trapped between their mutual pressure, brow knitted, she looked from her father to him and back again. For a moment, Jack felt pity. He almost hoped she would refuse. It was not often she refused her father anything.

She was not prepared to refuse him now. Reaching into the window pouch, she handed him the red-bound sketchbook.

With a sense of ceremony, Jack opened the book to the first page. An unmistakable likeness, almost a mirror image of Mr. Preston smiled up from the page. "Why, it is you, sir!" he blurted.

Mr. Preston craned to see. "Did I not tell you that one can recognize the rendering immediately? I thought the drawing very like."

It was very like, and very respectful as well. She had taken care to heighten emphasis on those features that were most attractive and gave little emphasis to those that were not. Jack turned the page with a sense of anticipation. How would Miss Preston have chosen to see him?

"Is this, then, your wife, sir? Your mother, Miss Preston?"

For a moment she looked pained, as if he had said something to hurt her.

Preston rose, swaying with the coach's movement, hunched in the confined space. "Perhaps it would be better, sir, if we changed seats, the better for you to see. Selina can identify the portraits as you turn the pages. You will know half of Chester in this manner before we arrive."

Jack had no choice but to similarly rise and switch seats.

Selina made room for him as he sat, but the edge of her skirt was caught beneath him nonetheless.

They realized the situation, their hands reaching to free the fabric at exactly the same moment. She jerked away and nervously smoothed her skirts.

"Beg pardon," he apologized.

"Think nothing of it." She concentrated on the sketches, her color high, her voice unsteady. "You see here my brother, Allan. He is fond of horses. Insisted he be sketched in company with his favorite mount."

Mischief, strong jawed and willful, looked up from both ends of a horse lead. Miss Preston's brother bore no resemblance whatsoever either to his father or his sister. The horse had good lines.

Jack leaned closer to Selina, turned the page, and as if by accident shifted his leg so that it brushed her skirt. It was he who drew sudden breath, not she. From the sketchbook, a graphite Selina stared up at him, perfectly rendered in every detail, her expression strangely wistful.

The real Selina reached across him, her arm brushing his, the scent of jasmine and roses teasing his nostrils, her weight shifting just as the coach hit a rut in the road, throwing her off balance, her hip against his, her thigh pressing his, her hand coming down smartly on the middle of the page she reached to turn, so that he felt the impact quite shockingly in the member of his body most likely to respond favorably.

"I am sorry," she gasped, righting herself, not yet collected enough to pull her thigh away from his. Her intent was to turn the page, and turn it she did, flipping away the image of herself as if it pained her. Her fumbling was rather more pleasurable than otherwise, yet Jack lived in fear that she might snatch away the book entirely, revealing in him something far more aroused than an expression in a self-portrait.

"I rather liked that last one," he could not resist saying.

"Tarporley, my dear," her father said. "We are almost home now. There is Beeston Castle in the distance."

She leaned away from him to gaze out the window.

Jack glanced out as well. A village street whisked past, a rose-filled churchyard, a medieval church. Beyond it stretched terraced hills; trees, green and dense; rocky outcroppings; what looked like a castle. It occurred to him that he had no home to return to. He had lost his home, his right to homecomings.

The Prestons were caught up in the view. Jack took advantage of the moment to flip hastily through a gallery of faces—men, women, and children—to the last page marked with graphite. He sought himself, knew she had captured him here in Oxford, outside the cathedral. Face-to-face with himself he stopped. He had been tossing his penny as he spoke to her father. The cathedral was roughed in behind them. She had focused the majority of her pencil's attention on their faces.

The drawing was remarkably deft; even his hand, caught in movement, the penny suspended above it, was well rendered. With little more than a few lines she had captured his mouth; his eyes, the fall of his hair, the set of his chin. Her discernment was startling, even disturbing.

In his stance, in the expression of his features, in the set of his shoulders, it was clear, painfully so, that he stood asking Avery Preston for a favor—a favor of consequence. From the start she had known, had recognized clearly enough that she might re-create her knowing on paper.

"What do you think, Mr. Ramsay?" She had turned from the

window and sat regarding him with the soulful depths of far
too observant a gaze.

"You captured me, Miss Preston." He closed up the sketchbook and handed it back to her. "Too well, I am thinking, far
too well."

Chapter Fourteen

Sshe had captured him. Selina did not know how to take such a pronouncement, certainly not when it came from Rakehell Ramsay, eyes guarded, the watchful look returned, as though he had revealed too much of himself to her and meant to keep the rest a secret. What did he mean, she had captured him? To her way of thinking, quite the reverse was true.

Selina puzzled the matter as the coach broke from the trees and wound its way down the lane that led to Little Moresworth, her home. From the midst of a small grove of oak, a gray-green slate roof and redbrick chimney thrust, crown for a beam-and-wattle monstrosity that ranged below, first one direction and then the other. The house revealing itself piecemeal through the trees offered up an answer of sorts.

She had captured a small bit of who Jack Ramsay was in her drawing. Like her view of Little Moresworth, it was not necessarily the best part of him, or even a part he wished her to see. How did she look in the eyes of this stranger? How did the place she called home appear to him?

Little Moresworth was a part of her, a part she did not wish to see rejected or ridiculed. Not the kind of dwelling place to which Ramsay was accustomed. Wings, windows, even extra floors had been added onto the original structure, an ancient farmhouse. She felt strangely protective of the place and hoped he would not judge it too harshly.

It was freshly painted, in the newly popular color scheme, the wattle washed in pure white lime rather than in the less expensive, traditional ochre shades to be seen elsewhere throughout Cheshire. The exposed oak beams, too, looked fresh and shiny, stained with glossy black pitch. It was a house dressed in the high-contrast costume of a French harlequin puppet.

Far more substantial than any puppet, Moresworth Hall had always resembled to Selina an unsinkable, if whimsical, Tudor man-of-war. Like the prow of a ship it rose three stories, higgledy-piggledy fashion, the top floor overhanging the other two, a long gallery of leaded-glass windows on the third floor catching the light.

A flock of geese and a pair of chickens pecked about the yard. Roses bloomed, and a bed of herbs. No formal gardens had ever been established. The Prestons had always been too busy for beautifications of that sort. Selina had never before noticed their absence, but having just passed through so much of England, where the architecture was modern, the landscaping a work of art, she considered Little Moresworth a trifle dowdy today.

"When was the house built, sir?" Jack asked her father. "Sixteenth century?"

"Earlier than that. Fourteen fifty-eight, to be exact. The wings were added half a century later, along with the third-floor gallery and the bay windows."

"Rare to see so much woodwork in my part of the country. Rare and beautiful."

It was rare and beautiful—from the familiar bold herring-bone pattern on the original structure, to a series of notched hoops and quatrefoils under the eaves of the add-ons.

Selina was pleased to hear Ramsay's praise. "The beam patterns at Moresworth have always pleased me," she said. "Each set of builders took pains to leave their mark."

He fastened his gaze on her. She should have looked away, should have guarded against revealing too much of her feelings. She could not. His stare was, for the moment, too compelling.

Barking the alarm, Shep and Hazard darted from the darkness of the portal that led through the bulk of the house, a passage just wide enough for a carriage to squeeze through. She should have looked away then, the dogs a distraction, swallowed up for an instant by the darkness of the passage. She did not. It would have been wisest. It would have been prudent. She expected to find that *he* had, when they broke free into the sunshine of the courtyard, horseshoes ringing on cobblestone. He had not. Their gazes were still linked, as though never parted.

"It is good to be home," her father said.

"It is," she agreed faintly. Breathless, she looked away as a flurry of welcome crowded from every doorway that opened onto the courtyard. Grooms, footmen, maids, and more dogs, tails wagging, descended on them.

"Good day, master, miss."

"Glad to have you back again."

"Did not expect you home so soon."

The coach door swung wide; a dozen hands helped Selina down from the steps. Baggage rained from the roof. The horses were led out of the traces. And through it all, Jack Ramsay was examined as curiously as if Selina had brought home the devil himself.

Mrs. Preston swept out of the house, arms wide. "My dear!" She enveloped first her husband and then Selina in an enthusiastic embrace. "Home so soon! You need not have raced back to Little Moresworth just because of a loom."

"Allan has fixed it, then?" Selina asked.

"No. You know Allan has no more aptitude for such things than you have for music."

Watching them, Jack Ramsay parted his lips, as if to say something. Selina silenced him with the slightest shake of her head.

"Allan could learn," she suggested, "if only he cared enough to apply himself."

Mrs. Preston's gaze darted uneasily from Selina to Jack, to Mr. Preston and back again. "But who is this you bring with you? Surely you have not given away your heart so soon, my dear?"

"No! Not at all," Selina blurted.

Jack laughed. "You flatter me, madame." He bowed, gracefully, saluted Mrs. Preston's hand and slid a conspiratorial look at Selina. "Alas, I am no more than Mr. Ramsay, your daughter's latest music master."

"Music master?" Mrs. Preston sounded amazed. "I am so sorry to have mistaken you for a gentleman, sir."

"A common error," Jack quipped.

"Mother! He *is* a gentleman."

"I am sure his manners are not to be questioned, Selina."

Selina frowned. "That is not at all what I meant."

Jack laughed. "Quite right. My manners, you have every right to question, Mrs. Preston."

Confused, Mrs. Preston tried to make some sense of it. "Have you come all the way from London, Mr. Ramsay? I am surprised Mr. Preston convinced you to undertake such a tedious journey."

"No tedium at all in such stimulating company. Your husband is a marvelous conversationalist, madame, and your daughter . . ." Jack Ramsay smiled as he spoke, his disconcerting gaze fixed on a discomfited Selina. "Your daughter and I have made splendid progress in our journey thus far. I cannot recall a pupil whose company I have enjoyed more."

"That does not surprise me, sir," Selina murmured wryly.

"Selina! You display an alarming absence of modesty, my dear."

"Not at all," Selina calmly contradicted her. "As I am the first and only pupil Mr. Ramsay has taken under tutelage, he can be quite free with compliments and I am equally free to question the sincerity of them."

Jack followed the footman bearing his cases, who had been assigned the task of escorting him to his room. Far larger than Jack had expected, Little Moresworth was a well-established property. It had not sprung up overnight, like a mushroom. Preston's forefathers had obviously worked hard, generation after generation, to acquire and maintain such a structure.

Not as spacious, nor as recently constructed, as his own family's ancestral home, it was perhaps better loved, better cherished. Certainly no one had gambled it away over cards for the past several centuries!

There was a quaint unevenness to everything about the house, and an abundance of exposed wood beams and carved brackets. There was a sense of solidity, of unshakable permanence so contrary to Jack's own state of mind that he felt dreadfully out of place.

He was shown to guest quarters, not the servants' hall, as he very well might have expected. Preston himself bustled up to demonstrate in cupboard, cabinet, and drawer, where his accumulated treasures were stored in the adjoining music room. It was a considerable and varied collection—rote, harp, gittern, and citole; mandore, lute, dulcimer, clavichord, and virginal. Preston had not stinted on expense for his finds. Inset with rare and exquisitely carved woods, laden with semiprecious stones: lapis; turquoise; agate, mother-of-pearl, and ivory; hand painted with landscapes, intricate geometric or flowered patterns, some faux marbled. Each piece was remarkable.

"There is a cello?" Jack said hopefully.

A cabinet was thrown open. "Stringed instruments are in here—cello, gambina, rebec, viol, and kits. You are free, of course, to play any and all of the instruments, to replace or repair any required parts."

Carefully, Jack lifted the weighty bulk of the cello free from the cabinet and reverently ran his hands over it as if caressing the body of a woman with whom he meant to be familiar. It was a painted piece, almost tawdry in an abundance of color and pattern, but appearance mattered not so much to Jack as did the song this cello might sing beneath his hands. He settled in a chair, rosined the bow, drew the instrument between his legs, and tested the bow against strings. He bent his head, his ears eager to hear the cello's voice, eager to test that voice with Bach's brilliance. Jack lost himself in the depths of sound, forgetting even where he was until he had built the rising notes of the prelude to a satisfactory finish and opened his eyes to find Selina and her mother observing him with intoxicated expressions, cheeks flushed, lips parted, eyes soft and shining.

"Bravo!" Preston shouted, breaking the spell Jack had cast so completely over the women. "I do like to hear beautiful music resounding in this room!"

"As it did when I was a child," Selina said softly.

Mrs. Preston was the sort of female, as his own mother had been, who reached out to touch the person she spoke to when she was much moved. She reached out now to pat his arm when she said, "Indeed, what a talent you have been blessed with, Mr. Ramsay! I hope you will agree to participate in the musicale with which we hope to raise money for the cathedral. It is in sad need of repair."

"Musicale?"

"Yes. Selina has not yet mentioned it to you? I must say, I am surprised! She is full of praise for your talent and tells me you have—in one lesson—taught her more than all of her previous music masters combined."

Jack stole a glance at Selina. There was more he would like to teach Selina Preston, much more. Mrs. Preston noticed the direction of his gaze. An observant woman, Jack thought. "What else does your daughter tell you of me, Mrs. Preston?"

"She tells me she hears the pattern of your thoughts in your music, Mr. Ramsay—the sad song of your soul."

Jack swung another look Selina's way. "She said that, did she?"

"Come now, no more sad music, Mr. Ramsay. I mean to give you a tour of the house and grounds so that you will know your way around." Mrs. Preston linked arms with him, and might have led him to the door had not her husband stopped her.

"Let Selina show him. I would hear news of the broken loom, Mrs. Preston."

Brows raised, Mrs. Preston looked from her husband to Selina. "If you think it best, Mr. Preston. Do you mind, my dear?"

"Not at all." Selina's voice was cool, her head held high as she crossed to the door. "Mr. Ramsay."

Jack relinquished Mrs. Preston's arm.

"Do not dawdle, Selina," Mrs. Preston admonished. "Dinner will be served as soon as Allan returns."

"Returns?"

Did he detect a hint of concern in the question?

"He has gone to the Roodee." Mrs. Preston's voice was sub-dued.

Selina pressed her lips together a moment, as if the information disturbed her. "Again? Despite his promises?"

"Yes. Shall we discuss it later, after you have shown Mr. Ramsay about?"

"Of course."

Intrigued, Jack followed in Selina's wake as she swept out the door.

The house rambled interminably, from the steaming bustle of kitchens lively with preparation for the evening repast, to the echoing Great Hall, where a vast table was being set for the entire household and the butler anxiously took Selina aside to ask if Mr. Ramsay's place was to be set above or below the salt cellar. Jack was relieved to hear her respond without hesitation, "As Mr. Ramsay's brother is a viscount, I should think we must put him above the salt, Saunders."

"Very good, miss." Saunders swallowed this tidbit of information blandly enough, but the heads of more than one of the footmen did a quick swivel in his direction. "Will the young master be joining us?"

She evidenced a trace of irritation in answering, as if she would not be convinced of her brother's intentions until he made them known. "Mrs. Preston tells me he will."

Linking arms with Jack, she strode with undue haste—or could it be anger?—out of the Great Hall, through two parlors, the chapel, the chancel, up the stairs into a prayer room, through a drafty great chamber appropriately called the Great Chamber, and past the faint dankness of several ancient garderobes, built into the wall of the moat.

"Still functional," Selina assured him.

It did not matter, none of it mattered so much as the growing tension between them, the uneasiness of her hand on his arm, the unsteady edge of her voice, and her inability to look him in the eyes as she pointed out to him three closed doors and identified them in a slightly choked undervoice as bed-chambers.

He wondered which was hers.

Through the guests' wing, where his things had been placed, back by the music room, past a small solarium green with plants, and up more stairs to the highest room of the house she led him.

"The long gallery," she announced as she opened the door. "My favorite part of the house." Her voice echoed the length of the sparsely fitted, high-ceilinged room.

The walls were oak, the floors lime and ash. Briefly the ceiling drew one's eye, its sturdy exposed beams echoing the spherical pattern one might witness on the exterior of the house. It was, however, the abundance of windows that distinguished this room from all others, row upon row of leaded glass on all sides of them, allowing the last of the day's light to flood the place. Set high above their heads in the longest of the walls, they offered a pale blue, cloud-strewn view. Windows. Of course this was her favorite room!

He did not care for the emptiness. It echoed an emptiness within himself he liked to forget. He appreciated, however, that they had the place to themselves.

She had nothing to say to him now that they were alone. Her thoughts, her glances, strayed elsewhere. To the Roodee, perhaps, and broken promises?

There was a painted panel at each end of the room, in the eaves above the leaded windows, gold-leaf and forest green against a wash of white. Jack held up his hand to block the glare of the setting sun. "What does it say?"

She answered absentmindedly, the words recited from memory. *"Destiny is to be found in the search for wisdom and truth."*

"Is it?" His voice was laced with a sarcasm that the walls threw back at him.

She ignored the comment. "It is Destiny you see depicted, sensibly attired, standing firmly on a cube. Balanced in one hand is an astrolabe. In the other a measuring device, calipers."

Bored, he slid the penny from his pocket.

"At the far end of the room," she said as she turned, her heel squeaking on well-waxed wood, "is the sister panel."

Curious, flipping his Welsh penny, he traversed the length of the room, the echo of his footsteps following him like a friend. The second panel depicted a blindfolded Fate. She wore a book like a hat, stood balanced unsteadily on a sphere, her clothes in disarray. Dangling precariously from a string above her head hung the wheel of Fortune. Beneath it went the saying *"Fortune relies blindly on chance and luck."*

Abruptly he halted the aimless progress of the penny—clenched it tight. Here was his life, his ruination, reduced to a platitude. His luck had run out, and with it his fortune.

"Mr. Ramsay." She said his name with purpose, as if she meant to follow it with words of great import.

Heels too loud on the flooring, he rejoined her in the center of the vast, barnlike room. It shamed him to think there was no question as to which of these sayings she must associate with him. He wondered if she meant, in some way, to lecture him.

"I must apologize, Mr. Ramsay."

So out of sync were her words with his thinking that he blinked with dismay. "Must you?"

"My father." She paused uneasily. "I am sure you must have noticed."

"Noticed?" He pocketed the coin—flexed his fingers. What about her father would she have him give note to?

"He throws us together, Mr. Ramsay. I will neither insult your intelligence, nor my father's motives, by explaining his intent. I am sure it must be apparent to you, as you have so clearly stated in the past your belief that I went to London with the hopes of snaring a titled husband."

He was stunned. She spoke of her shame, not his, her features heavy with regret. He wanted her in that moment, wanted to lie down with her on the cold wood flooring, that he might seek out the warmth and softness that so touched him in her words.

He fingered the hard outline of the penny in his pocket, pressed it hard against his ribs. "He means that you should win me, perhaps? That I should beg him for your hand?"

She turned her back to him, cleared her throat uneasily. "Perhaps."

"He sells you short, Selina." He circled her that he might observe her expression. "I boast no title, no money, no lands. I have, in fact, lost all that has been entrusted to me." He wanted her to know he was cognizant of his wrongdoing, that it preyed upon his peace of mind.

"The point is moot, sir." She met his regard with a wary look. "I merely wished to ease your mind, if it suffers the wrong impression. I have no such designs on your future."

"You mean, to put it plainly, that you would not marry me were I to go down on bended knee at this very moment?" He sank to one knee when she would have passed him, the floor creaking in protest.

Selina panicked. He was on his knees! A wholly inappropriate posture. Words of marriage tumbled from his mouth. Words she might have responded to with enthusiasm had this been her imagination working and not reality. Words, just words, empty of emotion, empty of meaning. He had no intention of seriously proposing to a mushroom's daughter.

"Get up!" she insisted, her words bouncing off the walls like rubber balls. Get up. Get up. "Cease this playacting at once. It does not please me in the least."

"You do not care for me?" Jack Ramsay possessed a look in his eyes Selina did not pretend to understand. He managed to sound both wounded and sarcastic as he rose from his lowly position. "Well, I cannot blame you. There is not much in me to love."

She scowled at him. "I do not know you, or your purpose, well enough to care or not to care."

"You have determined, then, that I have a purpose? That it runs contrary to your own? That we are incompatible, Miss Preston? As different, perhaps, as the panels picked out on the far ends of these walls?"

She turned her back and put some distance between them. There was something too intent about the way he looked at her. Helplessly she stared at Destiny and her astrolabe. "I suppose we are as different and as incompatible as the panels. Do you not agree?"

"Incompatible? I think not," he said, stalking her like a tabby after a mouse. The blue-gray of his eyes shone in a particularly fine manner because of the light from the windows, which lit his hair in far too distracting a fashion. His words did nothing to allay her uneasiness. "It is a law of physics, after all, that opposites are strongly attracted to one another." His voice was low, resonant, the voice of a cello.

As never before, he fit the title by which so many called him—Rakehell Ramsay. At any moment he might sprout horns. She must not, would not, fall prey to her desire for such a man. "Surely there should be common ground, sir, between two people who would discuss something so serious as marriage."

"In what way *common*?"

"Common mind, common sensibilities, common desires, and common faith."

"Common *desires,* Miss Preston? Speak to me, if you will, of your *desires,* common or uncommon."

Her mind raced. Was his hair so rich in color, she wondered, so smoothly silken that every woman longed to run fingers through it?

It perturbed her that he managed to make everything sound so seductive, so suggestive. It perturbed her more that every time she looked at him she was possessed by feelings she could designate as nothing short of desire.

"I desire . . ."

"Do tell." He leaned closer, his eyes bright.

She frowned, could not look at him and reply, could not reveal to him what sprang first to mind. Walking the length of the gallery she studied the faint scuff marks on the oak paneling. She had come here often with her mother as a child. Together they had bounced an India rubber ball against the walls when the weather was too dismal to go out of doors. Occasionally they had played at shuttlecocks or tennis. More than once they had discussed the painted panels at each end of the room, as she discussed them today with Rakehell Ramsay. At the east end of the gallery, the only wall where the windows had been set low enough to look out, she leaned her elbows on the sill, steadied herself so that she no longer felt as if she balanced on a rolling ball and stared a moment at the distant horizon. The silk mill could be seen from this window, and the distant walls of Chester.

"I desire," she said at last, "nothing extraordinary—to find contentment, love, spiritual fulfillment; to live a life of purpose, to touch the lives of those around me, to understand more clearly why I am here."

She could hear the solid contact of bootheels on wood flooring as he approached. The mass of him stirred the air as he took stance at the sill beside her. "You have no desire then, for . . ."

She looked up, concerned he had guessed her true desires, worried he might voice them for her, but no—

"A title?" he said. "A fortune?"

She laughed. "My father's desires, not mine."

"Marriage?" He was guessing; he could not read her mind at all.

Her feet were on surer footing now. "I should like to find love, a partner in life. Yes. Someone kind, gentle, steady, someone interested in salt or silk, perhaps." Anyone but him, she thought.

He laughed, a throaty sound that gave her gooseflesh. Stepping close behind her, he whispered, "Someone interested in mushrooms, Miss Preston?"

His mention of mushrooms, reminding her of the rift that separated them, steadied her.

"Very few mushrooms in London," he needled. "They all get eaten there."

Snappish and unhappy, she replied, "Do you eat mushrooms, Mr. Ramsay?"

"There is something very succulent in a lightly sautéed mushroom." He leaned in over her shoulder to say it, so close he stirred the fabric of her sleeve. "I would nibble it now, given half a chance."

"Sir!" She turned to glare at him, a great mistake, for in

looking into his eyes she was doomed. Penetrating and far too insightful, she fell into their blue-gray depths. For a moment she forgot to breathe. The ball of Fortune rocked beneath her feet. Her knees threatened to buckle.

His breath stirred her hair. They stood too close. Her skirt brushed his knee, shifting fabric and feelings along thigh, hip, and waist.

She sought to distance him, sought to steady her world in asking baldly, "Have you desires, Mr. Ramsay, other than the consumption of mushrooms? Why have you come here? All the way to Cheshire? I know it cannot be merely for the company of a mushroom and his daughter."

"You underestimate your attraction, Selina."

Heat fired in his gaze, igniting undeniably warm reactions in her body.

She turned her attention to the cool, wooded green of the horizon. She could not allow mere words—a look—to melt her resistance to his charm. "You avoid my question, sir."

He stepped away from her, turning his back to the view.

"Are you sure you would hear the truth?"

She frowned, turned to study the horizon of his bowed shoulders and lowered head. "Is the truth so dreadful?"

Flinging back his head that he might study the ceiling, hair licking like live flame at the crisp white of his neckcloth, he sighed. "I am not called Rakehell without reason." He turned to look at her, his eyes like wet agate, washed in the waterfall of light from the window. "You mentioned moments of clarity at the saltworks. Do you remember?" he asked.

"I remember."

"I am brine, Miss Preston, and would be salt."

Light shone full on his face. It was the truth he told her, but this truth confused her.

"What do you mean?" she said.

"Your father offered me sanctuary in which to crystallize."

"Did he?"

"Indeed he did. And you, Selina . . ."

The dangerous note was back in his voice. Her heart lurched. Even several feet away, she could feel the heat of him, stronger than the heat of the sun through the window. She backed against the sill, no room to maneuver, no room to escape his direct approach.

He smiled. "There is a strange tune that hums in the air between us whenever we engage in our private discussions. Do you hear it, Miss Preston? Can you feel it?" He closed the space between them, reached out to capture a lock of her hair. The shock of his touch hummed in every strand. She wanted to close her eyes, to sway toward him, not away, to encourage his touch.

Desire. She could not allow herself to fall prey to it.

His hand rose to lightly trace the curve of her cheek. "I long to play you, Selina. My fingers itch to see what sweet music I can coax from—"

She wrenched away from his practiced touch and pushed past him. Her bootheels rang out the song of her escape.

He called after her. "Would you leave the tune unplayed, Selina?"

On reaching the door, she turned. "I would learn music of you, sir, but the kind you suggest is too advanced."

He tipped his head, his expression sharply interested, as if he discerned the hint of deeper meaning in her words. "I bow to your wishes—your desires."

Panicked, she fled the room.

Chapter Fifteen

He watched her go, listened to the echo of the door closing smartly in her wake. What had possessed him to frighten her away? Was it Fate or Destiny led him to gamble away precious moments he might have spent alone with Selina? Why was he so hungry for more, always more? Jack turned to the window, stared out at the surrounding countryside, along the road down which he had come to Moresworth Hall. Why did he measure short the lives of those he loved?

"I desire," Selina had said, "nothing extraordinary."

He found her desires nothing short of extraordinary. He had never thought of life—desires—in such substantial and fundamental terms. He had been too consumed, too narrowly focused these many years, on his insatiable need to gamble.

What desires had he of substance? Was it Miss Preston he wanted, or her unshakable steadiness of purpose?

A vehicle broke from the trees, interrupting his thoughts. Fine matched bays pulled the eye-catching phaeton, the wheels picked out in red. The young man who handled the ribbons he recognized from a portrait in Selina's sketchbook. The elusive Allan. Home from the Roodee.

Jack returned to the guests' quarters, changed his clothes, and washed away the stains of travel in preparation for dinner. He wished he might as easily change his ways and wash away the stains of guilt and folly. The tour of the house had served him well. He found his way to the stairs, and might have made his way down them and through the parlor to the Great Hall, where dinner was to be served, had not voices slowed him—one of them Selina's—loud enough they carried into the stairwell.

"How can you so lightly go back on your word, Allan? So guiltlessly take my jewels to pawn? My mother's sapphires? They are all I have left of her!"

Jack paused on the steps, debating his direction.

"No nagging. Here they are, safe and sound. No harm done. Knew I'd have them back to you before your return."

"How could you know? Nothing is certain about betting. Did you depend on my father to redeem them had your horses run slow?"

Jack turned, his intention to backtrack to his room. This mention of betting stopped him.

"Well, I certainly never expected you to return so quickly from the husband hunt."

Too well, Jack recognized Allan Preston's defensive tone. In his own voice, in like situations, he had heard it.

"Never expected us? With a broadloom and a silk spinner down and no one here responsible enough to lift a finger in fixing them?"

"What? Did you expect *me* to do it? I know nothing whatsoever about such stuff. No interest in knowing, either, not when I am in the midst of a winning streak. Mustn't nag, Selina, not when I have just pocketed a great deal of gold and you have just pocketed your jewels unscathed."

"Dear God, Allan. Do you hear yourself? Your attitude sickens me. You risk far more than you realize, with no thought of consequences. Your mother worries dreadfully when you are gone to the Roodee. You age her with your disregard. All respect and esteem with which I once honored you is wasted on someone ready and willing not only to ruin his own future, but that of his family as well!"

She burst from the room as she said it, clutching a velvet bag, her movements energized by fury, her eyes flashing with anger, the same anger he had feared facing in the eyes of his sister and brothers. As sharply as if she had taken a dagger to him on their behalf, it pierced him.

He turned and took the stairs two at a time, the memory of her words blistering his ears as if they had been intended for him.

She followed, calling his name. He did not respond, did not feel at all inclined to do so, knowing she held him in such low esteem. He was throwing clothes into his cases by the time she caught up to him.

"Mr. Ramsay?"

"Enter," he said curtly.

She pushed wide the door, stood on the threshold observing. "You mean to leave?"

"I do," he said tersely. "I think it best."

"Where will you go?"

"That need not concern you."

"It does if you leave as a consequence of what I said to Allan. I can think of no other reason for this hasty departure. You should not have been subjected to such a display. I am sorry—"

He flung up a hand to cut short the words. "No apologies, Miss Preston. Please, I could not bear it were you to say you are sorry. You have no reason to apologize, no reason, either, to possess so much as an ounce of respect for me." He strapped shut the first case with vigor, anxious to be gone.

"You are wrong," she said softly.

"Very wrong," he snapped. "Have you only just now figured out how wrong?"

Her words angered him, her very presence was an irritation, not because of anything *she* had done or said, but because of all that *he* had done and said over the years that so closely mirrored the angry exchange downstairs. "I am worthy of your scorn, Selina. Far more so than your brother. Would you not agree?" He strapped the second case fast, lifted both, and made for the door.

She squarely blocked his exit, head high, eyes bright. "Not *my* scorn, sir. I would not presume to judge you on any behavior other than that I have witnessed. I find nothing to scorn in your musical talent, nor in your ability to teach, nor in having been rescued from ruffians by your hand. You have voiced your intention to stop your past pursuits and have shown no evidence of straying from that intention while in my company.

If you are deserving of scorn, sir, it must come from those to whom you have done injury, not me."

"What of my inappropriate advances upstairs, Miss Preston?" he asked, deliberately harsh, wishing her out of his way.

"You recognized them as inappropriate, and indicated that you bow to my wishes. Are you a man of your word?"

"I have proven none too reliable in the past." He meant to cow her, to drive her from the doorway by stepping toward her as he spoke.

She stood her ground. "I am none too interested in the past, Jack. Are you a man of your word today?"

Nonplussed, he stared at her. She called him Jack!

She stared back, gaze stormy, mouth pinched. "You promised you meant to teach me to play. Will you stay and see it through?"

He drank in the smell of her, drank in the heady idea that she wanted him to stay. "Do you desire it?" he asked.

Her eyes gave him answer before her lashes fanned down, shutting him away from the depths of her desire as she admitted quietly, "I do."

He stayed.

She was glad of it, and confident she had done the right thing in convincing him to do so, until he politely introduced himself to Allan before dinner. "Ramsay," he said. "Jack Ramsay. Your sister's new music master."

Allan looked him over, head to toe. "Ramsay, you say? Any kin to . . ." He frowned. "What is his name? I just heard it being bandied about at the track. A fellow referred to as the Rakehell?"

"Allan!" Selina tried to stop him.

He ignored her. "Lost his fortune at cards, I hear."

Ramsay made a bow. "And so I did. Gambling is a dangerous pursuit. What else have you heard of me?"

Allan exhibited increasing interest. "That's you, is it? I hear you are a remarkable gamester. That it was unbelievably bad luck you suffered at Fletcher's hand."

"I *was* a remarkable gamester. As for bad luck, I would say

I have experienced a turn of fortune that may prove to be the best thing that has ever happened to me."

Allan frowned, confused. "You are being accused of having killed an acquaintance."

"Said that, did they? More than an acquaintance. He was my friend."

Selina was dumbstruck.

Not so her brother. "It is true, then?"

Ramsay nodded gravely. "Am I accused of anything else?"

"There is some suspicion that you are the Gargoyle."

"The spy?" Ramsay laughed. "That last bit is balderdash, but the rest—largely accurate."

"You have killed a man?" Selina could not refrain from asking.

There was a weighty pause in which he met her gaze with a look of great seriousness, his expression difficult to read. "Yes."

She did not know what to make of him, of such an incredible admission of guilt. He had killed a man! Their exploration of the topic was cut short. Her father and Mrs. Preston joined them. Dinner was served. That the topic occupied his mind as much as hers was evident. His gaze met hers more than once over the serving dishes.

Allan leaned over at one point during dinner to whisper, "Brought a murderer into our midst, have you? And yet you would scold me for nothing more serious than pawning jewelry!"

"If you do not heed my warnings with regard to my mother's jewelry, I shall encourage this murderer to make you his next victim," she said tartly.

Selina had no desire to discuss the matter with Allan, and no opportunity to further discuss it with Jack Ramsay. Her family vied too enthusiastically for their guest's attention. He had killed a man, a friend, he had said! Unconcerned by such an admission, or perhaps drawn to him because of it, Allan insisted on showing Jack the stables that evening, and when Selina made her way downstairs the next morning it was to discover Ramsay gone, swept away in her father's company.

"A tour of the silk mill," Mrs. Preston explained. "Even Allan was talked into accompanying them."

Because Ramsay was a great gambler, because he had killed a man and Allan found him too fascinating! She wanted to voice her alarm and could not. Jack Ramsay had been prepared to leave. *She* had convinced him to stay.

"How wonderful it was to hear strains of music as I drifted off to sleep last night," Mrs. Preston said dreamily. "Did you hear it, Selina? Mr. Ramsay and his Handel aria? A sad piece, very moving."

"Sad? It was practically funereal. Heavy of heart it left me." She had heard—heard every note, wrenching and desolate— the covers pulled up to her chin because it felt as if by way of the music, the dangerous Mr. Ramsay had invaded her room. "I long to play you," he had said, and in playing his cello while she lay listening, he had come close to doing just that. Every tortured note coursed through her body, affecting the tempo of her heart, sending forlorn pulses vibrating deep into her very core. He wooed the grief deep within her heart without voice, without body. She wondered what it would be like to be her father's prized cello, propped between Jack Ramsay's knees, one warm hand stroking the sorrow in her throat, the other caressing the melancholy in her belly. His hands had killed a man—a friend, he had said.

Chapter Sixteen

How did one politely ask a stranger about the killing of a friend? Strictly proper etiquette, of course, dictated that one did not inquire. Yet Selina could not look at Jack Ramsay, could not entrust her hands to his in their gentle positioning on keys or strings, as the days passed, without wondering if they were, in truth, hands capable of great violence.

Ramsay took his position as music master rather more seriously than Selina had anticipated. He made, in the course of the first week, no attempt to explain the disturbing bombshell of information he had dropped so nonchalantly into her lap. Neither did he trouble her with further blatant overtures of lovemaking, though there was great opportunity for him to touch her, equally so for their gazes to meet in his instruction over the bodies of the violin and pianoforte. Other than the nightly musical invasion of both her bed and her dreams, he acted with surprising, even commendable, restraint. Nothing inappropriate or suggestive other than an occasional heated look, or the hint of suggestiveness in the way he phrased his instruction. His reserve caught her off guard. So prepared had she been to repulse his advances that the absence of need for such resistance left her restless, even disappointed.

It certainly disappointed her that there was so little opportunity for private conversation. Mrs. Preston made a habit, in the long, warming days that followed, of sitting in on the music lessons, needlework in hand. There was no opportunity for questions, polite or otherwise, as to how, why, where, and when one went about killing a friend.

Ramsay was no help. He seemed content to while away the hours speaking to her of nothing more intriguing than the placement of her fingers. He spent a great deal of his day talking horseflesh with Allan, discussing plans for the cathedral musicale with Mrs. Preston, or accompanying Mr. Preston in his trips to the salt mine or the silk mill. On Sundays he went with them to church.

His interests intrigued Mrs. Preston.

"Do you know I was convinced he meant to pursue you in coming here," she confided one afternoon when Selina sat in the parlor sketching a bowlful of bluebells and ox-eye daisies. "I did, in fact, live in fear, when he first arrived, that he would exercise a terrible influence on you and Allan."

"And now?" Selina did not reveal to her stepmother that she *was* influenced, and terribly so. She could not explain that with the subtlety of sound, Ramsay, every evening, seduced her. With the tender, aching stroke of his bow on strings, with a musical nakedness of feeling he otherwise kept clothed, he had repeatedly touched her. Unknowing, he left her trembling prostrate in her bed, possessed by the overwhelming desire to beg a Rakehell to play her, as he said he wished to, plucking from her the tune that hummed when he conducted his nightly serenade, in every inch of her flesh.

"I begin to think he might serve in quite the opposite capacity," Mrs. Preston said.

Selina, her fingers unsteady on her pencil, shook away the disturbing enticement of her thoughts. "What? How?"

"Well, who better than a ruined and reformed gambler to reach your brother, who seems determined to stumble down the same awful road to ruin? I have decided I must encourage him to spend some time with Allan."

"And how do you propose to do that? I have heard Mr. Ramsay refuse to accompany Allan into town on more than one occasion."

"I had hoped that you might help me, Selina."

Jack did not know what to make of it when Mrs. Preston turned to him over breakfast one morning and said, "You have yet to walk the walls, Mr. Ramsay. Allan and Selina must take you."

He understood soon enough what it meant to walk walls.

Those that surrounded Chester were a matter of pride to its citizens, encircling their city with history as much as with stone, brick, and mortar. A public walk had been built to top them, five feet or so in breadth. It created a queer sort of promenade.

"Does the prospect of wall walking bore you, Miss Preston?" Jack asked a yawning Selina as their trio made their way up the steps at the Eastgate.

"Bored, sir? Not at all. I am only a little tired."

"Bad dreams?"

"No. Not really."

"Sad music," Allan said.

"Allan!"

"Say it isn't so. Tell me my mother lies when she claims Mr. Ramsay's music set you to pacing last night. That she heard you weeping. That it is not the first time."

"My music?" Jack was stunned. The dark circles beneath her eyes were *his* responsibility?

She pressed a hand to her forehead. "It was a sad tune you left us with last night, Mr. Ramsay, an adagio by Bach, was it not? My mother used to play it when I was a child."

"I had no idea you could hear me, much less that it might keep you awake. I do apologize, Miss Preston."

"Think nothing of it, sir."

"But I can think of nothing else, knowing I have deprived you of rest, even driven you from your bed."

Selina laughed. An uneasy sound. "You make too much of it, sir. Please, let us change the subject. It is the walls we should be discussing, rather than my sleeping habits."

"Tell me about the walls, then."

Allan answered impatiently, as if the question were all too predictable. "Oh, you know. Romans started them and, of course, medieval kings refortified them. Towers were added, et cetera, et cetera, a drawbridge, the different gates."

"Chester served as a base for invading Wales." Selina tried to interrupt.

Allan waved her to quietude, pouring out the history in a rush, that it might be gulped rather than savored. "Yes, yes, and as you probably already know, we offered a hiding place for Charles the First during the Civil War, as a result of which Parliamentary forces blasted hell out of the walls trying to winkle him out. Then years of relatively boring stuff, during which the tumbled-down bits have been repaired and this walkway put in that everyone might be further edified by our enduring edifice."

Jack leaned over the recently capstoned edge of the wall, ran a hand along uneven reddish blocks, stared down at the rough-set gray stones touched with mossy green that Roman hands had first set in place. "Amazing!"

Far more amazing was the way Selina Preston looked at him today, as if she found him at least as fascinating as the walls.

Allan shrugged. "I suppose. Come along! Nothing to see here."

"This stretch *is* a bit tame," Selina admitted, hesitantly taking Jack's arm when it was offered, shyly falling into step beside him on the uneven pathway. "You can see, there, part of a ruined watchtower."

"It gets better beyond the Wishing Steps. Then you will see the river, and the Roodee," Allan called over his shoulder. He seemed bent on setting a brisk pace.

Jack was in no hurry. There was too great a weight of past moments here to rush the present. "Wishing Steps?"

"Yes. Have you a wish?" Selina asked artlessly, her eyes reflecting the cloudless blue of the sky.

He watched memory dawn as he said, "I do. You know I do. I wish to play you."

She blushed fiercely, dropped her hold on his arm. "I remember now."

They had reached the top of a flight of rather ordinary-looking stairs down which Allan had already plunged, heels clattering on stone.

"What does one do with one's wishes at these Wishing Steps?"

She began the descent in front of him, swiftly, as if in flight from the idea of wishes. Her explanation was a trifle breathless. "It is said that whosoever makes a wish and runs up, down, and up the steps again, without drawing breath, has his wish come true."

"If they do not drop dead of an apoplectic fit first." Allan's sarcasm drifted up from the first of several landings that separated the flights hugging the curve of the wall. "I recommend you save both breath and wishes for the Roodee. There are horse races being held today."

Selina slowed her pace with a sigh. "So *that* is why you agreed to come with us."

"Precisely!" Allan leapt briskly down the last three steps and turned to look up at her. "If you mean to scold, Selina, I shall part company with you for a nag of my own choosing."

"Go, then, if you prefer the company of racehorses." Her tone was as stony as the wall on which they stood.

Face flushed, Allan asked Jack, "With which sort of nag do you prefer to keep company?"

Jack kept his voice deliberately bland, his eyes on Selina, who with regal grace made her way to the base of the steps. He found her restraint admirable, as admirable as the heightened color of her cheeks, as noteworthy as the enticing sway of her hips. "Racehorses interest me very little these days," he said. "They have run away with far too much of my money in the past." Her lips, tight pressed as she feigned interest in an indifferent view, parted in surprise when he said, "Your sister, on the other hand, interests me immensely."

Allan shrugged and flung a last retort over his shoulder. "Suit yourself, but I would appreciate it if you refrain, in future, from addressing Selina as my sister. She is not my sister at all. She only likes to think she is."

Selina's mouth, as he left them, wore a wounded look.

"His case is serious indeed if he will not stay to guard your well-being after such a blatantly flirtatious remark," Jack said. "Do you feel uneasy having been abandoned to my care?"

"Uneasy?" Her gaze was direct, unwavering, as solid and unshakable as the wall on which they stood. "No, not at all uneasy. We two have been alone before, sir, in far more harrowing and provocative circumstances."

"You have determined, then, Miss Preston, that I am not a rapist, or . . . a murderer?"

She did not flinch from the remark, which he made with deliberate forethought. The intensity of her regard, instead, seemed bent on stripping him of secrets.

"I must admit to some surprise when first you admitted to having killed someone, and a friend at that. Time and consideration led me to the conclusion that it was highly unlikely that a murderer would speak freely of his victim. It was an accident, the death of your friend, was it not?"

He frowned, the pain still fresh. Could one reduce a killing to nothing more than mishap? "It was a tragedy. A tragedy of great magnitude," he said. "An ill-fated night in all ways but one."

"Do you want to talk about it?"

"No!"

"Forgive me." The very tenderness of her tone cut through him.

He could not look at her.

Her heels scuffed on stone. "I thought you might, given you had mentioned the matter at all."

"No. I would not burden you. Perhaps, instead, you will explain why Allan made such a point of disowning you."

"I thought you knew." Her voice was sad.

"Knew what?"

"That we have in common the loss of our mothers at a tender age."

Of all that she might have said to him, these words made him look at her again. "Mrs. Preston is not your mother? I had no idea."

She swallowed hard, frowned, pushed the words to the surface. "Mother died when I was seven due to complications of childbirth—a sister who survived the ordeal no more than my poor mother. Father married Mrs. Preston when I was nine. She was several years widowed, with an eight-year-old son."

"Common ground," he muttered.

"Yes. Stony though it might be. She has been very good, very kind to me."

"And Allan? Is he good and kind to you?"

"Allan?"

She smoothed windblown strands of hair away from eyes that gleamed a brilliant blue. With unshed tears?

"Allan and I were once quite close. He understood, as did no one else, the impact of my mother's death. We used to talk, about anything, everything. When he turned twelve, he suddenly shut me out. No more time for me. He never really bonded with Father."

Jack could not stop searching the beautiful blue depths through which she gazed at him. Pain lurked there—loss and loneliness, too—common ground she had long ago recognized while he had been too blind to see.

"Allan has no uncles, then? No male counterpart in whom he might find example?" He thought of his elder brother, Charles, whose example he should have followed more closely. Charles, whose fortune he had lost.

"No. He was, of course, very attached to his mother. He doted on her every wish once, but she can do little with him now he is grown. He seeks male company at the racecourse."

"Not the best of company, or places to seek it."

"No. Of course you would understand. Mrs. Preston was at wit's end until you arrived."

"Me?"

"Yes. She is uplifted by the fact that Allan spends time with you, convinced you could be the cure of him."

Jack laughed. "What can I do but stand as example of all that he should not aspire to be?"

"You cannot help him?"

"I cannot help if he has no desire to be helped."

"There is nothing you could say? You will not go after him to say it?"

He paused on the last of the landings, three steps separating them, his right hand fingering the shape of the penny in his pocket, eyes focused on the blank page of the cloudless sky. "I do not think you understand," he said very quietly.

"Understand? In what regard?"

It angered him that he should have to explain, but he wanted her to understand his history. "I am obsessed with gambling, possessed by it as one is possessed by a nightmare. I must guard against the lure of it with all vigilance—every day, every hour, every minute. It makes no sense to you, I am confident, that I should still crave what has brought about my destruction, but the longing sits in my breast, singing to me, like a siren. I cannot follow Allan onto the rocks if he would throw himself against them, no matter how much I would like to help you, help him, redeem myself. Do you understand?"

"I think I do." Her voice trembled. He wanted to kick himself for causing that faint vibrato.

Impatient with her, with himself, he said skeptically, "How can you?"

"I am not a complete stranger to obsession."

"No?"

"No." Her gaze slid uneasily from his. "I know what it is like to be drawn to something, to be mesmerized, even though one knows it is danger drawing one. Knowing it may destroy one's happiness, one's peace of mind. Even knowing it has already destroyed some part of me, because in falling victim even briefly to its lure, I give up some sense of self and self-control."

Keenly, he regarded her. "You show no signs of having fallen victim to aberrant behavior. Do you hide it too well, Selina, or have you stumbled on a cure? You must divulge what it is gives you such an outward appearance of strength and control."

She flung back her head, gazed at the sky, and responded in all seriousness, "I pray, sir. My weakness has been given into God's hands. He is my only anchor in a storm of emotion."

Chapter Seventeen

Jack Ramsay had no idea she referred to him in referring to her obsession. Selina had no intention of enlightening him. They had come to walk the walls, and walk they would. She moved away from the steps, away from the intensity of their discussion and the lure of his presence.

"I love the walls," she said, turning the subject as easily as she turned into the southern stretch of their walk. She focused her attentions on the weir interrupting the flow of the River Dee rather than on her heightened awareness of the man who interrupted the flow of her thoughts with no more than a sigh, the nearness of his presence, and the cool darkness of his shadow as he came to stand beside her. She drew a deep breath and caught a tantalizing whiff of his cologne along with the dank, musty tang of the river.

"I love to stand high above the streets observing life from a distance," she found herself telling him. "There is a helpful overview, an almost emotionless objectivity to be gained from the perspective of a bird's perch."

"A fence sitter, are you?" he teased, his changeable eyes more blue than gray today. Selina could not observe them with any sense of objectivity.

She laughed. "I suppose I am. And you?"

"Not I. Chasing after life is what I tend to do. Just as I have chased after . . ."

"Yes?" She held her breath, wondering what he might say next, wondering if there was a particular female he chased.

"Wishes!" he shouted, as he turned and took the Wishing Steps at a run, bootheels ringing on stone.

Baffled, she stood at the base of the steps, watching him race to the top, a man's body inhabited by the spritely spirit of a restless boy with hair like flame. She held her breath, just as she knew he did. Her lungs burned with a need for air when he came careening back down the steps and flung himself, gasping, into her arms, staggering, so that she caught him, briefly supporting his weight as he regained both wind and balance in the same instant and swept her into his arms, bending his bright head to hers.

He sought her mouth and kissed her—recklessly, ruthlessly—breathing heavily, his chest heaving against hers, his inhalations so forceful as their mouths linked that he took her very breath away.

Gasping, she pushed away from his unexpected embrace, away from her own joy in participating in that embrace. "What are you doing?"

He seemed pleased with himself. His eyes sparkled dangerously. "Proving that one does not have to run up steps for wishes to come true."

Voices drew their attention. A party of walkers emerged from the curve in the steps behind them.

"The Wishing Steps," a woman said, her voice carrying. And in the murmurs that followed, Selina heard the word *wishes* again and again, like water lapping on stone.

"Do you mean to disgrace me?" she whispered, feigning an anger that did not truly burn in her breast, though all rules of decorum dictated it should.

He laughed, as if he saw right through her pretense and fell into step beside her as she strode along the wall. Softly he said, no chance of being overheard, "No disgrace. Never that. I wished only to kiss you."

She had not often heard him laugh. She found that while his conduct did not, the sound delighted her. She stepped to the wall, that she might calm her thoughts in observing the peaceful flow of the river.

They were overtaken and safely passed, by the party from the steps, before she said with a sigh, "You must refrain from such behavior."

"Forever?" His brows rose, the woodland imp questioning

her resolve as he politely offered his arm. "You ask too much of me. Took you no joy in the exchange?"

"I . . . you fluster me, sir."

His knowing smile further flustered her, as did the affectionate tone of his voice as he said, "You are quite captivating when you have just been kissed, Miss Preston. I must make a point of provoking such a state more often."

He kept his voice low. They were in full view of a great many people on both sides of the wall, in the streets between the houses to their right, strolling along the ramparts dead ahead and along the riverbank to their left. He dared not accost her here with anything but words.

"Still, you avoid my question," he teased. "Took you no pleasure in kissing me?"

"A gentleman would not ask."

"A gentleman would not have kissed you. And still you have not answered." He leaned closer, his brows still risen, awaiting answers, deliberately provoking.

She would not lie to him; neither would she give him the satisfaction of responding in the positive. "Does the Rakehell consider the mushroom's daughter fair game for such liberties?" she asked instead.

He frowned. "You still see in me nothing more than the Rakehell, Miss Preston? And the Rakehell has insulted you? A pity. It was not a liberty I meant to abuse, but a form of homage I would pay to one who outshines the day."

"You are too glib, sir."

"Am I?" he asked it stiffly, his smile fading as quickly as the sparkle was doused in his eyes. His voice was gruff when he said, "Well, a Rakehell will live up to his reputation, will he not, Miss Preston?"

Silence fell between them as they made their way the length of the southern wall. It was an uneasy silence, interrupted only by the noises around them, and these grew more numerous as they passed a cluster of old mills crowding the far bank, water wheels at work, churning the river frothy with messy trails of corn and fullers' cloth refuse. Beneath them, within the city, rose a terrible stench as they passed the tanners' workshops of Skinner's Lane.

The ruins of a castle loomed red-brown to their right, reminding Jack of the conversation he and Selina had once shared with regard to the rebuilding of ruins. He was back to old tricks again, catching her and kissing her as he had, and to hell with the consequences. It had seemed appropriate at the time, but with tension between them now like a cello string wound too taut, the consequences of his haphazard approach were all too clear.

Their passage along the wall was a winding one. Single file they pushed past more and more people. A crowd stood thick along the wall as it faced west, staring out over a brilliant green sward, where the thunder of galloping hooves filled his ears like remembered music.

Jack approached the site, hands clammy, his breath short, the pace of his heart quickening with anticipation. Ruthless and impatient, he pushed his way through the gathering, craning for a glimpse of the track and horses below.

Flags, like colorful birds tethered to tall white poles, whipped gaily above tents and pavilions. Top hats and parasols clustered upon the grass like multicolored mushrooms. Mushrooms brought to mind Miss Preston, who forged a path ahead of him, pushing industriously through the crowd as if pleased to put him behind her.

He let her go with trepidation, with the feeling that he had lost his hold on something dear in losing hold of Miss Preston's arm. And yet he let her go, thrilling to the sight of a line of nervous horses as they danced to the starting line, satin flanked, ears at the prick. Their anticipation was contagious.

Expectancy surged through Jack's veins like an excess of spirits. He would watch one race, only one. It could not hurt just to watch. After all, he hadn't a penny on him to risk in betting. And yet a strange foreboding, almost a sense of terror, squeezed at his heart and lungs, as if he had forgotten how to breathe and suddenly drew a lungful of the purest of air, had been deaf to sounds suddenly heard, had been blind to colors suddenly made clear. Here was the Roodee, spread before him like a mouth-watering banquet. Poisoned food! Look but don't taste. The oldest race-track in England. Hard to believe he had waited so long to see it. He had thrilled to the name every time it was mentioned in the Preston household. He thrilled now to its brilliance. All else was forgotten for the moment as he inhaled the intoxicating smell, a forgotten joy, the odor of sweated horseflesh, sun-baked manure, and the crushed-grass greenness of trampled turf. A fine bouquet, heady and full of promise.

Every track he had ever been to was the same—great grass gaming tables. This racecourse, however, mounted like a pendant in the silver of the river on three sides, resplendently green in the day's brilliant sunlight, glittered like a rare jewel. Jack was dazzled, completely mesmerized, lost to everything but the Roodee, until a hand clapped him familiarly on the back.

"Jack! Can it be you?" The voice was unmistakable.

"Rob!" Jack whirled to clasp his friend in a back-pounding embrace. "Or should I call you Bertie now?"

Rob pummeled his shoulder and stood back to look him over, his expression bright. He growled happily, "You do, and I shall never speak to you again. I have escaped both the unhappy harridan and my fitful, wailing offspring for a fortnight. You do me no favor in reminding me I must eventually return to them."

"But what do you do in Chester?"

"The races, of course. What else is to be enjoyed in the god-forsaken north? I bring Hugh with me. You must join us! Just like old times."

Hugh broke through the crowd, his face lit with smiles, his breath rummy. "Jackie, old boy! Here you are! All of London is wondering where you had got off to. I suppose I ought not be surprised—you at one end of the country—Charles at the other."

"Charles? He is returned?"

"You had not heard? Setting up shop in Brighton, he is, making ready to receive a great shipment of Far Eastern goods, the details of which he enthusiastically fills everyone's ears when he is not attempting to sell one some part of what little remains of his estate. Quite the huckster is your Charlie. People have begun to avoid him like any salesman's dog. Call him Rash Ramsay, they do."

"Tsk-tsk." Rob made a buttoning motion over his lips. "Tongue runs away with you, Hugh."

Hugh nodded and pressed finger to lips. "Right. Mum's the word. Jack won't want to hear all that rot. What you *will* want to know is that I have not forgot my debt to you."

Hugh dug into his pockets, fumbled forth a purse, pulled out a wad of soft.

"Debt?" Jack was sobered, too keenly reminded of his irrepayable debt to Charles. He frowned at the money, frowned as he looked past Hugh, his gaze settling on a dear and familiar face that deserved no frowns at all. Selina. All smiles, she had broken through the crowd behind Hugh.

"The mushroom ball money!" Hugh blurted, stashing the fistful of cash in his waistcoat pocket as if it were a handful of hankies.

Too late, Jack opened his mouth to say something, anything, to stop Hugh.

"Bet you a monkey. Surely you remember five hundred pounds? I declared you would not be caught dead at such an insipid gathering, much less stay to play cello."

Selina reacted as if she had been struck, her mouth snapping shut, all smiles gone, her complexion first blanching and then flooding with a surfeit of color as she turned her back on them.

"No!" Even as he cried out she lost herself in the crowd, the high crown of her straw hat visible for no more than a moment.

"Yes! Yes!" Hugh patted his bulging pocket philanthropically. "Your lucky day, eh? Found money! Must place some of it on a likely filly running in the fourth."

"Indeed! We must all test our luck." Rob threw an arm around his shoulders, herding him in the direction of the track. "Come along! No time to waste."

Jack wrenched away from him as roughly as a man breaks away from the hangman's noose. "Must go!" he gasped. "So sorry. Must go!" He could say no more, offered no further excuses for his abrupt departure, could only free himself from staying hands and plunge into the obstruction of the laughing, carefree crowd that knotted and tangled in his path, as if maliciously intent on blocking his escape.

Chapter Eighteen

He chased after Selina, in pursuit of all that was dear to him. He chased after her hat—it was all he could see of her—a distinctively tall-crowned French hat of satin straw banded three times in blue ribbons that matched her blue spencer. He had to catch up to her, had to explain. White foxtail feathers bobbing, it was not a hat one might easily hide, not even in the crowd that separated them. He fixed his eyes on it and pushed after her. Only once did his gaze stray, when the crowd, in unison, voiced a groan over the fall of a favorite.

For no more than a heartbeat he turned to assess the situation—tumbled horse, tumbled rider, both picking themselves up. The animal, riderless, lathered, trailed after the bunched pack of horses still chasing after the prize, quirts flailing as the finish neared. A heartbeat's distraction. A heartbeat too long. When he returned his attention to his pursuit, the hat was not to be seen.

It was nowhere to be found along the wall ahead of or behind him, nowhere in the crowds moving toward the racing stands, where Selina might ostensibly have headed to locate the wayward Allan. Tall crowned hats, yes, and bobbing feathers, but none of the right configuration and color. Panic washed over Jack. Had Selina come to harm without his escort? Had she been spirited away, never to be found again and all his fault, his responsibility, more dire consequences due directly to his carelessness?

He raced from one side of the wall to the other, pushing ruthlessly past anyone who stood in his way, the sounds of the racetrack fading behind him. The crowd thinned the farther he moved along the wall. Had she flown away? Been trans-

formed? Had she taken off the blasted hat? No! Thank God!
There, it was—she was—descending the steps that led from
the walls at the Watergate. She meant to lose herself in the city
center, not on the crowded Roodee!

With all haste he made his way to the steps, craning his
neck to get an occasional glimpse of her—of her hat—as she
headed past a row of old warehouses, up the steady incline of
the street. Two at a time he took the steps, pausing only for a
moment to look up when from above him came Rob's concerned, "Jack? What's the hurry? Money lenders after you?
Devilish rude to tear off that way."

"Sorry, Rob. No time to explain. Must catch up to her."

Like a wheel of pale, pockmarked cheese, Rob's face peered
down from the wall. "A her, is it? All's forgiven, then. You
will look me up later?"

"Of course."

Rob waved his hand theatrically. "After the wench. Tal-
lyho!"

Jack did not have to be told twice. Yet as if fate exacted a
price for his having taken his eyes off of her, for the second
time, when he reached street level, again she was gone.

Of all people who might have strode past the stained-glass
windows of Trinity Church, Selina did not expect to see Jack
Ramsay. But even through tinted glass, grayed with generations of dirt and neglect, there was no denying it was him. The
bright, swept-back curtain of his sunlit hair caught her attention. She had found his hair eye-catching from the start. Still
did, silly fool that she was! What did fair hair matter, if the
thoughts within the head ran foul? Furious with him, with herself for falling prey to his charms, Selina abandoned her original intention of asking a gentleman of the cloth for escort
home, paralleling instead Ramsay's progress the length of the
church. She would meet him at the far door and . . . and what?
Give him a tongue rattling? Screech at him like a fishwife?
Shame him with a flood of tears? All or naught, the appropriate response would surely come to her.

She had expected him to be lined up, posting bets on the upcoming races. Too many years of disappointment in Allan's broken promises led her to suspect nothing more of a gentleman who readily confessed his obsession with gambling. Ramsay was, after all, a man who had gambled over her father's ball, over the playing of a cello, over the disposition of his brother's inheritance. It was more than likely that he gambled with her affections as well. Had he made a bet that he could coax kisses from the lips of the mushroom's daughter? That he could make her fall in love with him?

He had already done that.

Separated as they were, by more than walls and glass, separated by rank and fortune, by the very different ways in which they viewed the world, they walked the length of the church. She could not separate herself from the truth. She was smitten, completely taken in. She had grown to admire, even respect him, to trust in his intentions to mend his wicked ways. What did a young woman in love say to the man who bet on breaking her heart? When they came to the end of the windows, he walked on, unknowing, while she stood in the doorway, berating herself.

How could she have been so gullible, so readily deceived? Had she misjudged him and his attentions to her completely? Where did he go, if not to bet on the races? What had him in such a hurry? She was surprised he left his friends behind so soon after having encountered them. Full of surprises today, Ramsay was, and the surprises left her breathless, wounded, and unwilling to call out to him, to insist he honor his responsibility as escort and protector of her safety.

On impulse, anger and pain driving her, she quit the church. She would catch up to him and ring a peal over his head. She would hold him accountable.

It did not immediately occur to her the consequence of her own folly in so doing, but it was not long in impressing itself upon her. Dodging horsemen, wagons, barrows, and foot traffic, she skirted the annoyingly plentiful piles of horse dung amongst the cobbles and—even more annoying—the excremental sort of persons who were not to be avoided no matter where she walked. A young woman alone was assumed to be the kind of female who begged looks from strangers. Look upon her they did, as if she strutted wares like any other hawker on the increasingly crowded street.

Head high, her expression deliberately aloof and emotionless, she did her best to ignore the turned heads and leering glances suffered from virtually every man she passed. The women, no better, scowled and smirked and looked her up and down, their eyes full of negative feeling and ill will. To be regarded so hatefully shamed her. There were shopkeepers and vendors among them who had known her by name as a child. The little girl was now a grown woman, however, and they did not recognize her, the slate of their memories wiped clean by too many telling years spent in a distant school and in her tour of Europe.

Happily, fearlessly, she had trekked the Rows in the company of others on a hundred shopping errands in the past. Today, business swelled by the racing crowd, the singsong calls of the hawkers touting their goods and prices, this place seemed too strident, too loud and pushing. The manner in which she was brushed and bumped and pressed in upon by those who shared the walkway was far too familiar. In broad daylight, on this busy thoroughfare, she was afraid. Her skin crawled. Her cheeks burned. The covered double-decker walkways of medieval Rows, a place of nooks and crannies, of upstairs and down, of too many windows and doorways from which one might be observed, even spied upon, seemed sinister in a way she had never before recognized.

What was it Allan had called the spy with whom Ramsay's name was being linked—the Gargoyle? Could it be Jack deceived them with regard to that as well? The idea was too intriguing to dismiss, too ludicrous to be believed, and yet, so jumpy and nervous did her progress leave her that she began to suffer anxieties that, as she stalked Jack, she was herself stalked. On several occasions she whirled to scan the street behind her.

Small wonder, really, that she felt as if someone followed her. Virtually every man in and along the street observed her passage with bright-eyed interest. Some were not content with staring. Several made so bold as to nod, to tip hats, to wink at her! A carriage slowed in the street. Another obnoxiously persistent fellow leaned out of the downed window to call to her.

"My dear girl. Whatever do you do, walking the streets?"

Selina had been ready to find him rude, but then both voice and face fell into place in her memory. Mr. Harvey! A business associate of her father's. He had been in the habit of bringing her licorice whips when last she had seen him.

Relieved beyond words, smiling, she turned toward him.

He smiled congenially in return. The carriage door was flung wide, the step let down.

Happy was she to take advantage of the offered safety of the gentleman's carriage.

"Come, come," he beckoned, beaming, from the window. "Shall we order up a Shaftesbury, sweeting? Perhaps stop at an inn for a bite or two before we go about burying me own shaft right up to the hilt? You are a toothsome morsel. There's a sovereign or two in it for you."

Shocked speechless, insulted in a manner she had never before so much as imagined, Selina backed away from the step she had almost set foot to, away from the carriage that had almost swallowed her up.

"You do not recognize me, do you, Mr. Harvey?"

With a puzzled lift of bushy brows he looked her up and down in a highly disconcerting manner.

"Have we had commerce before, then, dearie?"

"We have."

"I thought there was something familiar in your countenance. Have I slighted you in your usual fee?"

"We have had commerce before, sir, but not the sort you suppose."

With that, she turned her back on him and put the horrid man and his dreadfully improper offer behind her.

He refused to drive on, however. His horse was coaxed into a shambling walk, easily keeping pace with her progress.

"Come now, puss. Do not play the coy mystery. Name a price and a place that pleases you. We'll conduct this business to both our satisfaction."

She pretended he was not there. What other response had she? She fixed her eyes on Jack Ramsay instead, willing him to turn and look behind him, to save her from this Hell of humiliation. He did not turn, however, did not save her, did not sense her desire for his assistance at all.

Mr. Harvey's coaxing came to an end in a burst of temper. Directing his driver to whip up his team he shouted from the window angrily, "Cunning tease of a cunt! You may put on airs and scrape the sky with your nose, dearie, but you're no better than a three-penny stand-up when lights are out and skirts raised."

As he raged, Selina ducked into the doorway of the nearest shop, cut to the quick, knees weak, her face burning with shame, humiliation, and rage. Through the window, a tear-blurred image of the carriage rattled up the street, past a wavery image of Jack Ramsay who turned at last, to see who caused such a hubbub.

It was a scarlet-nosed, Friday-faced woman who roughly grabbed Selina's elbow and rudely shoved her out the door of her stinking leather-goods shop. "Out wit' you. I won't have your kind in my shop, messing with the wares."

"My kind, Mrs. Barnes?" Selina laughed. She had to laugh or burst into tears and she would not so disgrace herself in front of this dreadful, uncaring woman, from whom her mother had once bought carriage rigging and quirts.

The woman's eyes went round. "Who are you, then, that you should know me name?" she demanded. "I am a decent, God-fearing woman."

"As am I!" Selina retorted. Head high, she set off in pursuit of Ramsay again, determined now to catch up to him, to demand safe conduct, spy or no, liar or not. Her task was not an easy one. His pace was brisk, and while he did pause for a brief peek into every shop window or door he passed, she could not catch up to him without running or shouting out his name, which she was loath to do.

She was pleased to see him stop to gape at Bishop Lloyd's carved animals: a dancing bear, an elephant, two monkeys, and, from the posts that supported the Rows, glaring owls and bearded giants. As she closed the distance that separated them, Selina wondered if Ramsay recognized the carvings from the sketches he had once given compliment. Did he think of her at all in this strange detour on which he had embarked?

It was not a game of chance he wanted. He had passed up the rattle of dice and the slap of cards in any one of a half dozen pubs and roadhouses into whose doorways and windows he peered and then passed.

Could it be he was, after all, a spy? The Gargoyle? Why would a spy be hunting in Chester? The idea, too titillating to ignore, had her questioning the very next person Jack stopped to speak to.

He was a butcher. There were several of them in the Row, and the flies that hung about their shops were almost as thick as the unpleasantly rank odor of sheep fat and aging sausage. This particular butcher stood in the doorway to his empty shop, wiping his hands on a bloody apron and calling out to the passersby that he had fresh rack of lamb and breakfast chops, very lean.

"What was it that gentleman asked of you?" Selina inquired politely.

The butcher's gaze fixed first on her face, and then somewhere above it before he laughed, tapped the side of his nose and said slyly, "As if you did not know, my dear."

"I do not know," she said. "I would not inquire if I knew."

The man laughed. "It were a hat he asked after."

"A hat?"

"Yes, a lady's hat, tall, made of French silk straw, and banded thrice in blue ribbon. Your hat, my dear. Lost your swain, have you?"

Selina blinked in dismay! He had been hunting her all this time?

"My guess it is not the hat he is after so much as the young lady beneath it."

Selina blushed, pleased by the idea, greatly relieved.

"I would not be averse to having a piece of such a millinery treasure myself," the butcher said, reaching for the ribbons beneath her chin with his smelly, blood-stained hand.

"Whatever do you think you are doing?" Selina would have jerked away had he not made free to grasp her waist. In response to this uncalled-for familiarity, on top of the gauntlet of humiliation with which she had thus far contended, without hesitation, and with admirable force, Selina kicked him.

With a yowl, he jerked away from her, hopping and cursing, yanking hard at the ribbons still tangled in his grasp, knocking askew the much-discussed hat.

"You deserve far worse for your insolence," Selina muttered starchily as she untied the snarled ribbons beneath her chin and left him to nurse his shin in solitude.

Had he passed her in the street? Was she hidden away in some shop? Jack scanned the gallery. Had she outpaced him? The odd stacked arrangement of the rows of galleried shops in this part of the city were the devil of a place to go looking for someone who had no inclination to be found. Covered walkways too thick with shade to be revealing, further shaded the interiors of a myriad tiny shops, upstairs and down, into which a whole scarlet-coated regiment could duck without anyone the wiser. To further complicate his search, dozens of noisy street hawkers blocked both his passage and his view with the goods they offered for sale along the wooden walkways.

He could not ask them all if they had seen Selina. It would take too much time, and he suffered the most dreadful premonition that a young woman on her own in such a rugged setting must be found quickly, or not at all. He stood thus, in the street, not far from the old stone cross that marked a crossroad of two major thoroughfares. Where to go next? Whom to ask?

A down-at-heels old wattle-and-beam building caught his eye, tucked between the row of more modern brick butcher's shops and a shaded area where fishmongers had set up baskets full of their richly odiferous wares. The building was yet another mellow ochre and brown edifice, its beams sagging with age. A painted board posted on the wall beside the railed porch proclaimed it the abode of a glazier, who was at work framing a window in the cramped space beneath the porch.

Jack had always thought of Selina in connection with windows. Perhaps this glazier was a good omen. Certainly the words boldly carved into the bowed beam supporting the weight of the upper story offered hope. In block letters, it read, GOD'S PROVIDENCE IS MINE INHERITANCE.

Heart aching, Jack paused a moment to offer up a prayer for providence. Selina's providence. He prayed that she be kept from harm. In approaching yet another person to ask if she had been seen, Jack knew he was the greatest and most worthless of fools in having lost her in the first place. For a moment Jack longed to lose himself in the bottom of a glass of ale and the slap of cards on baize. And yet he could not and still live with himself; he would not again forsake his responsibilities. The consequences were too grim.

The glazier, who had finished framing the window he worked on, carried it out of his work space that he might add it to a stack of windows leaning against the wall. Jack blinked and held up his hand, first blinded by the glare of the sun reflected in the surface of the glass, and then intrigued by the reflected view of the church tower across the street—a boxy thing, none too distinguished, and yet undeniably a church.

Of course! She would go to a church. She felt safe in churches. Hope renewed, he turned at the sound of a man shouting oaths. The butcher he had spoken to was clutching at one leg and hopping up and down on the other. Red-faced, he shouted, "Wicked little slut!"

The recipient of his foul epithets walked, head high, hat in hand, along the walkway toward Jack, her eyes fixed not on the blustering butcher, but on him.

Selina held her hat out to him. "I believe you have been looking for this?"

He leapt forward, as if to grab it, but took possession of her hand instead, his grasp so fervent the hat was knocked to the ground. "Where have you been?" The look in his eyes was as intense as his hold on her. "I have been desperate to find you."

His joy in seeing her was moving. There was a terrible warmth in the way he was looking at her. She had seen it once before, in the woods, when he had rescued her from the poachers. Such concern, coming, as it did, so close on the heels of having been verbally and physically abused by so many others, provoked unwanted tears. She blinked to keep them at bay.

He seemed unwilling to blink at anything, unwilling to lose sight of her even for a moment. He looked at her as if he wanted to see all there was to see of her, as if he wanted to draw her closer by the very power of his gaze, as if he would not hesitate to kiss her right here, in the middle of the street, in front of God and everybody.

"I have been right behind you, sir." Her voice quavered as she gently extricated her hand from his. "You had only to turn about and there I was."

The glazier had stopped his work to stare at them. The butcher had hopped to the edge of the walkway.

Selina had no desire to become an object of interest again. She had had quite enough of spectacle for one day.

Jack bent to pick up the fallen hat.

"I see you have found Providence House," she said.

He returned the hat to her with a flourish. "I have been blessed by Providence in discovering you."

His voice was too loud and still he gazed at her with such unmasked joy that it left her feeling overheated and breathless.

Several of the fishwives watched them, heads bent together, mouths moving. The glazier had yet to return to his task. She dared not look at the butcher. She wanted a sense of normalcy, of less heightened emotion. In an effort to achieve just that she said, "It is called Providence House because out of all the dwellings in the street only this one was spared from death's touch during the great plague."

Jack was not to be distracted by history long past. "I thought I had lost you. That you had come to some harm."

With a gaze that devoured and a touch that cherished, he linked arms with her.

"Is it not a wonderful story?" she asked softly, her gaze shifting uneasily from his.

"You ran from me, Selina." His voice was low, wounded.

"From the protection of my escort. Why? In truth, it was a dangerous thing to do."

She frowned and would have pulled her hand from his had he allowed it. The memory of what had driven her to flee his protection still pained her. "I thought . . ." What had she thought? He wanted truth, did he? She would give him truth. "I thought it would be difficult for you . . . getting past the temptation of the Roodee."

His lips twitched uneasily. Deep in the gray-blue of his eyes she recognized a trace of fear.

"It was. It is. You are right." His fingers tightened on her arm.

"That was why I went back. Why I . . ."

"Overheard Hugh. I know. I saw the unforgettable expression on your face."

She managed to free herself from his hold in reaching up to place her hat upon her head.

"I would explain," he said.

"No. Please, no explanations." The hat blocked for a moment the concern in his eyes. Hands atremble she pulled at the ribbons beneath her chin, tilting up her head to tie them. She looked him directly in the eye to say sadly, "I thought I knew you."

"You do!" he whispered, his mouth tragic.

She shook her head as she tied the bow, her hands clumsy, her heartbeat erratic. "I am no longer convinced."

"My heart aches to hear you say so."

His every word sounded so genuine, so affectionate, so desperate for approval. It shook her.

"I must reeducate myself where you are concerned," she insisted, determined to be strong, determined to use her head and not her heart.

"You do know me." There was something desperate in his tone. "As I am, not as I was. But who I was still lives within me. That other me was tempted, is tempted, will be tempted, by the Roodee, by the click of dice, by the thunder of hooves, by the very sound of a deck of cards being shuffled, and by unexpected appearance of old friends with bad habits, once shared."

"What stops you?"

"Stops me?"

"Yes. What stopped you today? You were free enough to stay with your friends, to be or do whatever it is you truly desire, as opposed to what I might wish you to be."

"Free to stay? I quail to think you hold me in such low esteem. Do you think me so unaccountable, so unaware of consequences? I could not in good conscience leave you to wander the streets, and such streets as these. Alone. Unguarded. Do you think I would have been able to live with myself had any harm come to you? Come. Tell me. Your opinion of me is more important to my progress than you may realize."

"It would be wiser in you," she said, "to conduct yourself in a manner that fosters your own good opinion of yourself than in trying to please me."

"Do I not please you, then, in any form or fashion?"

She was unprepared for his question. No response leapt immediately to her lips. "I am . . ." she began, and stopped herself. She dared not reveal that she was far too pleased with him. He was not after all, a spy, a liar, a wicked man unredeemed. He had come looking for her! To reveal her relief and joy would be unwise. She said instead, "It would please me if you would be so good as to accompany me to Chester Cathedral."

"But of course. You mean, perhaps, to pray for my soul?" The words were biting.

He offered up his arm, as if offering up a challenge. She took it.

"No. I mean to introduce you to my mother. It is largely because of her, after all, that you were invited to Little Moresworth in the first place."

Chapter Nineteen

Introduction to a woman long dead was not an occurrence to which Jack was accustomed. It could be accomplished by way of a short stroll past a number of shops offering milk, wheels of cheeses, and crocks of freshly churned butter; up a set of steps and though a narrow passageway with signage that proclaimed it Godstall Lane. At the end of the lane loomed the cathedral, red sandstone, with rows of arched stained-glass windows and a square tower, blackened with soot and age.

They stopped to buy flowers.

"Mother loved flowers," Selina said, dipping her nose to the bouquet. "Almost as much as she loved music. It was she who used to fill the music room at Little Moresworth with beautiful sounds. My fondest memories of her as a child are of the songs she used to play. She was rather good at the spinet. I never felt I could, or should, fill her shoes in that regard. Perhaps that is why I have resisted so long the idea of learning to play any instrument. Too well, I remember sitting in her lap, watching her fingers move so deft and sure along the keys."

"I received my first lesson on the harpsichord at the age of five, sitting in my mother's lap, my fingers following hers," Jack said, the words sticking in his throat.

"What a lovely memory. And so like my own!" Eyes blue as a winter sky met his for a moment, shining with unshed tears.

"Yes," he agreed, his gaze settling on a marble angel, pale as snow, even in the shade that had begun to gather between the west front and the south transept, where a host of townspeople had, in neat rows, been laid to rest. The exterior walls of the cathedral had a dirty, sad, downtrodden look. The angel had begun to gather moss and a cap of bird droppings. He did not tell her that he held fast to the lovely memories, that they might outweigh the ugly.

"Do you miss her still?" The question hung unanswered between them as she knelt beside a well-tended gravesite and went to work replacing blooms withered almost to dust with the fleshy beauty of fresh ones. A pair of doves cooed gentle music as she worked. It seemed not to matter that he did not respond. "I miss Mother," she said. "I can go days, sometimes weeks without thinking about her absence, and then, in the most unexpected and palpable manner, it hits me afresh—the sadness, the pain, the sense of separation and lost potential."

He stood frozen behind her, fingering the Welsh penny, unable to respond, his heart pained beyond measure by thoughts of an icebound day and an overturned carriage, a foggy dockside and the look of surprise in Nicki's eyes as he realized he had been shot and by whom.

She seemed content with his silence. "Her absence leaves me singularly lonely at times," she murmured, her voice as soft and as sad as the cooing of the doves. "As if a piece of me were missing. I suffered that feeling this afternoon in walking through the Rows alone. A foolish thing. I should never have left your protection as I did. Mother would not have been at all pleased with me."

He agreed with her in all but that he held himself responsible for her having left his protection.

She rose and with her rose the doves from their nearby perch, with startled cries and a rattle of wings. "Come," she said, briskly brushing grass from her skirt. "You must see the inside of the cathedral, for it is with a mind to its repairs that Mrs. Preston's musicale has been put together. You did say you would play, did you not?"

"Yes, I did, but before we stray too far from the topic, can you tell me, do you understand in any way why God would take her from you?"

Her hands fell still. She turned, her eyes following the flight of the startled birds as they circled, chose safer perches, and settled themselves to cooing from new heights. "I have asked myself that question many times."

"And found you answers? What grand pattern is to be seen in taking a mother from her children?"

She took his arm, led him out of the shadows, her hand a comfort. "I found a sort of answer, a hint of pattern, in imagining the deed undone."

"Undone?"

"Yes. I set my mind to contemplating the consequences had Mother not died. You see, Mrs. Preston would probably still be a lonely widow grieving the death of not only her husband, but her son as well."

"Allan?" He frowned, confused.

"Yes. Father insisted that both Allan and I be exposed to cowpox, as was prescribed by Dr. Jenner's findings, soon after he and Mrs. Preston were wed. She feared her son being exposed to any illness, no matter how mild. Father prevailed, however, after three days' ongoing discussion."

"He has the gift of gab, your father."

She smiled. "Yes. We were both inoculated, suffered a brief bout of illness, and were protected thereafter from a severe outbreak of smallpox that left a great many of the local children dead."

"And you?" He stopped her before they entered the darkness of the cathedral.

"Me?" She looked puzzled, the oval of her face in the frame of her tall-crowned bonnet a perfect, coral-tinted cameo.

"How has your life been changed?"

She sighed. "Well . . . I am confident I would not have received the wide and varied education I have enjoyed. It was at Mrs. Preston's instigation that I was sent away to an academy for girls. She, too, who fostered my enjoyment of drawing. She is quite good at it herself. I do not think I would have been given the freedom to travel Europe and there would have been no Season in London. Mother thought Father tried to make too much of me, even as a child, just as Mrs. Preston does, but Mother would have cajoled and pleaded with Father with far more energy. She liked life to be simple, stable, contained—and she always got what she wanted."

With a flick of the wrist, he drew a line between them. "We . . . should never have met, then?"

"Probably not," she admitted. "There would most certainly never have been a mushroom ball." She unlinked her arm from his and preceded him into the dim coolness of the cathedral.

"A great pity that would have been," he said, voice echoing too loud in stone-bound heights. Momentarily blinded by the change in light, he paused and lowered his voice to a whisper. "I shall never forget your ball."

She turned, pale skirts brilliant as she passed through the stark, diamond-paned squares of light bleeding through the windows that lined the nave. "Really? You did not find it completely ridiculous?"

"No."

"I am glad. I thought perhaps you did, because of . . ."

"The dashed bet."

"Yes."

"A stupid bet, made before ever I had set eyes on you."

"Does that render it any less offensive?" She breezed ahead of him, her whispers echoing sibilantly, her slippers making hushing noises on the crumbling, uneven flooring.

"No, I don't suppose it does. It was another foolish mistake among many I have made. Can you forgive me? Can you imagine the deed undone?"

She tipped back her head, as if to study the soaring arches and groined ceiling, both stained with age. A pair of pigeons roosted in their heights. A wash of light from a second story of pointed arch lancet windows, some cracked or missing, illuminated her face with an uneven light. "We should never have met that night had the bet not been made. Am I right?"

He had to nod. It was true.

"Indeed, my ball would have been a dreadful failure."

Ruefully he said, "Ironic, isn't it? That a man who had just proven himself a complete failure could turn your ball into something less than one with nothing more than music."

"But what music," she said softly, her gaze dropping from

more lofty pursuits to study his face. "I carry the memory of it still, within my head."

"I must confess," he admitted playfully, "I have the fondest memories of hearing *you* play for the first time."

Her laughter fluttered above them. "Oh dear. You must make an effort to erase all memory of those dreadful sounds."

"Ah, but that particular memory appeals to senses other than my ears, Selina."

She blushed.

He pressed the point. "I have been thinking we should undertake lessons of a more advanced nature."

"Advanced?" She eyed him warily, chin rising. "You would suggest such a thing here?"

"Yes." He chose his every word with care. "For I should like, above all else, to play with you."

"Play with me?" She had the look about her of a sinner waiting to be struck down by a bolt from above.

He ceased his teasing. "A duet. For the musicale."

"Oh!" Her relief was profound. "The musicale. Of course."

He smiled. "What else?"

"The last of the series is a Christmas pageant," she said, rather than answer his facetious question. "If you think we would be prepared to play anything but the simplest of tunes before that, you are the most optimistic of instructors, Mr. Ramsay."

"I am optimistic," he agreed, smoothly taking possession of her hand, "where you and I and the making of music together is concerned."

Small wonder Mrs. Preston meant to raise money, Jack thought. The stone pulpit and a throne of medieval origin were both in sadly worn condition. No musicale, not even a series of them, could begin to cover the expensive and expansive changes required here.

At an oak table they armed themselves with candleholders, for the use of which tuppence was requested by a placard next to a slotted box. She provided the necessary pennies, insisting the candles were absolutely necessary to properly view the carvings in the choir. She was right. The wood might be blackened by the

smoke of decades of candles, but the Gothic canopies and pinna-
cles soaring into the arches that framed the row of carved
choirstalls like tiny, airy angelic houses with incredibly high-
pitched roofs, were worth a well-lit look. Carved figures marking
the bench ends bore a thorough examination as well.

"I recognize this fellow from your sketchbooks," he said,
patting the carved hat of a bearded, booted pilgrim with a
walking stick clasped in hands that were far bigger than his
feet. "But where are the seats of pity? I should like to see the
fox in monk's clothing."

With a pleasant smile, she flipped up one of the wooden seats
in a row of hinged chairs to reveal an intricately carved wooden
brace, hanging liplike at the edge, and suggested, "We shall require the light from both candles to examine them properly."

Candles thus in hand, they made their way along the row of
upfolded chairs, forced into close company. Selina bent to examine the carvings, eyes aglow with the reflection of twin candle flames, her cheeks pink with pleasure. Her beauty, inward
and out, captivated Jack's attention even more than the pity
seats, which had considerable charm. With intelligence and
wit, Selina explained the meaning of a number of the scenes
depicted. He heard her, heard and enjoyed the lilting cadence
of her sweet voice, but he absorbed none of what she said, too
absorbed was he in watching the golden play of candlelight on
her face and hair.

"I mean to capture all of the misericordia in my sketchbooks
before I am done," she said with such conviction the words actually registered.

She paused beside the beautifully detailed rendition of a
mother pig suckling a row of tiny carved piglets, a gleam of
expectation in her eyes, as she awaited his response.

He smiled back at her, pleased more with the sense of accord
between them, with the amazing sense of connection they
shared in the history of their lives. Pleased, too, with the rather
blasphemous thoughts provoked by the gleaming enticement of
shining tendril kissing curls at cheeks and forehead and the lure
of lips he wished to kiss far more than her curls. Here, of all the
beauties in the cathedral, he found something to worship.

Such ungodly thoughts brought a guilty smile to his lips. Pupils expanding, she must have read something of his admiration, of the growing desire he felt. A blush heightened the color in her cheeks. She backed away from him, her gaze intent on her candle, on examining the next of the carvings, on anything other than his eyes. She did not look at him again until they came to the fox in monk's clothing.

"What is it the maid gives Monsignor Fox?" he asked, as he maneuvered his candle, the better to see.

"What would a fox in monk's clothing require of a maid?" She leaned closer, that the carving might be better illuminated.

He paid no attention to the fox, far more interested was he in the maid beside him, far more hopeful that she would turn to examine him with as much interest as she exhibited in carved wood.

"I once thought of you as foxlike," she admitted softly.

"Oh? Why? Was it no more than my coloring?"

"No, not your coloring at all, though it does lend itself to foxishness." She turned to look at him, really look at him, her eyes playing over his hair, over the freckles on his cheeks, with an expression of such delight that he stopped breathing for a moment, afraid that the slightest of movements would make her look away.

"Why foxlike, then?"

She seemed embarrassed to admit it. "You seem clever, deceptive, and two steps ahead of the hunter."

Her eyes—sky-blue orbs that captured all too accurately the world as she saw it—captured him now, saw him too clearly, too keenly. Never before had he been examined with such a depth of understanding. She knew he longed to kiss her, here in the candlelit stillness of the church. He saw the recognition in her eyes.

"And how do you see me now? Am I nothing but a hound, after all?"

She made no immediate response, just stared at him with far too piercing a gaze. It did not fall away or retreat even as he leaned slowly, inexorably, closer to her.

From his eyes to his lips and back again, her all-seeing, all-knowing gaze did stray. She closed her eyes at last only as his head sank to hers, and the promise of her mouth became reality, a soft, warm, yielding reality cut abruptly short by the intrusion of a bootheel crunching on broken tile and the discreet clearing of a throat before an all-too-familiar voice drawled, "A church is the last place I expected to find you, Jack."

Selina drew back with a gasp.

Jack closed his eyes, unable to believe his ears, unwilling to believe his brother's ill-timed appearance.

"Roger?"

"You were expecting someone else?"

Of course it was Roger, as finely dressed and foppish as was usual for him. His coat, immaculately tailored, fit him like a glove. The collar was high and buckram stiff. Its appearance tended toward the fashion for a military look, but for the excessive width of its lapels, the narrow cinching of its waistline, and the extravagance of swallow tails. His waistcoat was striped silk. He affected today a single patch beside his mouth, a wig of curls, a silver-rimmed monocle, and a walking stick with a chased-silver knob in the shape of a rose. Every inch of him bespoke the dandy.

He advanced languidly in their direction, the quizzing glass raised in a yellow-gloved hand, as if he were absorbed in nothing more interesting than the canopy of carved wood above them. The glass dropped briefly to examine Jack as he rose, lingered a moment in an examination of Selina as Jack helped her to her feet. "Not your usual haunt, Jack," he purred.

"Nor yours."

"No." He waved his quizzing glass broadly. "But then, it had never occurred to me to put the church, or its benches, to such good use." He doffed his hat and bowed to Selina. "Roger Ramsay, madame. At your service." He swept up her hand, planted a flamboyant salute on her knuckles, and, with a dashingly dangerous gleam in his eyes, inquired. "You are?"

"Selina Preston," Jack hastened to intrude. "Selina, my brother Roger, whose appearance is, more often than not, unexpected. What the devil are you doing here, Rog?"

"You are Mr. Ramsay's brother?" Selina asked, polite but curious. "I am pleased to meet you."

"The pleasure is all mine," Roger drawled, his gaze traveling lazily from Selina to Jack and back again. "I do beg your pardon for interrupting . . ." He paused, brows arched as if anticipating some sort of denial that he had interrupted anything.

Selina blushed and said nothing.

Jack glared at him for so pointedly discomfiting her. "Something devastatingly important, I trust?"

"But of course," Roger said sweetly. "Do you mind giving us a moment alone, Miss Preston?"

"Not at all." She seemed, in fact, relieved. "You will find me?" she asked Jack.

Jack nodded, almost as reluctant to let her out of his sight as he was to hear Roger's news. It was undoubtedly urgent. "What dreadful event have you ridden the length of England to inform me of?" he muttered.

"I do apologize for the interruption. You were making most promising progress with your brazen little minx."

"My what?" Jack's voice echoed.

A pigeon flapped protest in the heights of the groined ceiling. Selina turned, her face a picture of concern.

He waved at her uneasily and lowered his voice to a heated whisper. "She is no such thing!"

"Credit me with a little sense, Jack. I have followed the two of you all the way from the Roodee. She was in shameless pursuit of you the entire length of Watergate. Cooly turned away two other offers, I'll have you know."

"Offers? What do you mean, offers?"

"Turned up her nose at a prosperous fellow in a carriage who tried to take her up, and gave short shrift and a stiff kick to a butcher who made so bold as to fondle the wares before he had paid for the privilege."

"The butcher? Damn the nerve of the man. I shall make mincemeat of him."

Roger put his quizzing glass to use again in a languid perusal of Miss Preston. "How can you afford the tart? She is no doubt as expensive as she is pretty."

Jack longed to snatch up the offensive glass, to wipe the lurid appreciation from Roger's face. "Another word impugning Miss Preston's honor and I shall be forced to dislocate your arm, Rog. You know not of what you speak."

"*Au contraire, mon frère.* I am known to be an expert in the field."

"Not in this field."

Roger shrugged. "As you will. Defend the lady. She must be something rare indeed to make such a champion of you."

"She is," he said, filling his eyes with the sight of her on the far side of the cathedral, the tall-crowned hat removed, her fair hair gleaming like spun gold. Like a holy votive illuminating the darkness of my soul, Jack thought, and breathed deep the musty candlewax smell of a town's mingled sorrow and joy. "What business brings you, Roger? Not the championing of a lady's honor, I take it?"

"Ah, but you are wrong. It is exactly that. Rupert, you see, has run away—figuratively speaking, mind you—to Gretna Green."

"Rupert?" Jack was stunned. "Surely you jest."

"No. And that is not the half of it. Rather proud of our younger brother, I am. Takes courage and enormous conviction to embark on such a mad escapade. Rather clever of him, as well, to have snared a bird by the name of Fletcher. Don't you agree?"

"Fletcher? Any relation to Lester Fletcher?"

"His niece, I believe. Isn't it rich? I find it immeasurably apropos that our brother, the poet, should unknowingly render you the favor, and Lester Fletcher the poetic justice, of winning his niece's heart."

Jack's gaze followed Selina as she strolled the perimeter of the cathedral. "I confess, I am confused."

"Yes. I have always thought so."

Jack ignored the dig. "You mentioned a lady's honor. Are we to rescue this Fletcher girl from Rupert's amorous attentions?"

"Gad, no! As I understand it, her brother Miles, the very one who has inherited all of the money you lost to his recently deceased uncle, has already set out on that very errand. It is Aurora we are to rescue. You see, Rupert has abandoned our dear sister at the Earl of Norfolk's annual sheep shearing, a gathering made up of so many gentlemen and so few females that she is, doubtless, in danger of unwanted attentions."

"You did not go straight to her?"

"No. It occurred to me that a modicum of misbehavior might be turned to our advantage."

"What? You mean to see Aurora married as a result of some indiscretion?"

Roger smiled—a cat in the cream—drew a lawn handkerchief from the pocket of his waistcoat and polished at his quizzing glass. "That would be a happy ending, now, wouldn't it?"

Chapter Twenty

She watched them from the far side of the cathedral—watched Jack, his posture one of a man under siege, his hands as active as his mouth in expressing his unhappiness with the news his brother brought. News he was not inclined to share with her.

It was rather a good thing that Allan was in a talkative mood on the way home to Little Moresworth that afternoon. Selina certainly had nothing to say in the face of a silent, brooding, strangely distant Jack.

His kiss was still warm on her lips, but his eyes when he looked at her had lost all of their former heat. The two of them had spoken of nothing of any substance since Roger had bid them both adieu. He had mentioned seeing Jack the next morning. Jack had nodded, then asked her to show him anything else of merit to be seen in the cathedral with a decidedly distracted air.

There were no more attempts to kiss her, no more badinage between them, and when she looked into his eyes she was met with a chillingly distant thoughtfulness, a trace of sadness.

He took to tossing his coin before they were done. Damn the thing! A sure sign he was bored.

Just when she thought she knew him as well as she knew the road they bumped home along, there came a fresh obstacle. Lord, how he confused her! That his brother stood somehow in her way was undeniable. But how? And why?

". . . invited me to London, they did," Allan was saying, his face alight with the prospect.

"Who?" Selina had the impression he had already said who,

but she had not been listening. Whoever it was had provoked in Jack Ramsay a most perturbed expression.

"Ramsay's friends, Hugh Stuart and Rob Galdough," Allan repeated. She could hear the echo of words already spoken.

"You met them at the races?"

"Yes. Ripping good company. We had a jolly time. They mean to make a circuit of several excellent racecourses, thought I would like to come along. Brought them luck today, or so they kept telling me."

Jack was frowning. Sensitive to his moods, to his every change of expression, Selina assumed he was in sympathy with her own unspoken objection to Allan's scheme. Bad habits he had mentioned in the street. Old friends and bad habits.

"You picked winners, then?" she hazarded. "You were lucky?"

Allan patted his pocket. "Time and again. An eye for it, they said I have, almost as good an eye as Jack Ramsay, they told me. He was the best they had ever known."

Jack's frown deepened. "A pity," he said.

"A pity you were once the best? How so?" Allan asked.

"No. No! You mistake my meaning." Jack looked at Selina then, rather than at Allan, his concern evident in the intensity of his expression. "A pity you have decided to go to London just now. I had hoped you might see fit to accompany me to Norfolk."

"Norfolk?" Allan was intrigued.

Selina was stunned. He meant to go to Norfolk?

"What's to be seen there?" Allan asked, with no notion how she hung on Jack Ramsay's answer.

"A sheep shearing." Jack chuckled, the humor never reaching his eyes, still locked on hers, with a look so delving and serious she felt he meant to convey something of importance.

"A sheep shearing?" she repeated, too stunned to ask outright for further explanation.

"You have heard, perhaps, of Coke of Norfolk's annual gathering?"

"Heard of it? Who hasn't?" Allan asked contemptuously. "Best breeders of livestock in the whole of England are bound to be there—sheep, cattle, horses, and pigs. None of which interests me in the least but the horses."

Jack nodded. "I thought you might enjoy dropping in on just such a gathering."

"But when do you mean to go?" Selina choked out the words. "I had no idea you meant to leave us."

He focused on her again with a sadness undeniable. "I did not, until this afternoon, know I should be going myself."

"Your brother?"

"Yes." There was more he wanted to tell her—she could see as much in his eyes—but with Allan's attention now fixed intently on his every word he said only, "We have a rather pressing need to be going there together."

"When?" Selina softly echoed Allan's next question.

Jack's brow knit. "In the morning," he said gently, and could not look at her as he said it.

She felt as if he had knocked all the breath from her lungs.

"I should very much like to go with you," Allan said earnestly.

Ramsay no longer stared at her. His focus transferred. "Do, then," he suggested, with a firmness that convinced her it had been his intention all along to sway Allan to such a decision. His blue-gray eyes bore into hers again.

"Your father will not object, will he?"

There was an urgency to his question, to the way he looked at her, as if he sought an ally in convincing her father that Allan should go with him.

"But I have promised myself to your friends." Allan's voice was full of regret. "I am loath to disappoint them."

"No trouble," Jack said firmly, his voice, his very posture stiff with purpose. "I shall have a word with them."

Chapter Twenty-one

As night claimed the day and one after another of the candles illuminating the windows of the courtyard winked out, Jack took up a bow, as was his habit, and played, as he had played every night since he had come to Little Moresworth—that he might sleep. Music both soothed and stirred him. It wiped clean the errors he had yet to right and voiced the melancholy longing that surged like a leashed animal within his breast.

He played tonight with the thought that Selina Preston listened. He knew she listened—she had told him she did—and so he chose to reach out to her in the dark through the strings, by way of a poignant overture by Bach called "Air," expressing the night's longing, sadness, and regret. From the first pensive, lingering note, he told her everything he hesitated to voice in words, the gentle, aching throb of the music melodically mirroring the ache within.

This might be his last opportunity to so express himself, the last night they spent beneath the same roof. The music room had never seemed more lonely, his bedchamber less beckoning.

He had no idea how long she stood in the doorway, clad rather irresponsibly in nothing more than a muslin nightrail and beribboned camisole, but at some point before he struck the final dolorous note he became aware of her presence and the faint, teasing scent of her perfume. She was, inexplicably, there. His heart sang with the risk she took in braving his private quarters as night fell.

With the last note of the overture he began a melancholy adagio, also Bach, the notes sweetly tragic on the strings,

achingly lamentful. The piece spoke keenly to him. He hoped
it spoke to her as well. Finished, the notes fading, his fingers
momentarily stilled, he kept his head down, afraid she would
go if he acknowledged his awareness of her. He did in fact
start a third piece and would have played on until morning, but
despite all precaution she stirred, might have faded back
through the doorway, had he not stilled the bow and said,
"Don't go."

She hesitated, her nightshirt wafting about her ankles,
caught in a draft as wavering as her resolve.

"You came to listen? Come in. Listen."

She stepped forward, not away, came to a stop in the doorway, against the jamb of which she leaned, as if for support.
Her cheeks glistened with tears.

"That was beautiful." Her voice trembled. She wiped at her
tears with the corner of her camisole.

"You could not wait to tell me so tomorrow morning?" His
own voice seemed too husky.

"I came to ask you . . ."

"You came to ask me what?"

"Why do you go?"

"To rectify a few of the many wrongs of which I am guilty."

"Oh." She stepped through the doorway, almost as ghostly
as her gown. "That is a good thing."

"Depending on your definition of good. I go for several rea-
sons, chief among them family business. Does it matter that I
go?"

"I hope you will do as your own heart and mind dictate."

"And your heart and mind, Selina?"

"What of them?"

"Have I reason to hope . . . to believe there is some chance
for more between us than music?"

"The music is a powerful bond, sir."

"So it is. I had hoped we would be engaged in playing a
duet by Christmas. Something cheerful. The Boccherini min-
uet is coming along nicely."

"I should like that," she said.

"Shall we play together now? One last time before I go?"

She bent to pluck up a stool, her nightrail clinging seductively to buttocks and thigh as she bent, the beribboned neckline of her short, quilted camisole bed jacket loose enough that for an instant he glimpsed the swell of cream-white breasts.

"Yes." She sounded nervous. She clutched the stool as if it were some sort of barbaric weapon. "But a tune, sir, we have never played before."

"What tune is this?"

"You offered once . . ." She paused, took a deep breath, licked her lips, let the rest of her sentence out in a frantic rush. "To play me."

"Yes. You found me impertinent, and rightly so."

"The idea has lodged itself in my brain and will not leave me alone. I have no peace because of it."

"And what will bring you peace, Selina?"

Her mouth moved, as if to say something that would not form itself into words. She pressed her lips tightly together, closed her eyes, and blurted, "Will you play me, sir? Before you go?"

He was silent, taken aback by her request, unable for the wisp of a moment to believe his ears.

"I fear I cannot oblige you, Selina . . . if . . ."

"Yes?"

"If you continue to address me as sir."

She laughed uneasily. "And if I call you Jack instead?"

He smiled, but not too broadly, afraid luck would run out on him. He set aside the cello and his bow. He rose to take her arm, found she shivered at his touch. "I should be more than happy to oblige. The stool?"

She handed it to him, her movements clumsy. He settled it on the floor between his knees, patted the top of it invitingly. "Sit."

She sat stiffly, her back to him, her posture rigid, hands clasped in her lap. Her fingers shook.

He found it difficult to believe that good fortune seemed so ready to sit itself down in his lap. Leaning forward, he briefly closed his eyes, drank in the clean, sweet smell of her: jasmine, roses, soap, and, underriding it all, a musky, feminine scent. She was as aroused by this illicit late-night tryst as he! He exhaled heavily, with satisfaction, his breath stirring her hair.

She shied nervously—jumped and started without ever having been touched. He rose from the bench, crossed the room quietly, gently closed the door. Her eyes seemed darker, wider than usual as he returned to the bench. She shivered as he carefully settled himself behind her, his knees on either side of her hips.

"Second thoughts?" he asked before he allowed himself the luxury of touching her.

She shook her head. "No."

He clasped her shoulders, the fabric of her quilted camisole cool and crisp. "Relax, then. Lean back."

She shivered, leaned rigidly against his chest.

"Are you cold?" He rubbed his hands the length of her sleeves. "Do you fear me?"

"Fear you?"

"You tremble."

"I fear the pull, the force that sings between us."

He nodded and leaned close to whisper, "Like the memory of a note just played."

Her shivering increased.

"Why fear that pull?"

"I am concerned I make a fool of myself."

"Never that. But you are not given to taking risks, are you, Selina?"

"No. I am not."

"You will not gamble, then, on the possibilities inherent in your feelings for me?"

"The risks are great."

"What risks? Name them."

"That I lose my heart unwisely. That you toy with me. That you pretend to love a mushroom's daughter in order to lay claim to her riches, while caring nothing for her heart."

"Anything else?"

"Yes. I am a woman. I risk my good name, my self-respect."

"I see."

"Do you?"

"I see you do not trust me, nor have I given you much reason to do so. I see that my reputation does me little good and a great deal of bad, for it now stands squarely between us, and I would not have anything stand between us."

"No?"

"No. Not even this thin fabric." His right hand slid lightly down the front of her camisole, catching, tugging at the ribbon ties. She shrank from his touch. Her hands ice-cold, she reached up to halt his progress.

"Are we not in tune with each other, Selina?" His left hand rose to her throat. High on her neck, just beneath her ear, he traced a teasing fingertip path.

Her eyes closed. She swayed beneath his hands.

He drew a series of lines, from earlobe to jaw and thence to the neckline of her nightrail, each stroke plunging a little deeper into the humid valley between her breasts. Her breath labored an uneven rhythm as his right hand tugged free the confining ribbons, while with the left he pushed apart the fabric. Deeply she inhaled as he stroked a line across her breast, deliberately skirting the stiff, rosebud peak of her nipple. Back arching, her breast rose to meet his palm. A moan sounded deep in her throat.

"The song begins," he murmured. "It is the sweetest of tunes." Skimming the surface of her nightrail, he ran his right hand lightly across the faint curve of her belly. Another gasp provided his fingers a more concave surface down which to ride the planes of her torso.

He reveled in her throaty response to his every touch. Gently, slowly, beat by beat, pulse by pulse, he teased the melody from her. Masterfully, rhythmically, he played, lovingly stressing a sharp series of gasps and moans from her throat—just a few surprised staccato exclamations at first, then a rapid tempo cadence of "yeses" as he plucked, prodded, and probed strings in her that had never before been sounded. In perfect, lyrical pitch, she sang solo beneath the stroking ministration of his touch.

He would have built her crooning moans to a crescendo, his

fingers having tested the fabric that guarded the soft, springy mound of hair between her legs and found it humid with her desire—had she not whispered, "God, help me!"

God help her? God help him. What was he doing on this night of all nights when he meant to ride away with the dawn?

"You must go!" he admonished, rising abruptly from his bench—so abruptly that in reaction she slid clumsily from the stool, her eyes wide with surprise and unguarded desire.

"Go?" she repeated weakly, disbelieving.

"Yes, go," he said gruffly. "You asked God for help, but *I* offer it up to you. Go!" he said. "While I still have self-control enough to bid you do so. The consequences, otherwise, could be dire, my dear."

Clutching her camisole around the pale beckoning bliss of breasts and shoulders, she stumbled up from the floor, tripping over the hem of her gown with a muffled cry—of relief or disappointment he could not be certain. He closed his eyes, listened to the drum of her bare feet on the wooden flooring, heard her break into a run when she had cleared the door.

"No. Don't go!" he wanted to call after her, but she was already gone, and he could not run after her.

She ran from him, from her own aching desire, ran, feet skidding on polished wood, fumbling to tie loosed ribbons, the night air chill on burning skin. Twice she paused. The first time she turned around, almost ran back to him, so great was her yearning, so enticing the unfinished song of lovemaking they had left half played. The second time, her body humming with the memory of his touch, burning with desire unsated, she could not resist. With a sob, her heart beating so erratically she thought she must stop breathing, she turned and went back.

He stood quietly in the music room, his back to her, leaning in a tortured stance against the frame of an opened window. The sweet perfume of rain-washed air wafted through the room. A sigh, heartfelt, hissed from his throat, along with a single soft oath. He ran a hand through his hair. It gleamed wetly, like rich, moonlit silk.

Heart in her throat, Selina turned away from the sight of

him, away from the idea that she was prepared to fling herself at him no matter the consequences. She turned, only to be faced by the sight of the doorway to his bedchamber, the door ajar, beckoning.

Overheated, Jack had flung open a window to cool his head. The rain, the fresh smell of it, the distant patter in the courtyard below, the occasional pelting flurry of drops that struck his face, did well to cool him, if not his thwarted desires. He leaned out of the window, allowed the misting drops to wet his hair, drank in the sweetly musky odor of freshly wetted rocks, grass, and dirt in the courtyard below. Rain chilled, his hands, when he pressed them to his forehead and ran them through his damp hair, smelled of Selina—jasmine, rosewater, and the rainy musk of her desire. He cupped them to his nose, drank her in, inwardly kicked himself for insisting that she return to her own lonely bed rather than keep him company in his.

And yet, had he to do it all over again, his response would be the same. Consequences. Accountability. He could no longer ignore such concepts. Too many times had his life been drastically altered by way of forgetting them.

Without thinking, the shape of familiar comfort in his hand, he slid his found penny from the pocket of his waistcoat and flipped it high, moonlight gleaming on copper. The penny brought back memories, reminding him of a night he did not want to remember—a night it had not rained but sleeted, the sound thin, crisp, and cold.

That night had smelled of pipe smoke, roasted cheese, and stale ale. His mother had complained of the stench. She had paced as he now paced—anxious to be gone from the stifling confines of the noisy, overcrowded inn in which they had been forced to seek shelter by ice-bound roads and exhausted horses.

"We must leave in the morning, Jack," she had said so decisively that Jack, an impressionable seven-year-old, had believed that indeed they must.

"Rouse Mr. Stapeley," he had been directed early the next morning. "Tell him the sun is up. The snow has stopped. I want to be on the road before the hour is out."

Obediently, he had hunted out old Mr. Stapeley among the half dozen sleeping forms curled up on the common room floor, close to the warmth of the fire now reduced to white ash. In stepping over and around the snoring men, he had found a Welsh penny token, big and copper, the markings strange to him—plumes in a crown on one side, a ship and castle on the other. VIRTUET ET INDUSTRIAT, it read. Virtue and industry abandoned on the floor.

"On the road?" Stapeley repeated querulously as he rose, snuffling and bleary-eyed, to rub a clear spot on the nearest frost-fogged windowpane. "But the roads, Master Jack. We risk bruising the horses' knees. Tipping the carriage. You and I, my boy, we must do our best to dissuade Lady Ramsay from such a course, don't you see?"

Jack was easily led, and impressed with the wisdom of any man with so many lines weathered into his countenance. Nodding agreeably, he had padded back up the stairs, happily flipping his found penny and trying to predict crown or castle.

His mother was not impressed with him or his penny. She insisted Jack follow her downstairs to see how one went about directing one's coachman to obey one's directives, no matter how much they might disagree with one's wishes.

Her mind was made up, no matter that Stapeley begged in a most subservient and humble fashion, ". . . not to risk the safety of the boy, marm, or the horses."

She was no more than a little swayed, as the innkeeper and his wife both took Stapeley's part in the discussion, advising her, "Best stay put at least one more day, and let the sun work its magic on the ice."

A headstrong woman of decided opinion, she did not like to be thwarted. "What say you, Jack?" she had asked as he sat flipping his penny. "Shall we toss your coin on the outcome?"

Happy to be included in such an important decision, Jack had nodded. "Crown or castle?"

"Crown we stay, castle we go."

Stapeley had nodded, dubiously morose. "If that's how you think it best decided, marm." He turned to Jack with a squinty wink. "It's crowns we'll be wanting, lad."

Jack had nodded, sobered by his role. He had tossed the penny well enough, only to fumble the catching of it.

A hundred times he had replayed the moment in his mind.

The penny, bouncing off the tips of outstretched fingers—such a simple thing—gave rise to restless nightmares.

Beneath the oak sideboard it had rolled. On hands and knees he had scrambled after it, lying flat on his stomach, desperately scrabbling, the coin just out of reach.

"Get up from the floor," his mother had insisted. "You dirty your waistcoat. We are going, Mr. Stapeley. I'll have no more argument on the matter."

"But mother. Crown side up." Jack had run after her, the penny fetched from beneath the sideboard with the assistance of a poker. "Crown side up! We ought not go!"

She would not listen, had become quite irritable with him, had, in fact, snatched his penny out of the air, the hundredth time he flipped it, when at last they had begun their careening way along the slick roads. Her voice strung high with nervousness, she said, "Do please put that away," the very instant before the wheels slid into a nasty patch of ice, horses squealing in terror as the coach overturned in a steep ditch.

The memory left him exhausted, weary, and sad, the penny clutched in a hand now tainted by the metallic tang of copper. One-handed he tossed and caught, over and over, a moment in time that had made the difference between life and death. He had, these many years, held himself entirely accountable for his mother's demise, for the clumsy inability to catch a coin. He had never admitted his guilt to anyone. He had clutched it tight to his chest, this feeling of responsibility—his and his alone. With no one had he shared culpability, until now, on this moonlit, rainy night, when for the first time he admitted that his mother had figured greatly in the enactment of her own tragedy.

As had Nicki.

Chilled, he shut the window. How would his own tragedy play itself out when he left with Roger in the morning?

Breath caught, like a fluttering moth in the trap of her ribs, Selina waited. Shivering, despite the layers of linen between which she had slid—perhaps because of them—she listened as he entered the room, lit a candle. The wavering glow, the match's sulphurous smell, intruded on the drapery-hung bed in which she lay trembling. Anticipation, fear, and unmet desire kept her silent. Waistcoat and breeches, she heard them slide to the floor, heard the wardrobe opened, the clothes hung away. Cold air wafted. The shadow of danger loomed huge on the bedcurtains before they were flung wide, that candlelight and Jack Ramsay, nightshirt clad, might invade her safe haven.

For a moment, mouth dropped open, he stared at her.

"Good God! Selina! What in Heaven's name . . ."

"My being here has little to do with Heaven." Her voice shook.

He smiled, his expression far more tender than ever she could recall having witnessed, his eyes full of concern.

"Do you mean to send me away?" She sounded childlike.

"Would you go if I sent you?"

"I will not sleep, knowing that you go away tomorrow. My bed is too big, too empty, too cold."

"It would be better, safer, did you go. It would be obedient, wise, and prudent." His voice held warning, but his eyes kindled sparks. There was a combustibility to his question, a flicker of mischief to the set of his lips as his smile grew. It set to blazing the growing conflagration between her thighs. She ached with the heat.

"I will go," she whispered. "Will be obedient, wise, and prudent, as I have my whole life been." She lifted the linens to slide from under them. "If you so desire it."

As she vacated the sheets, he slid into them, the firm, guiding strength of his hands catching her about the waist, waylaying her departure, drawing her back into the warmth, against the heat of his chest. "My desire has nothing at all to do with your going," he protested thickly, enfolding her in his arms, fitting their bodies together like nested spoons. "As you should well be able to judge."

The stiff proof of his desire was not to be denied or ignored. It throbbed hotly against the thin muslin covering her backside. "Quite to the contrary," he said, cupping her breasts, "it was my newfound appreciation of consequences . . ." Down her torso his hands glided. Lower still they slid. ". . . that provoked me into asking you to go. Those consequences still concern me." His fingers teased, touched and gently probed, only the thin layer of muslin between them. "I need not question your desire. You are deliciously wet with it, Selina." He nuzzled her ear, her neck, her shoulder. "But I would ask you once more if you are sure you wish to share my bed, knowing I leave in the morning. I can promise to warm you, my love, as you have never before been warmed, but it will not be a restful night, and I cannot say when I shall return."

He fell still, awaiting her answer. The weight and warmth of his hands withdrew from any contact with her body. She could feel the rise and fall of his every breath at her back, could feel the tension in his thigh against hers, could smell the very odor of their mingled desire rise from beneath the sheets. There was a feeling of rightness about the closeness of their bodies, a sense of home, of warmth, of love on a level she had never before experienced. Yet, fear and longing washed over her in overwhelming waves, each threatening to drown the exhilarating fire of her desire. The dangerous bulge of his need against her backside, the searing wet throb of white-hot longing where he had so recently touched her, terrified.

"You do mean to return?" she asked.

"Ah, my love." He ran the palm of his hand lightly the length of her spine. "If this is how you would receive me, how could I stay away?"

Like a tuning fork, just struck, she vibrated to his touch, to his every word. The unsteady ball of Fate rolled beneath her feet, dizzying her. She had but to thrust her feet once more from the sheets to find solid ground. Either way, he would leave her in the morning and she would be left with her longing—a longing so intense she turned to face him in the warm nest of the bed.

"I love you, Jack. May I stay?"

Chapter Twenty-two

Selina awoke before dawn, clad in nothing but the radiant, throbbing glow of her euphoria. The night had passed in a haze—warm, ecstatic, blissful. She had never experienced such an intoxication of ardor, lust, and sensual pleasure. Effervescent and fiery, it raced in her veins.

Shameless! She had been absolutely shameless! She stretched like a cat, glorying in the memory, exulting in the warm sex-scented tangle of legs and linens. Jack! Dear Jack. His face, smoothed of all lines as he slept, was beautiful in the graying light of the coming dawn. He had the look of a fallen angel, a sleeping wood imp, a drowsing boy—yet even in repose the raging fire that had consumed her might be witnessed in his brows, lashes, and flame-red hair. Most compelling, his mouth—a tender, silken, magical mouth. Nuzzling, kissing, licking, suckling, nibbling, it had cooled the burn between them at times, that the fire might more slowly, more completely consume her. Her flesh tingled with the memory of Jack's unstinting ardor, urgent, plundering, and pleasurable.

Tugging at the sheets, she unveiled the beautiful molding of his bare shoulders, marveled at the strangely wonderful sight of her naked breast comfortably nestled against his chest. Her nipples throbbed, as did the more private part of her that she had freely, even flagrantly, given up to the unexpected power of her carnal needs, more than once in the heated course of the night. Despite the lack of sleep, she pulsed with energy, wanting nothing more than to throw herself at him again, to meld her body to his.

It was the sight of blood on the sheets that stopped her, sobered her.

Like a scarlet letter, here was her sacrificed virginity for all the world, certainly all of the staff, to witness. Panic and pain seized her, as it had ever so briefly in the night, chasing away the warmth, the bliss, the glow. Jack had soothed her in the night, had explained that her pain was a temporary one. He could not soothe her now, not even had he been awake to try. The loss of her virginity was not a temporary ill. It was devastatingly permanent. The servants would be stirring soon, might be up and about already. She must not be caught in Jack Ramsay's bed with the blood of her lost innocence staining the sheets.

Shaking with chill and her own audacity, Selina slid from beneath the weight of the arm in which Jack cradled her to his chest, untangled her legs from his, and stole away from the soporific warmth of the Rakehell's rumpled bed. Managing to locate all of her cast-off clothing, she threw it on and crept, without waking him, from the room.

She had naively begged the Rakehell to seduce her, had lain willingly—nay, wantonly—in his arms while with gentle seductive finesse he took her maidenhood! She had reveled in their lovemaking, had trustingly opened herself up to him, frankly professed her love to him, had received sweet words, honeyed looks, the tenderest arousal in return. But in the stealthy trek returning her to the safety of her room, she realized that Jack Ramsay had made her no promises. He had never said he loved her.

In the chill light of dawn, guilt and a panicky shame filled her, chasing away all trace of mindless bliss. How to face the man this morning after such intimate exchanges as they had shared? How to face the world? Would she read regret in his eyes? Contempt or scorn? Would everyone she encountered be able to read the drastic changes she had undergone?

Carefully, she bathed herself, sponging away the smear of blood, the musky smell of their lovemaking, the wet desire that still lingered between her legs. A few tears salted the bowl of cold water, so raw, swollen, and unfamiliar was she with herself, inside and out.

She did not want to be in love with the Rakehell—did not want to say good-bye to him, to witness, deep in his gray-blue eyes, that he had no intention of returning to the foolishly wanton mushroom's daughter. This morning, more than any other she could recall, she felt very much a mushroom's daughter.

She missed Jack Ramsay this morning, as she covered her nakedness with the trappings of who she had been the day before. They were yet to be truly parted and already she felt the yawning chasm of distance that separated them. She loved him, foolishly, irrevocably, wholeheartedly. Her body still thrummed with the pulse of her love for him, and yet she questioned, as if it were a fantasy of her own making, that he loved her at all. She had to admit the truth of his never having said to her as much, an admission she wanted to face even less than the man this morning.

What a fool she had been! A reckless, naive fool. How many such foolish girls had Rakehell Ramsay debauched? Did he make jest of his conquests in the company of his friends? Was she to become the latest gossip? Would Allan soon catch wind of her folly? Good God, what had she done?

She was almost glad Jack was soon to be gone. No, not glad. There was a wrenching tug in her heart when she considered the prospect of him abandoning her, perhaps forever. But, as it was easier to imagine him capable of the seduction of a mushroom's daughter than the loving of one till death did they part, it seemed right and proper that he should go.

Unable to bear the idea of facing him, she took up her basket, asked one of the maids to inform her father that she had gone to the woods to study mushrooms with a footman for escort, and took herself out a side door, happily convinced she had eluded all parting embarrassments with Jack Ramsay.

She never expected him to see her from his window upstairs, never expected him to leap down the stairs two at a time in pursuit of her, never dreamed he would silently, finger to lips, relieve the footman of his burden and send him back to the house, that a Rakehell might follow her into the dripping, rain-drenched dampness of the woods instead of a servant.

It was appropriate that she happened on not just a mushroom this morning, but a fairy ring of mushrooms. "How enchanting," she said, thinking she spoke to the footman who had followed her out of the door.

"As enchanting as was the night," the Rakehell said, his all-too-familiar voice whirling her around in astonishment.

"You!"

"Yes, me," he said. "I missed you this morning."

"Oh. Did you? I did not wish to wake you; you slept so soundly."

He grinned. "The sleep of contentment."

How did one reply to suggestive remarks, when one could no longer pretend innocence? "A damp morning," she said lamely.

"Not so deliciously wet as was the night."

She blushed and backed away, feeling vulnerable, uncomfortable with his blatant reference to what they had done.

"Last night was a mistake," she said firmly.

His brows rose. "Never say so. Last night was too extraordinary to be a mistake. Never deny your courageousness in coming to me as you did."

"It was not at all courageous, but foolish, weak," she said uncertainly. "I will not make such a mistake again."

"I certainly hope with no one other than me." He put down her basket and stepped toward her. Wicked purpose sparkled in his eyes.

"Stay where you are." She backed away from his advance.

"Oh, but I cannot." His voice was throatily seductive. "I must go away for a while, but before I go I would wish you farewell."

"You can speak from where you stand, can you not?" She backed up another step, bumped up against the low-hanging branch of a tree, turned her head to see what she had run up against. Her hair caught in the leaves. Then his fingers caught in her hair, tangling in the curls, not painfully so much as provocatively, as he freed her from the grip of the tree.

With his touch, with the soft, seductive way in which he looked into her eyes, his thumb tracing a line along her neck, all of the feelings of the night before came flooding back. His touch warmed her like sun on snow, melting her resistance, fueling her desires. She knew he meant to kiss her. She ought to have fought him off, ought to have put up a protest, should have turned her head that her lips might not meet his, but she dared a look instead. In looking she saw that while there was undeniably pride of conquest in his gaze, there was more, far more. With tenderness, heat, and desire his eyes devoured her, delved into her, seeking answers in her gaze as avidly as she sought them in his. Shifting, his gaze sought only one answer and that one had to do with her mouth, which he glanced at with such heated interest she tipped up her chin, the better that he might see it. Leaning into the hand that cupped her head, she allowed the gentle pull of his fingers in her hair to guide her head toward his.

The kiss brought her to tears. She pulled away, might have fled had he not taken gentle hold of her hand before she could make good her escape and clasped her to his chest, his words almost desperate. "Do not run from me. Not again. Can you not feel how wrong it would be to part any sooner than life demands?"

"It is you who goes away!" Her voice, almost a wail, came muffled from his shirt front.

He was silent for an instant, stroking her hair.

"Yes. Does it trouble you? I like to think it does."

She looked up angrily and pushed away from his hands. "You enjoy troubling me? How many troubled hearts have you left behind you?"

"Never one to which I so longed to come again."

"And do you mean to return?"

He laughed. "Do you promise to play a duet with me upon my return?"

"A duet?"

His eyes glittered with anticipation.

Her cheeks flamed, along with various unmentionable parts of her body. She sniffed, turned her face away from the kiss he directed at her lips. It glanced off her temple instead. "You mean will I throw myself into your bed again?"

He laughed, cradled her chin between his hands, and planted a kiss on the tip of her nose. "You are too harsh, Selina. Too cynical by far, if you believe you must throw yourself at me in any way. I see I must make a point of throwing myself at you when next we meet."

From the direction of the house they could hear Allan calling and a quick, distinctive whistle.

"My brother," he said. "Time I was going." He opened his arms. She flung herself into them, and as he clasped her close one last time he whispered, "Fare thee well, my little mushroom. I shall return. I give you my word. And as proof of my pledge I give into your keeping my most precious possession." He pressed into her palm a penny.

Chapter Twenty-three

As suddenly, as unexpectedly, as he and his music had come into her life, Jack was gone, but for a worthless Welsh penny token Selina tucked daily into the bosom of her dress, that she might hold some part of him close to her heart. The music was silenced, and Allan gone, too, leaving stillness, emptiness.

Selina's greatest concern, the bloodstained sheets, were remarked upon, only in passing, by Mrs. Preston.

"I am alarmed," she said, "to think any of my younger staff of females was so foolish as to have been taken in by a gentleman of Rakehell Ramsay's notorious reputation. We can only hope the silly slattern, whoever she may be, has not got herself in the family way."

Selina forbore admitting herself the foolish slattern. It had never crossed her mind to fear a pregnancy along with the loss of her innocence. Now the thought preyed upon her daily as the matter of the sheets was avidly speculated upon by the servants, all the young women in the household being held under suspicion, except—at least not within her hearing—Selina. Eventually, new gossip supplanted the old. The matter was dismissed and, to a great extent, forgotten, by all but one. She could not forget, would not forget, no matter how hard she tried.

And she did try. In the first week of her loneliness she applied herself to practicing the violin, haunting Little Moresworth with the tunes Jack Ramsay had once played. Her footsteps, too, haunted the long gallery, where, floorboards creaking, she paced, pausing again and again at the window, to peer up the road, watching for signs of horse or carriage. To her drawings, as well, she devoted her energies. They had always, in the past, filled her with purpose and contentment. No longer. Flowers she drew, and in drawing them, she thought of the flowers she and Jack had taken to her mother's gravesite. Portraits she tried, but her pencil seemed capable of rendering only one face. Mushrooms she gave up on entirely. They brought to mind Cannock Chase, where Jack had saved her from the poachers, and the fairy ring she had found on the day Jack had left. To the chapel at Little Moresworth she went every evening, head bent, to pray for peace, for sleep, for forgiveness. But it was not enough, none of it, not nearly enough.

Her days passed like the ticking of a metronome, all too predictably, their very regularity filling her with restless ennui. Nights were worse than the days. She lay awake, unable to sleep, the memory of a single reckless night a torment, her loneliness overwhelming.

Indeed, the more she practiced the duet she and Ramsay were to have performed at Christmas, the lower she sank into a sense of melancholy. Her attempts in Chester Cathedral to sketch a misericord of a young man offering a ring to a princess resulted in an outburst of tears that echoed quite miserably in the high ceiling.

The second week was marked with a letter from Jack. Briefly, it lifted her hopes. Addressed to Mr. and Mrs. Preston, the main thrust of its message was to thank them for their hospitality. There was only one part of the letter that Selina might interpret as meant specifically for her.

> *I miss the sweet contentment of days spent happily at Little Moresworth. They are honeyed memories by contrast with the present bitter time. Too much salt, perhaps.*

So impersonally was the affection thus conveyed that she could not be pleased. He did end the missive *"Ever yours, Jack Ramsay,"* but he made no mention of returning.

Impatient with her own discontent as the second week of her loneliness began, Selina discussed with her father an idea, long held, that she should be more involved in the business of producing silk. He fought the idea. He always had.

"I do not want you to smell of the shop," he said. "That is not why I invested so heavily in your education."

In the end, however, he was swayed by her frank admission, "I am lonely, Father. Time weighs heavy on me."

To the mill, therefore, he took her—into the reeking steam of the boiling degumming vats, past the pungent brightness of the dyeing vats, through the rattle and hum of the winding, throwing, and warping areas to the weaving room. Even there, the stink of the process by which the silk was produced hung on the air. It clung to the fibers of her clothing, imbued itself in the very strands of her hair.

"How do you accustom yourself to the odor of this place?" she asked the stout woman who had been given the task of explaining to her, in detail, the silk-weaving process.

"Odor?" The woman's brows rose. "What odor, love?"

Her father laughed. "Inured to the stink," he said. "Come often enough to the mill and you will soon lose all awareness of it as well."

Selina tried to ignore the stench. She tried to drown it out by soaking her fichu in rosewater, but it was only in focusing her attention on the method that transferred her designs to the Jacquard looms that she became oblivious, for any length of time, to the odors at the mill. She had watched the cards being cut and laced together in the past. It was a fascinating bit of magic. Soon she was seated amongst the artisans, learning the method herself.

Her days filled with new sights, sounds, and smells, but the nights were by contrast emptier, lonelier, than ever. The house seemed unearthly silent without Jack's evening serenades. Her ears seemed perpetually pricked for music that never played. Her arms longed to wrap themselves around remembered warmth. Her flesh, most particularly her breasts, ached with longing for a lost lover's touch. She understood, as never before, how much her father must have missed her mother when she had died.

No further word from Ramsay, no word from Allan. Her despair, her sense of abandonment, grew daily. A letter, at last, from Allan. To Hertfordshire they had gone from Norfolk. A wedding. Jack's sister to be married. A lovely girl. Headstrong and passionate. An excellent rider. She and Allan had talked horses. Jack had given her away. At the bottom of the letter, in Jack Ramsay's bold hand, a single line. "Brick by brick, the ruin rebuilds himself."

Allan promised to write more later, but the third week slipped away, a wordless passage of days. No letters. Selina grew nauseous, sick with the idea she had been taken in, completely betrayed by her own desire. She ceased eating with her usual healthy gusto. She lost all energy—lost weight—wanted nothing to do with her sketchpad. The odor of the dyes at the silk mill seemed to grow worse rather than better. The wine posset at bedtime prescribed by Mrs. Preston made her retch.

The weighty feeling that something vital to her happiness was missing grew daily in its urgency, until it occurred to Selina that something other than Jack *was* missing these many weeks. Her monthly course, the flow she had always considered a female curse, now mocked her in its very absence. She tried hard to convince herself she had miscounted, miscalculated the meaning of the cessation of what had come to her so regularly in the past. She did not want to believe herself in the family way, did not want to face the choices and decisions such a change of circumstance must thrust upon her. Another week flew by. Still no blood. There was no one to tell, none on whose shoulder she could cry, on whose counsel she could depend.

She stopped going to the mill with her father, too overpowered by the smell of the place, the constant motion and noise. He asked her why, reminding her it had been at her request he first took her. She could not explain to his satisfaction, could not break his heart with her growing shame. Nor could she burden Mrs. Preston with her perfidy—with the consequence of bloodied sheets. No one would find cause for gladness in her momentous, indeed, her daily burgeoning news. Panic, fear, and continued changes in her body—growing nausea, fatigue, the tenderness and swelling of her breasts, strange cravings for gooseberries and cock-a-leekie soup—these things were hers, and hers alone.

Her melancholy feeling brewed like a storm, darkening the heavens, troubling the clouds. It ran in rivulets along misted windowpanes. It took her out of doors one wan morning, the skies still awash, a basket over her arm, a sketchbook tucked beneath the confines of a hooded cloak. Into the woods she wandered, free of escort, no clear goal in mind.

Past the spot where she had stood beside a fairy ring, enchanted by a promise, a penny, and a kiss, deeper into the trees, into the darkness of her own unhappiness she stumbled. Her cloak sodden, the hood dripping tears, beneath the damp sigh of Wych elms, silver birch, and oaks she wandered, the smell of mold, decaying leaves and wet earth so intense she stopped to retch on more than one occasion. What she sought—answers, she supposed—she knew not until she happened upon them, as if they had been waiting for her, a cluster of yellowish white parasols, glistening with rain. *Amanita phalloides*!

She knelt beside them, heedless of the wet, the mud, the ruination of her dress—knelt as she had so many times of late, to pray. But this was no altar and it was not God she sought in genuflecting before the unholy potential of these pale, perfect angels of death. Poetic irony was what Jack Ramsay might have called it. A fitting solution for the mushrooming problems of a mushroom's daughter. She lost track of time in pondering their dark promise. With a freshening breeze, the trees whispered to her, stirring her to action. A shaft of sunlight brought to a gleam, like a diamond, a raindrop poised on the lip of the largest mushroom.

It was beautiful. She would thrust it in her mouth quickly, no time to think, no time to change her mind. She would bite down fast.

Her mind made up, she reached out to pluck it, only to be stopped by a butterfly. An ordinary brown butterfly, it was not at all spectacular in size or coloring, but it was caught for a moment in the same light that made a diamond of the Death Cap. Delicate and meandering, it wafted lightly past her fingertips, distracting her. She turned her face into the strengthening sunshine. Raindrops jeweled the vaulting of breeze-stirred branches above her head. Red and green and blue, the flickering, prismatic light seemed, for an instant, to pour through stained glass. Selina smiled. She knelt in Nature's cathedral. The rain-washed air smelled sweet, pure. Drinking in a great lungful, she stood and turned her back on death. Head bowed, she closed her eyes, shamed to think she had considered taking not one life, but two. As she stood, stilled by the dire consequence she had just avoided, another butterfly touched her with its delicate beauty. Deep in the pit of her stomach it fluttered. Awed, laughter bubbling at the back of her throat, she pressed both hands to her stomach and waited expectantly for the next faint brush of wings.

Eighteen weeks to the day since he had ridden away, Allan rode cheerfully into the courtyard one warm July morning with a great clatter of hooves and cries of "Where is everyone?" as if all should have known he meant to arrive, five massive animals in tow—a fine roan colt and four fillies. Bought, he said, from one of Coke's guests

He was a young man changed, full of plans for his future. He wanted to be a breeder. "Not racehorses, mind you, but dray horses, for there is, I have been informed, increasing need for the stoutest sort of beast here in the north."

Plagued by the need to know when Jack Ramsay meant to return—if he meant to return—Selina found opportunity to speak to Allan alone that afternoon as he exercised the colt on a lunge line.

"You seem changed, Allan," she said, hoping he would not recognize how much she, too, was changed.

"Do I?" he asked with an eagerness that surprised her. He slowed the colt that she might join him at the hub of the great wheel the roan's massive hooves and heavily feathered fetlocks cut into the meadow. "Ramsay turned me around."

"Ramsay?" she breathed the name as if breathing in hope, savoring its sound. The green smell of crushed grass was strong. The horse turned them around, around and around.

"He did it intentionally. Showed me my paces, as surely as this colt learns his. You see, I thought he and his brother would be rowdy companions, that we would have a bang-up time of it, that I would become a regular knight of the elbow."

She stopped spinning, stopped to stare at her feet. There were harebells growing in the meadow: harebells, goatsbeard, and honeywort. They swayed beneath her feet like waves beneath a boat, green waves. The world around her kept turning. Allan and the horse kept circling.

"I thought a Rakehell would show me the ins and outs of the devil's books and the ivory rattlers, Selina, but he revealed to me something far more important."

"Oh?" She wanted to throw up, to walk away, to breathe air untainted by the stink of horse and crushed green things, but more than any of these she wanted to hear about Jack.

"He showed me his shame, Selina!"

"His shame? What shame?"

The roan had begun to sweat. The smell of it, of crushed grass, oiled leather and fresh droppings almost overcame her.

Allan took no notice of her greening complexion. He had no idea how close she came to vomiting on the gleaming tips of his boots. He was too caught up in what he had to say. Quick, short little breaths she took, all the time insisting to herself she was not going to be ill.

"Shame brought upon himself and his family by way of his gambling."

She swallowed the taste of bile, swallowed the shame that swelled panic far swifter than it swelled her breasts and belly—tried to listen.

". . . witnessed enormous courage in Jack Ramsay. Great self-sacrifice. I saw him beg his siblings' forgiveness for playing fast and loose with their lives, their money, their futures . . . saw him walk his sister down the aisle."

The horse rocked and reeled as it ran.

". . . muttering their ill opinion of his gambling habits."

His voice, as he turned, went from her right ear to her left. His meandering enthusiasm wearied her, the pounding thump of the horse's great hooves seemed to shake her very foundations.

". . . cordially gave her away to the very man who had in his possession all else he valued in the world."

If only she could stop the whirling.

"It was at Jack's insistence that the wedding took place where it did."

If only Allan would stop the horse.

". . . hoped his brother-in-law would be more readily accepted in the neighborhood."

If only Allan would stop talking.

"Admitted he had shot his friend. In court. The place packed with his peers." Allan's enthusiasm was almost as sweated as the horse. "Turned me around, it did."

Around and around. As though from a distance, she heard him talking. As though she viewed them from another woman's eyes, the meadow—harebells, goatsbeard and honeywort—came spinning out of a growing darkness to meet her.

"Selina. Wake up, Selina."

The offensive odor of smelling salts jerked her back to a nauseated state of consciousness. She waved them away.

"Please, they make me sick."

She opened her eyes to find Mrs. Preston armed with the vial, and a cool, damp cloth with which she dabbed at Selina's forehead. Allan hovered at her shoulder. They were in her bedroom. She lay on the bed.

"You fainted." Mrs. Preston sounded worried.

Selina tried to rise. It was her stomach, not her head, that turned. She sank back against the pillows. "I am still faint."

"It is the heat," Mrs. Preston assured her with such loving concern, Selina wanted to weep. "Perhaps if you rest a bit without the confinement of corset and clothes . . ."

"That's my cue to go," Allan said with a cheeky grin.

Selina flung out her hand to catch his arm, which was not at all within reaching distance. "Will you come back in a minute?" she called to him, her voice weak. "There is so much we have left to talk about."

Mrs. Preston helped her from her dress, unlaced her. Selina was glad that, as yet, there was nothing much in her figure to betray her situation.

Allan returned, as she had asked, to find her more comfortable, in nightshirt and camisole bed jacket, propped up against the pillows, a cotton throw covering her legs, and drapes shrouding the room in an artificial twilight.

"Feeling better?" he asked.

"Much." She patted the edge of the bed. "Sit. Please, and tell me more of your adventures."

He sat, his eyes roaming the room. "This reminds me of the times we shared as children. Each of us unburdening our hearts in the evenings when we could not readily fall asleep."

She nodded. "Those were good times. To no one else could I reveal so many of my sorrows and fears."

"What sorrows and fears would you reveal now, Selina?"

She took a deep breath, pushed back the matter that sprung first to mind and said with a great deal of effort, "Begin at the beginning. Tell me about Norfolk."

Allan did not have to be asked twice.

"Holkham Hall, Sil, a marvelous place. You must make a point of seeing it someday. A bloody great mansion, chock-full of artwork and statuary. Greek and Roman stuff. Land for miles. Coke trying all the latest techniques. He had made arable great stretches of wasteland. Sheep—I have never seen such beautiful creatures. And the noblemen I was introduced to—dozens of names you would recognize—all of them interested in improving their land; wool production; or the size, weight, and hardiness of their stock. They were so knowledgeable. Driven—like your father—to make improvements in their lives. Left me feeling small—quite insignificant as to my accomplishments."

"The valor of virtue and industry," she whispered.

"What's that?"

"Something I read on a penny. The Ramsays went there for their sister?"

"Aurora, yes. A lovely girl. Red hair and freckles, with a

temper to match. She was ready to flay Jack alive when we arrived.

"For losing his brother's estate?"

"That and for expecting her to assume responsibility for selling off the livestock, to which she was attached."

"*She* needed rescuing?"

"Seemed capable of taking care of herself, but she had been abandoned. Another brother, Rupert, who had been acting as her escort, ran off to Gretna Green, you see, with a young lady name of Fletcher. Grace Fletcher."

"Any relation to the Fletcher who won the Ramsay inheritance?"

"Yes."

"But I thought you said it was Jack's sister who married a Fletcher."

"She did. He did. They did. A humiliating occasion for Jack, the wedding."

"Humiliating? How so?"

"It was held just down the lane from the country house and grounds that Jack had lost to Fletcher. Hard for him to see the place again. Pained him, too, to be the subject of so much gossip. However, not half so painful as the gossip he stirred in London."

"Because he had shot his friend?"

"Everything about the trial was a scandal. Some chaps in the Navy had been caught stealing goods—hemp, canvas, lumber—offloading them at a pier. Officers, mind you. Well-connected young men. According to all accounts, it was the Gargoyle that nabbed them."

"What had that to do with Jack?"

"Well, I had no idea until Jack was called to testify. Seems he was the one who had gathered evidence against the thieves. He, and a lamplighter he refused to identify, had witnessed the thefts at the pier the very night Jack lost his fortune to Fletcher—the same night he appeared at your come-out ball."

Selina grabbed Allan's arm. "Is Jack the Gargoyle, then?"

Allan frowned. "He never admitted as much, but gossip was rife. People believe his very visibility on the evening in question was an attempt to throw suspicion of the Gargoyle's identity in another direction.

Selina sank back against the pillows.

"Do you require smelling salts?" Allan asked.

"No, no." She waved away the idea. "A bit of a shock to think we harbored a spy, a master of subterfuge."

"I know. Shocked me as well. So much so, I simply left the courtroom without so much as a good-bye. Headed straight out of London, my head reeling with all manner of thoughts, about how little we may know someone—their depths, their strengths."

"Their capacity for secrets," she said.

"Yes."

"Is he ever coming back?" she asked faintly.

"Shouldn't think so. He said nothing to that effect, at any rate. Are you in love with him, then?"

"I am, Allan," she admitted, her voice very low. "I carry his child."

Chapter Twenty-four

Allan was in a mood to ride off at once in pursuit of Jack.

With a few quietly uttered words, Selina gave him pause. "You mustn't. I threw myself at him."

He did not want to believe her. He argued, "He could have resisted your advances."

"And so he did, the first time."

"There was a second time?" He looked at her askance. Then it seemed he could not look at her at all.

"I made it impossible for him to refuse me."

"Good God, Selina!"

"I know, Allan, I know. It was entirely irresponsible of me."

"Rash, Selina, and you are not wont to rash acts. What do you mean to do? Does your father know?"

"No. Nor does your mother. Nor would I have them know."

"And Ramsay? Has he been informed? Did he know while I was with him?"

"No."

"You must tell him."

"Must I?"

"He does love you, does he not?"

"I thought he did. Now, looking back on it, I may have simply seen love because it was what I wanted to see."

"He should be told, Selina."

"Why? So that my name can be bandied about London in the latest gossip associated with the Gargoyle?"

"So that he has the opportunity to make things right. He did seem to me to be a man bent on setting things right when last I was with him."

"But you tell me he evidenced no intention of returning."

Allan spread his hands. "He never said as much. Shall I write to him and inquire?"

"No. This is my doing Allan. I must write to him."

And so she did, directing it to the London address.

> *Dear Jack,*
>
> *It has been too long since we last had word of you. Allan, safely returned to us, informs us that there is great speculation with regard to your background and occupation. I fear said occupation may keep you from us. Tell me please when next we might expect to see you. I have news, urgent news, of such a private and personal nature that I dare not entrust it to the post. It would greatly ease my mind if I knew that I should have opportunity to reveal it to you face-to-face with all possible speed.*
>
> > *Sincerely yours, Selina.*

Again she waited. She had grown accustomed to waiting.

Like the inks in the dyeing vats at the silk mill, the green, cerulean and yellow of summer changed to olive, ochre, russet, and brown. No new word from Ramsay. Selina resigned herself to the idea that she might never hear word, despite his promise to return. If Jack was, after all, the Gargoyle, he had every need to fade from the limelight, to lead a quiet, secretive, watchful life.

Arabella came to visit, full of good news and smiles. "I am to be married," she exclaimed before she had even stepped down from the coach that had brought her so far. "Baldwin is his name. Do you remember? I met him the night of your ball—the night Rakehell Ramsay played cello."

"I remember," Selina said. She remembered all too well.

"The Ramsays never cease to amaze people. Who would have guessed Jack was the Gargoyle?" Arabella hugged her, her mouth never ceasing in its outpouring of joyous chatter. "You are looking well, Selina. Not at all thin. Positively glowing. Country life agrees with you."

"And you, Arabella. Are you really in love?"

"I suppose there can be no other explanation. Banns have been posted, a dress must be made—something silk, I have decided. Something special with a pattern by my dear friend Selina's own hand. I have not forgot the dress you wore that night we first met Rakehell Ramsay."

"And what of the Rakehell?" Selina tried to sound nonchalant as she linked arms with her friend and led her into the house and up to the guests' quarters that could not help but remind her of Ramsay. "Has he done something of late to shock you? I have heard about the thieves he exposed."

"Old news, my dear. Now you must admire my ring." Arabella waved the hand on which she wore her new engagement ring, a band of mixed stones. It glittered bravely. Selina praised the beauty of each stone. "*R* is for ruby, *E* for emerald, then garnet, agate, ruby, diamond. He spells out his regard for me!" Arabella enthused. "It is the latest fashion in engagement rings. Isn't it romantic?"

Her attitude soured by a cynicism born of personal experience, Selina assumed Arabella or her father would be paying for the ring, soon after the wedding, when bills came due; but she hesitated to question her friend's blithe trust in a penniless gambler. Her own judgment where such gentlemen were concerned was highly questionable. Thus far, her hand was bare of any sort of promises, paid for or not.

"The Rakehell has gone to Brighton," Arabella said airily, her change of topics almost as dazzling as her ring.

"To Brighton?" Her letter might never have reached him!

"Yes. His brother, Charles, has opened up a business there. It is very sad. A viscount reduced to shopkeeping. They have all gone into trade, these Ramsays." She frowned a moment, considering. "Except Gordon, who is drunk too often to form the idea of gainful employment much less to engage in it, and Roger, who had too little life left in him, I would suppose, to engage in strenuous labor." She seemed suddenly to recall that Selina's family's wealth hinged on trade. "Not that there is anything wrong with going into trade. I am sure I wish the Ramsays well in their endeavors."

"What sort of business is it?"

"Antiquities, if I have it straight. A joint business venture between Charles Ramsay and Miles Fletcher, of all people. All of London was agog that those two should become linked not only by marriage, but by a partnership as well."

"Does Jack Ramsay mean to join them in the business?"

"I have heard nothing to that effect. He remains in Brighton, you see, as a favor to his brother Charles, who left suddenly for the Orient. On business, I am sure, but there is the oddest gossip going around that he has fallen in love with a governess turned lady's companion—that he is so head over heels in love with the creature that he must chase her all the way to China. Is it not delicious?"

"Terribly romantic, but I am still unclear just what it is Jack Ramsay does in Brighton."

"The Rakehell is minding shop." Arabella could not contain her amusement. "Can you picture it, Selina? Does he play cello for the customers, do you think?"

Selina did her best to look amused, but what she wondered more than anything was if Jack had received her letter, and if so, why did he not reply?

Arabella had chosen the pattern for her wedding silks and was on her way back to London by the time a letter from Jack finally arrived. So bulky one might almost call it a parcel, it was addressed to Mr. Preston, and contained small, cut samples of some exquisite Oriental silks. It's text focused primarily on the subject not of his return to them, but on a suggestion. His brother Charles, now well connected in the Far East in matters of trade, might be able to provide silkworm casings in whatever quantities were desired, at a better price than Preston currently enjoyed. Several pages of pricing and shipping information were enclosed.

In the letter—it went on for pages—came explanation at length of the trip to Norfolk, Aurora's wedding, the trial, his elder brother's departure for China in pursuit of his love, and his younger brother Rupert's current state of bliss, also due to marriage. If weddings were contagious, he quipped, he might soon be married himself.

At the close of the letter, he directed salutations shared with all of the Preston family, whom he sorely missed, most especially Miss Selina Preston, of whom he was reminded every time he played the cello. He hoped she still practiced. She must, by all means, be ready to play a duet with him by Christmas. He looked forward to returning to them for the Yuletide holidays, barring any more family crises. She still kept safe the small token he had left in her hands for safekeeping, did she not?

"So, he comes back to us at Christmas for no more reason than a duet!" her father happily teased, well pleased with the letter in its every aspect. "To what token does he refer, Selina? You never mentioned Ramsay having left something with you."

Blushing to think that she had been left with more than one token of the Rakehell's affection, she explained, "It is a penny."

"A penny?" Mrs. Preston repeated.

"Yes. A good-luck talisman he was in the habit of carrying. It did not seem worth mentioning."

"What an odd thing to leave in your possession."

"Yes, I suppose it is."

"We must hope he brings you something more valuable for Christmas, my dear," her father chuckled. "Perhaps a ring if he catches this wedding sickness his family falls prey to. Would that please you? Are you pleased he means to return to us?"

"Pleased?" She sighed. "Yes, though Christmas seems a distant thing." She would be six months advanced by then!

"Well, I mean to reply immediately to his letter. Is there anything you would care to add before it is posted?"

There was. Selina carefully penned the lines at the bottom of her father's brief reply indicating his interest in the silkworm casings.

Dear Sir,
Your penny is safe. I keep it close to my heart, along with another small something you did leave me, a token of es-

*teem far more precious than the penny, I urge you to return
to us with all haste. It will be well worth your while, I as-
sure you. Can you not come to us before Christmas? I desire it above all things.*

A reply was nine days in coming. It was directed to Miss
Selina Preston. She opened it with shaking fingers.

> *Dear Selina,*
> *I am touched by your desire for my hasty return. Were
> my own wishes and needs the only ones involved, I would
> be at your side even now, but with every intention of offer-
> ing retribution to a brother I have most foully wronged, I
> am committed to stay in Brighton until such time as
> Charles and his new wife return from their journey over-
> seas. I look forward with much anticipation to being re-
> united with you, in December.*
>
> > *Yours always, Jack.*

Selina cried when she read the letter. She did not like to
beg, but she sat down again to write, with every intention of
conveying more clearly to him her necessity. And if he did not
come? She had considered the consequences.

She ran a hand along the tight bulge of her abdomen. Consequences indeed!

Jack bent his head over the cello he had brought with him to
Brighton, ran his hands over the curved body of the instrument, as he did every night before he played, his thoughts elsewhere. Far away they were, in Chester, and the cello beneath
his hands did for an instant become, in his imagination, a
young woman hungry for his touch, so hungry she crept to his
room in the dead of night, so hungry she had written messages
to him that vibrated with the depth of her desire. Gently, lovingly, his every touch a caress, he began to play.

"Your worm casings have come." Like a stone thrown into
the stillness of a pond, Miles Fletcher poked his exquisitely
coiffed head around the door frame. "And another letter." He

entered the room, peering through his quizzing glass at a battered square of folded paper. "It would appear to have been misdirected first to London. The postman did apologize."

The bow slid from the strings of the cello. Jack made a grab for the letter. "And does the silk look promising?" he asked hopefully as he broke the wax seal.

Miles shrugged. "I've no idea what's considered promising when it comes to silkworms, Jack. Shall I send them by the mail to this Mr. Preston of yours so that he may be the judge?"

Immersed in Selina's delayed letter, he shook his head. There was an almost frantic hunger to the wording of this missive—an urgency he could not ignore.

> *Dear Sir,*
> *While pleased to hear you mean to rejoin us at Christmas, I write to inform you that the Yuletide season will be too late to bring me comfort in my current exigency of need for your company. I had hoped to see you sooner. I hold myself accountable—completely responsible—I would have you understand, for the urgency of my expectation. Perhaps you will recall favorably, as I do, the tune we played so sweetly in parting—a song that lingers, that swells, even now, within me. I cannot play on alone. Soon, I fear, I will no longer be able to disguise the effects of our music. Then everyone must know the true depths of my affections for you.*
> > *Come as soon as possible,*
> > *Selina.*

Twice Jack read through the words, before he said, with a slight frown, "Would you mind awfully, Miles, if I delivered the things personally?"

"Not at all," Miles agreed cheerfully. "Kind of you to connect us up with the fellow."

"If things work out as I hope," Jack said softly, "we shall have close ties with him indeed."

Unbeknownst to Jack, the most important letter Selina had yet penned to him, and it was, in fact, not so much letter as invitation, arrived even as he set off along the road to Chester, via hired coach. A crate full of silkworm casings and three carefully packed objets d'art that Miles had politely requested he deliver along his way were entrusted to his care. To London, then Oxford, and finally, Derby, he headed. This last detour, Miles promised, would take him no more than a day out of his way, unless of course, it rained.

It rained. And while that made little difference from Brighton to London and from London to Oxford, where the macadamized roads were little affected by the moisture, from Oxford to Derby the coach was several times bogged down. From Derby to Chester, the roads were well-nigh impassable. The day out of his way became three, then five.

A full ten days later than he had intended, bone weary, his boots, leggings, and coattails mud-spattered, Jack arrived in Chester. He paused at a roadhouse there, his intention to bathe and shave himself, to change clothes and make himself entirely presentable, while the carriage was washed down and the horses changed, before continuing on to Little Moresworth.

The clerk behind the counter winked at him, waggled his brows and said, "Come in time for the wedding feast, if not for the wedding, have you?"

Too tired to guess what the man meant by such a remark, Jack peered down at the mud on his boots and wondered if they would ever come clean again. "Wedding? What wedding?"

"You did say you were going to Little Moresworth, did you not?" The clerk looked confused.

"Yes. Is someone getting married there?"

"Aye. Quite a scandal, that. A great crowd of gawkers have set out this morning to witness the oddity, though where they will fit them I do not know. It is only a tiny chapel they have. A quiet affair it was meant to be, I think."

"But who is to be married?" Jack asked with a rising sense of panic."

"The son."

"Oh," he sighed with relief.

"Yes. To the daughter."

"What?" Jack could not believe his ears.

"Not related by blood those two, and so it is to be allowed. A queer turn, nonetheless . . ."

Jack heard no more. He was already on his way out the door, in a mad dash to the mews, where his horses had just been led from the traces.

"A hack, lad," he called to one of the stableboys. "I must have a horse, immediately."

"None to be had, sir." The boy shook his head. "All gone, they are, to carry them as have gone to Little Moresworth for the wedding."

With an oath, Jack swung onto the broad back of one of the muddied and sweated carriage horses. Leather straps trailing, he set off at a gallop for Little Moresworth.

Selina meant to marry Allan? He could not fathom it. The day had turned into a nightmare.

Chapter Twenty-five

M uddy, unshaven, and road-rumpled, Jack arrived at Little Moresworth to find a great, well-dressed crowd gathered outside the gates, on the grounds, and in the courtyard. Abandoning his lathered horse, he attempted to push his way through a body-jammed doorway, but was turned away by the sheer numbers who pushed him back with cries of, "Here now, lad. No way to turn up at a wedding, without so much as a bath or a comb through your hair. You'll not go tracking mud in now."

Had he cleared the door, there was no making his way up the packed stairway that led to the chapel anyway. No way to so much as let Selina know he was there, short of screaming her name into the stairwell. He would have begged private consult with her had he recognized a single face among the crowd, but they were strangers, all of them.

He was not to be stopped. By way of the back door at the far end of the house he climbed the narrow back servants' stairs to the familiar music room, where he flung open a cabinet, grabbed cello and bow, and rather than attempt to push through the massed crowd in the hallway, raced up the flight of steps that led to the long gallery.

Selina felt faint. The chancel was crowded and hot, as was the chapel beneath them, the hall leading to it even more so. The smell of packed bodies preyed unkindly on her too-sensitive nose.

"Will you open the windows?" she asked Allan, fanning herself vigorously and wishing she had had better sense than to pick a heavy, silk damask for her wedding gown, a fabric chosen more for its drape than for comfort's sake. Beneath it, she had squeezed herself into the confines of a corset. No sense letting the world know this wedding was even more scandalous than supposed.

The windows were flung open. Allan returned to her side, his hand a welcome support at her elbow.

"Better?" His voice, his eyes, were concerned. God, how she had depended on him these last few weeks!

She nodded.

"Chin up," he said bracingly. "We have only the vicar to delay us now. You need hold off on fainting only until he is done with the vows."

Chin up, therefore, she studied the biblical texts that had long ago been carefully lettered in black paint on the upper walls of the chancel and suffered great pangs of guilt and wonder that so far from the path had she strayed that she should be willing today to wed her own brother.

"Allan." She gave his hand a squeeze. "Are you sure you want to go through with this?"

His smile was as tragic as any other he had conjured up in the past few days. "This is the best of a bad situation, Selina. You know it is. Come now, cheer up. Let me see your dimples. We are watched by a great many curious people today. We must put a good face on it."

"Vicar's here," Mrs. Preston said, her gaze lingering on Allan's face, her expression unduly sad for a wedding day. "Shall we begin?"

"Get the damned thing over with," her father muttered, taking Selina's arm. "A bad business, this. Not at all the marriage I had envisioned for either one of you, Selina."

Another of the waves of guilt Selina swam in crested, threatened to topple her. As they passed the window Selina's gaze sought relief in the far horizon.

"A breath of air, Father," she begged. "I feel faint."

"Small wonder," he growled, but obliged her in stopping at the window.

Selina leaned against the casement, her dizziness heightened in staring down at the mill of people below, who, spying her, whispered and stared, or pointed, waved and called out to her. For a moment she considered the idea of jumping headfirst onto the bricks below, to end all of the whispering, the side-long looks, the dreadful speculation that had been aroused by the much disliked announcement that she and Allan meant to wed, by special license, with no delay. The bricks had a brutal look, harder to face than her father's disappointment, harder than a future with reputation ruined in a community that would be quick to calculate the true reason for this hasty marriage when her baby came due.

The vicar, who had been much mashed by the crowd along the stairs and in the hallway, wiped beads of sweat from his upper lip, asked if all parties were indeed set on the same course, and when he had ascertained by nods and low-voiced assurances that indeed the wedding was to take place, began the painful ceremony of linking Selina and her brother forever in the bonds of holy matrimony.

She swallowed hard, tried to shake away the roar in her ears, succeeded only in dizzying herself further, and heard hardly a word that was uttered, as the world closed down around her in a muffled sort of blackness in which nothing but Allan's concerned face might be observed. So disoriented was she that she thought she heard music—a cello. It drifted in and out of her consciousness like a whiff of remembered perfume.

The vicar directed all of his attention in her direction, as if awaiting some sort of response. Allan was staring at her, too, his dear face pinched with concern. "Selina? Are you all right?" he whispered.

"What? Yes, I thought I heard . . ."

"Of course you did, my dear, I shall just repeat it for you," the vicar said with great patience, "Do you, Selina Preston, take this man, Allan Preston, to be your—"

"No!" she said. She definitely heard faint music.

"What?" The word was a chorus, Allan, the vicar, her father and Mrs. Preston all wanting to know what she meant by no.

"Do you not hear it?" she asked Allan anxiously.

Allan frowned. "It?"

"The music. A cello?"

Allan shook his head, but her father wore an arrested look as he tilted his ear toward the ceiling. "Yes," he said, confused. "Rather a sad piece for a wedding."

"Bach," said the vicar.

Selina waited to hear no more. Lifting her heavy skirts, she pushed past the vicar, thrust her way through the room and into the hallway, ignoring the questions that might have slowed her, the looks of curiosity. Dragging the weighty train of her wedding gown she raced up the stairs to the long gallery. Tearing open the door, panting hard, she slid across the polished wood floor, skidding to a stop before a dirty, disheveled Jack Ramsay. He did not so much as raise his head to look at her, did not slow the sad course of his bow, even when she stood before him, gasping for air, gasping with relief and exhaustion and stays too tight for her condition.

"You came," she almost wept.

"I did," he agreed, his voice low, harsh, "but not to wish you joy. I've no joy in me to offer you. I came to retrieve my penny." He raised his head to look at her, his expression haggard, his manner brusque. "If you will be so kind as to return it to me."

"Selina!" Allan burst through the door to the gallery, his voice echoing the length of the room.

"Ah, the happy bridegroom." Jack spit out the words as if they fouled his mouth. His hands never ceased their work in wrenching sorrow from the strings of the cello. "How does it feel, Allan, to be a married man?"

"I wouldn't know," Allan said uneasily.

"I would," Jack said gruffly, "and I envy you your wedding night." The cello cried roughly in his arms. "Will she sing the same sweet, bawdy tune for you, my boy, that she carolled for me?"

Selina flushed with shame. Allan's face went red. "Why do you think I marry her, Jack? I know well enough that she has ruined herself with you. But spawn of a rakehell or not, the babe deserves a father, does it not?"

Head bowed, Selina pressed palms to her stomach and stifled a sob.

The cello fell silent. "You *are* pregnant then?"

Allan made a guttural sound of disbelief. "Why else would she have begged so insistently for your return, man?"

The cello fell away unheeded, the noise as it slid to the floor almost as unpleasant as the sound of Selina's weeping.

"You carry my child?" There was a trace of disbelief—of wonder—in the question.

"No one else succeeded in seducing her," Allan said waspishly.

Selina choked back her sobs, waving at Allan with a tear-dampened hand. "Please, Allan. Leave us a moment."

"Leave you? Are you sure?"

"Yes."

Grumbling, his stride impatient and angry, Allan quit the room.

"Your letters said nothing of a child!" Jack's anger seemed to rise with him as he stood and pulled several sheets of paper from the pocket of his coat. He waved them furiously under her nose. "Nothing of this wedding!" His rage echoed the length of the room.

She did not flinch, back away or raise her voice. "They did. The last letter I sent to you informed you of my intention to be married, and thence to Belgium for the birth of the baby."

"I never received such a letter," he growled, his voice quieting, if not his ire.

"You have a handful of my letters there. Could you not discern my need of you in any of them?"

He paced around her, reading, his manner that of a man done an injustice. As he read, his pace slowed, came to a halt. "Hints! No more than hints couched in the most guarded of terms." He slapped the pages. "The truth staring me in the face, all along."

She sighed. "I am sorry the letters were not more plainly worded, but as they were to be sent by post . . ."

He raised a hand to stop her, sighed heavily, looked her keenly up and down and said, softly, "Yes. I see. I am sorry to have been so obtuse."

She felt like sobbing again to hear his anger cooled at last, but she would not allow herself the release of tears. He would think her foolish and tiresome if she kept blubbering.

They stood a moment, awkwardly silent before he asked, very softly, "How are you?"

The warmth in his gaze, the loosening of the set line of his mouth reached out to her like the beloved refrain of a remembered song.

"I am tired, moody and all over swollen," she snapped, unwilling to forgive him so quickly their angry reunion. She walked to the window. "When I am not fainting or puking, I am voiding my bladder. How do you think I am?"

"You look wonderful," he said, coming up behind her, encircling her in his arms. "Started a baby, did we?"

She sagged against him, free at last to let go of her fear, her panic, her loneliness in the idea of facing a future without him.

Comforting hands stroked her shoulders, her back and sides. "Hiding the truth beneath corsets, are you? How can you breathe?"

"With great difficulty," she admitted. "I have been close to dropping all through the wedding."

"We must get you out of them," he whispered naughtily in her ear.

She turned to find his eyes bright, his manner confident.

"Is the vicar gone? Will you agree to an annulment? Will Allan? If he doesn't, you realize I shall have to shoot him."

She laughed, the sound broken by a sob. She dabbed at her eyes impatiently. Her voice shook only a little when she told him, "We are not yet married."

"What?"

"I ran out in the middle of the service when I heard the cello."

He laughed. She rejoiced to hear the sound of it.

"Stood up poor Allan, have you? Well, then, my dear. We must go down and finish the thing, mustn't we?"

"Must we?"

"Indeed." No longer laughing, he sank to one knee, as he had in this same room, oh so long ago. "You once said you had no designs on me. Do you remember? You said you did not know me, or my purpose, well enough to care, or not to care for me. You believed we were incompatible."

"I remember."

"I determined on that day, in this very room, to change your mind."

"Did you?"

"Yes. Resolved I must have you, Selina. Wayward, penniless Rakehell that I was. Never intended to seduce you. Quite to the contrary. Certainly never meant to get you pregnant in order to win your hand."

She smiled and bent to kiss him. "You are forgetting, sir. 'Twas I did the seducing."

"So it was," he admitted with a grin, and kissed her soundly before they went together downstairs, that the vicar, indeed the entire gathering, might be amazed by a wedding that began with the scandal of one husband and ended with quite another.

Acknowledgments

My thanks to those who graciously offered their expertise:
Margaret Singh checked the cello details,

Marilyn Lewis patiently explained and listed the misericords
of Chester Cathedral,

John Stafford-Langan offered Welsh penny token facts,

The Chester Heritage Center along with the Chester and Mac-
clesfield tourist information centers sent me all kinds of great
information on silk, salt, wall-walking, the Rows, and a great
old house, Little Moreton.

Last but not least, thanks to my husband, George, who brought
me a copy of *The Story of Chester* by James Williams.